CHRISTINA
SKYE

is code for romance and adventure!

CODE NAME: BIKINI
"A fun, antic read."
—*Publishers Weekly*

"When it comes to sexy suspense and high-tech
adventure, the Code Name series delivers big time."
—*Romantic Times BOOKreviews*

"Fast-paced action, flashes of humor, and futuristic flavor
typify this romantic action-adventure. Fans of the
'Code Name' series will enjoy this delicious addition."
—Kristin Ramsdell, *Library Journal*

CODE NAME: BLONDIE
"Romantic thrills and adventure from the expert."
—*Romantic Times BOOKreviews*

"Skye is terrific at writing fast-paced adventure romances…
a tantalizing addition to the compelling Code Name series."
—*Booklist*

CODE NAME: BABY
"Thrilling…fans should eagerly await the next in the series."
—*Publishers Weekly*

THE DRAYCOTT LEGACY
"Christina Skye's delightfully haunting Draycott Abbey
tales…pass the test of time, as they remain some
of the better romantic fantasies available."
—Harriet Klausner

CHRISTINA
SKYE

TO CATCH
A THIEF

HQN™

ISBN-13: 978-0-373-77307-7
ISBN-10:   0-373-77307-2

TO CATCH A THIEF

Dear Reader,

Some characters you never forget.

Some stories grip you from the first word, locked deep in the heart. For me, that love struck with a great gray cat, a brooding English abbey and its aristocratic guardian ghost, Adrian Draycott.

I've walked through eight books and two novellas set at the abbey now. Each story brings more secrets and the heady scent of rich heritage roses climbing up tower and parapet.

Dangerous magic.
White-hot passion.
Undying love.

How could any writer resist?

And just to keep the tension hot, I've brought a rugged Navy SEAL from my Code Name series to the abbey, locked in pursuit of a vicious enemy.

I hope you enjoy the adventure.

See you at the abbey.

Christina

Acknowledgments

In a world where distances loom large and the handling of books can become vastly impersonal, one group of people makes a daily, hourly difference in the reading experience.

It is my greatest pleasure to thank those extraordinary people here. I refer to all the extraordinary booksellers who cherish and protect the children of a writer's heart.

You know who you are. But you may not realize how far your influence extends and how deeply you touch the lives of readers every day.

I hope you will accept my heartfelt thanks for all the thousand things you do to care for every new book you unpack from a box or straighten on a shelf.

I also want to send a special nod to Cindi in Wisconsin, Ellen in New Jersey, Sharon in Pennsylvania, Marcy and Tom in Oregon, Beth Anne in Colorado, Sharon in Ohio, Rosemary and Margaret in Australia, Kellie in Hawaii, Terry in Chicago, Penny and Janet in Indiana, Molly in Louisiana, and Phyllis, Kathy and Vicky in Arizona.

You are all totally amazing.

That's why this one's for you.

TO CATCH
A THIEF

PROLOGUE

Draycott Abbey
Sussex, England
May 1622

THE BOOK WAS THE KEY.

All its dangerous secrets lay inside fragile yellow pages. He had to hide these secrets now, while twelve guests slumbered over their spilled port, with wigs askew. Their sleep would not hold forever, and he must act before their greed and suspicion returned.

In the shadows across the elegant room, the Earl of Wetherton mumbled in drunken dreams, his heavy goblet cracking as his wrist sent the glass flying to the floor.

Motionless, Viscount Draycott studied the ornate walls of the house he knew and loved beyond all logic. As the last candle guttered out, the cynical aristocrat stood in a bar of moonlight, cradling a fine leather book. The weight of history pressed down, filling him with excitement.

And finally with dread.

Such a treasure, a notebook from the hand of Leonardo da Vinci, carried too many secrets. According to the man who had lost the notebook, it was cursed. Equally cursed was the exquisite piece of art now hidden upstairs in his suite. But the memory of the luminous beauty of the art made the viscount forget the danger.

A sudden movement at the drifting curtains made him slip back into the shadows. Who came in stealth through the darkness?

But the figure was only a great gray cat, slipping up the stairs with black-tipped paws, as quiet as the night. Behind the cat the viscount saw a new maidservant, her eyes wide as she crossed the hall, a basket of freshly folded linens in her arms. A cat and the new maid.

But his worry would not be gone. Men would kill to hold the art of Leonardo da Vinci even if the art was cursed by its creator.

The abbey's lord was a careful man, a generous man, and the weight of duty drove him hard from the moon-touched Long Gallery to the library and to the shadows of a stone staircase above his wine cellars.

The cat was somehow before him as he took the stairs in hurried steps, a lantern held high to mark his way. The worn notebook did not move, cradled at his chest for safety.

Maledetto con gesti e' parole.

The words burned like poison in his head.

Cursed by hand and tongue.

Cursed to dream and want, all who hold this book.

Up the stairs a chair fell with a clatter. Drunken voices echoed through the sleeping house, calling his name. *No more time.*

Quickly he pressed at the wall, opening a niche between stone and mortar. In the small, snug opening he shelved the notebook.

For now, the sketch that had come from the hand of Leonardo da Vinci would hide in his own chamber inside a similar wall recess. He would make a safer hiding spot for it later.

The abbey's lord could do no more. A prize won in a turn of cards, the sketch caught at his heart. Da Vinci's hand was clear in every stroke and curve of the Mona Lisa's face, all distant grace and soft seduction.

According to the notebook, the sketch was the artist's final study before he began his painting. As was his custom, the Italian master often chose chalk to sketch the details of all he would later attempt in oil, and the notebook recorded his process of creation.

Both were priceless. Together they provided an unmatched look into the mind of a genius.

But there was no time for the viscount to linger. Upstairs boots rang out and petulant voices shouted for more port. Draycott felt a sudden disgust for his dissolute guests.

They were not real friends. He knew that any one of them would kill for the notebook and the art it described. The worn leather cover taunted him. His hands shook as he sealed the niche.

Here the notebook and its secrets would rest. With luck his descendants would have the strength to preserve this treasure, keeping it safe along with the priceless sketch it described in such intricate detail, capturing all da Vinci's agony of creation.

Frowning, Draycott raised the lantern for one last look. All was sealed. No signs of cracked stone or shifting mortar gave away the notebook's hiding place. By all appearance the wine cellar wall lay untouched, ancient as the house.

It was done.

But the weight of the curse remained.

Maledetto.

Draycott Abbey
Summer 1785

THE WALL WAS EMPTY.

Plaster spilled from a gaping hole, wood beams broken crudely. Blood stained the silk wallpaper where the thief—or thieves—had worked in painful haste. Boot tracks crossed the white snow of fallen plaster, vanishing at the far window, where the curtains fanned out like searching hands.

Adrian Draycott scowled at the hole in the wall. He cursed as he saw the broken recess, the hiding place of his family's da Vinci masterpiece. Now only a carved and gilt frame remained, its pieces discarded on the marble floor.

The thief had come by night, moving straight to this room while Adrian was in London on estate matters. No one had heard the furtive steps. No one had seen the knife that slit the wall and dug to find the hiding place of Leonardo's chalk study.

Now the elegant smiling face, accursed in its glory, had vanished. The eighth Viscount Draycott closed his eyes, breathing hard in the shock of the theft. Yet even then he felt something close to relief.

Maledetto con gesti e' parole.

The words drifted, twisting like smoke.

Cursed by hand and tongue. Cursed to dream and want.

The still-hidden notebook had recorded Leonardo's curse long centuries before. Both sketch and notebook had been stolen from Leonardo's studio by a charming servant ever alert to the chance for profit. For his crime the servant had earned the artist's curse. So had all others who came in contact with the stolen possessions.

Adrian Draycott ran a hand across his eyes. Well did he know the bitter pains of great loss, of trust betrayed. That pain he kept well hidden beneath a cold, languid facade. He cared for no one and nothing—only his beloved home.

The great gray cat pressed at his boots, tail raised, eyes alert. The viscount bent low, smoothing the warm fur. "So here ends both the tale and the curse, my friend. The art is gone, and though I should feel fury, I do not. I am…relieved. Let another poor fool carry the curse's weight. The Mona Lisa's smile is too cold and enigmatic for my taste."

The cat meowed, brushing against the viscount's boot. "I almost wish they had taken the notebook, too. In truth, I care not for this curse it carries."

The cat's eyes moved, keen in the spring night. Slowly Adrian turned, facing the open window that marked the thief's retreat.

Drops of blood stained the broken sill.

Maledetto.

"No matter," the viscount muttered, trying to believe his words. "The curse cannot hold power here. Not after so many years. It is done. Over."

Adrian Draycott prayed it was so. But the cold wind through the tall windows and the prickle at his neck argued otherwise.

CHAPTER ONE

The Isle of Skye
Scotland

SHE WAS COLD and tired and hungry. Her blistered feet ached and right now all Nell MacInnes wanted was a hot bath and a steaming cup of Earl Grey tea, followed by a warm bed to rest her weary body.

She closed her eyes, listening to the buzz of quiet pub conversation around her. The little inn nestled up against a pristine loch with towering mountains on three sides. The locals were far too polite to intrude on Nell's reverie, and when she dumped her mountain gear and backpack on the floor, sinking into a worn wooden chair, no one raised an eyebrow.

It was heaven to be warm and dry after six days of climbing the nearby peaks, battling rain and wind on every ascent. If not for her climbing partner, Nell might have curtailed the trip three days sooner, but Eric's enthusiasm was hard to resist. No doubt he would appear from his room upstairs within the hour, after taping his badly sprained ankle.

Warmth began to seep into her bones, as gentle as

the low burr of the Scottish voices around her. Scotland was truly heaven, she thought.

"And I'm telling you it was no such thing as my imagination, Angus McCrae. A grand fish it was—bigger than two arm spans, I'll tell you this."

Over the muted, good-natured argument about a lost fish, Nell heard the pub's front door open. Cold wind snapped through the room as two men entered, scraping booted feet. "Where is the American man, Angus? We need the climber called MacInnes."

Nell stiffened at the flawed description. Who wanted her now, when all she craved was one precious night's rest? No one from San Francisco even knew she was in Scotland.

The man at the door wore a muddy parka and broken-in boots. A satphone was gripped at his chest. "We've bad weather up on the hill and I need the American—assuming the man's as good as I'm told."

Nell took a short, wistful look at her half-eaten shepherd's pie and the cup of tea, but a request for aid was never refused.

She gulped the rest of her tea and stood up. "I'm the American named MacInnes."

"You—a woman?" The man looked startled.

Nell nodded, used to the surprised glances after twelve years of climbing on four continents. "How can I help you?"

"A team of young climbers has gone missing on Blaven, and there's bad weather already, with more due through the night."

Blaven.

Nell recognized the name of the dark peaks that girded the valley on three sides. "They're on the peak now?"

"Aye. They were expected down three hours ago and no sign of them yet. We have just now received word that they're stranded." He raised the satphone, his eyes grim. "A German climber saw them scattered out over the south slope like lost sheep. They did not answer his hails, and at least two had the look of being hurt." His voice fell. "Badly hurt."

Nell thrust her arms into her waterproof jacket, already making mental notes. "How many are in the group and what level of climbing experience? I'll need to know the exact coordinates where they were last seen, too." Even in a blizzard, the GPS would help Nell track those missing.

"I'm assembling that information now."

Nell unzipped her pack, assessing her resources. "I'll need drinking water and dried high-energy food, along with a more extensive first-aid kit."

"I will have it prepared for you, Ms. MacInnes, and our thanks to you for your help. My SAR team is under-staffed, all but myself sent over to assist in the recovery of plane crash victims on Uist. A terrible thing, that. I only wish I had two more people and I'd climb up myself."

"No, you're right to stay here. Someone experienced needs to be available to coordinate resources and guide the authorities. Besides, I'm familiar with Blaven." She smiled crookedly. "I worked SAR here myself nine years ago during my summer vacation."

The man looked pleasantly surprised—and a little relieved. "So you know the Cuillin, do you now? I'm glad to hear it. There are those who take our Cuillin lightly. Some of them do not live to learn their error, I'm afraid."

"I won't make that mistake, rest assured." Nell's voice was firm. She had seen enough dazed climbers and shattered bodies during her rescue summer to know just how fast conditions could change up on the nearby peaks. Within minutes an exhilarating climb could turn into a zero-visibility nightmare. "What's the weather prediction up there?"

"Northerly gale force eight. Snow already falling on the summit. Temperatures dropping to minus nine Celsius."

Nell made the conversion to Fahrenheit quickly, taking the bottles of water and zippered food bags that the local SAR coordinator handed her. "One more thing." Ruefully, she looked down at her feet. "I'm afraid I'll need dry socks. These are fairly well soaked after walking down through the rain all day."

Without a word, every man in the now silent pub bent down and began to unlace shoes or unzip boots, hearing her quiet words.

In seconds hand-knit socks appeared on every table.

Nell smiled at this instant generosity.

She cleared her throat. "I appreciate your help. What I meant is, I have special climbing socks up in my room. I'll do better with my own gear, you understand."

"Of course." The local SAR man said a few words of explanation in Gaelic. The men around Nell nodded. The socks vanished back on hidden feet.

She started toward the stairs to her room, calculating exactly how much she could cram into her pack and what injuries the lost climbers might have incurred. There was only so much possibility for medical intervention on the top of a mountain with limited supplies.

"One word, miss. Your partner—he will be going with you, will he?"

Nell shook her head. "Not with a sprained ankle, he won't. But Eric will stay in contact. He can help you down here with backup arrangements. I'll tell him the situation."

Nell knew her friend would insist on joining her, sprained ankle or not, but he'd be no help with an injury that had kept him limping for most of the day. She'd have to make the climb alone. She didn't need any amateurs slowing her down.

"I'll be down in two minutes. If someone can drive me up to the trailhead at the end of the loch, it will save twenty minutes."

"A Land Rover is already waiting for you, miss." The local rescue coordinator ran a hand through his hair. "I'd much prefer to go up the hill with you, truth be told. It's a fair nasty stretch across the south slope in weather like this."

"I'll be fine." Nell was calm, with years of climbing experience, focused on planning her route. She was used to facing the worst. Climbing a rugged peak in nasty weather wasn't half as bad as the other shocks that life had thrown her.

HE WATCHED her shoulder the heavy pack and then adjust both padded straps, working with the intense focus of someone used to carrying heavy weight well into the pain zone.

The woman clearly knew what she was doing, Dakota thought, slouched out of sight inside a dusty delivery truck parked up the road from the inn. The bug in her backpack was working perfectly, allowing him clear access to every word she said. So far she'd made no slips. Her conversation with her climbing partner had been full of good-natured bantering and reminiscences of earlier climbs.

No talk of art theft or organized terrorist activities, the Navy SEAL thought cynically.

His orders were absolutely clear. Close surveillance and assessment of all contacts made by Nell MacInnes. She'd done something to land on the government's highest priority watch list.

Better than anyone, Dakota Smith knew that SEALs didn't get called up for aimless threats. Nell MacInnes was up to her slender neck in trouble.

With or without her father's help, she was suspected of participating in the theft of one of the most valuable pieces of art ever to enter the National Gallery. Dakota's job was to find out who she was working with and locate the stolen Renaissance masterpiece before it vanished forever, traded through a shadow network of international criminals, sold to finance the activities of an elusive terrorist group active on American soil.

The SEAL's eyes narrowed on the woman's back as she climbed into a battered Land Rover, accompanied by the head of the local search-and-rescue volunteer team. Dakota wondered what made her tick, what drove her back out into a pounding storm after six days of strenuous climbing. He doubted it was simple selflessness. No, he figured that Nell MacInnes enjoyed walking on the edge, tasting danger. She looked like a classic thrill seeker, which would also explain her involvement in a complicated, high-stakes robbery.

Not greed. She didn't drive a late-model Maserati or own a string of houses. Her apartment back in San Francisco was neat but small, and her only hobby appeared to be climbing. Yet appearances could be the most unreliable thing in the world, Dakota knew.

Still, he wondered about that brief note of resignation he'd heard in Nell's voice back at the pub. The confidence had faded, along with the high energy, and she had sounded tired and worried, as if she genuinely cared about the missing climbers.

Forget about the target's emotions, a voice warned flatly as Dakota pulled onto the road, following the Land Rover at a careful distance. He'd track her up the brooding slopes of Blaven and make certain she came down in one piece. But he'd break his cover to save the other climbers only if it was absolutely necessary, mindful of his orders to stay well under the radar until all Nell MacInnes's shadowy contacts were bagged and tagged. The mission came first.

Always.

After parking down the slope from the small trailhead, Dakota pulled on an all-weather parka and a fully stocked backpack, then fingered his shortwave radio. His contact would be waiting for an update. "Teague, are you there?"

"Yo." Izzy Teague's voice was clear, despite an edge of static. "I've got the topo map on the screen in front of me. I checked with SAR and got the coordinates. You'll have a straight ascent for an hour, followed by a fairly strenuous climb through shifting rock when you near the south face. A chopper is on its way over from the mainland, but the weather may prevent a landing until tomorrow."

"So I'm on my own," Dakota said calmly. "Fine with me. I don't need anyone slowing me down or asking questions."

"Watch out for yetis up there," Izzy said wryly. "I'll keep a bottle of Glenlivet on ice for you."

"You do that. Alpha out."

The dark face of Blaven was veiled in clouds as Nell set off up the rocky trail. The Land Rover headed down to the inn. The first wet flakes of gale-driven snow lashed at Dakota's face as he started up toward Blaven's brooding darkness, Nell already out of sight before him.

FOR SOME REASON she couldn't shake the sense that she was being followed. For the third time Nell stopped, peering through fingers of clouds, looking for other climbers behind her.

Only rocky slopes met her sharp scrutiny.

Of course you're alone, idiot. Any climbers with good sense are inside huddled before a roaring fire right now.

But a climber didn't turn away in an emergency. Rules of the road.

Rules of life, too.

Turning back into the cutting wind, Nell nursed her aching right knee and chose each step, careful not to trigger a slide in the loose rock. Her face was cold, wet from the wind driving up from the sea. She estimated she'd reach the missing climbers' last coordinates in another twenty minutes. If the weather didn't shift, she could begin guiding them down off the peak immediately.

But Nell was prepared for a dozen unknown variables from shattered morale to shattered ankles. Any one of them could hamper a fast descent.

No point tilting at windmills, MacInnes. Every rescue was different, so she'd tackle each obstacle as it appeared. She eased her pack lower on her shoulders, trying to stay loose.

Once again she was struck by the twitchy feeling that someone was down the slope in shadow.

Watching her.

Blaven face.
One hour before sunset.

WIND RAKED Dakota's neck.

Icy rain howled over the cliff overlooking the restless Sea of Hebrides.

Visibility was down to zero and already the storm was driving intermittent gusts of nearly sixty miles per hour.

Over the slope Nell MacInnes had made contact with the frightened climbers. Thanks to the howl of the wind, Dakota could only pick up one word in three, but from what he heard, Nell was dealing with the rescue quickly and by the book.

She assessed injuries, boosted morale and passed out dry trail rations and chocolate, then radioed down to the SAR leader to have transport with a medical team waiting at the foot of the mountain. The climbers were teenagers from an international school in London, and their leader, a burly ex-naval officer from Brighton, was clearly out of his element. Why he had tried the ascent was still unclear, but Dakota knew the speed of weather changes on Skye could take anyone by surprise.

He fingered his transmitter. "Alpha to Teague."

Instantly static crackled. "Pizza to go. What can I get you, Alpha?"

"I figure a large cheese with double pepperoni is out," Dakota said dryly. "So I'll settle for backup medical response at the lower trailhead. One girl up here has full-blown asthma with signs of respiratory distress."

"Roger that. I'll wander on by to help and make sure it looks like a coincidence. What about the other climbers?"

"There are seven in all, plus their leader, Ian Westlake. He might have had a heart attack. He's holding on, but he's no help to anyone. Nell's about to try guiding the able ones down and I'm going to meet her on the slope to help out."

"Copy that. Better get the lead out, Alpha. That storm is picking up speed."

Bad news, Dakota thought. "Roger. I'll check back in ten. Alpha out."

The SEAL stared across the slope. To his right a steep cliff fell away in a vertical drop straight down to the loch. To his left a lower ridge vanished into the notched teeth of the Cuillin range.

There would be no climbing down tonight.

They were on their own. No rescue chopper could land in this wind, even if any were available in this remote corner of Skye. Dakota had to help Nell hold the kids together, dig in on the ledge for the night and wait out the storm.

In exactly eight minutes he rounded a turn and saw the little group, huddled beneath a ledge. Nell was snapping out crisp orders to a gangly teenager in a brand new parka.

"Hamilton, get your pack lashed over that boulder. Then I want you and Meyerson inside your tent in sixty seconds."

"Yes, sir. I mean ma'am."

Once the boy's pack was secure, he joined his terrified partner in the tent that had been pitched and tethered around stones in the lee of the wind.

What lee there was.

Another icy gust pounded over the ridge.

"Wu, secure your tent. Hernandez, get that lantern ready to help him."

Dakota watched Nell work beside the kids, making temporary shelter. She was using their last names, which created distance and the comfort of hierarchy, making orders easier to give and follow.

He noted that two other boys were working to secure another tent to nearby boulders, with packs tied down near the tent entrance.

"Good job," Nell called. "Now all of you get inside."

So where were the wounded ones? Dakota wondered.

A tent flap opened. A slim girl crawled out, looking for Nell. "I found that radio you asked about, ma'am. "It's—"

"Wilson, go back inside and take cover. This wind is—"

The rest of Nell's order was swept away in an icy gust that screamed over the ridge, caught two unsecured backpacks and threw them into the teenage girl, knocking her into a spine of sharp granite. As her scream was swallowed by the wind, Dakota dove forward and caught her waist, pulling her away from the cliff edge. She moaned brokenly as he lifted her into his arms. Blood streamed over his fingers from a gash down the side of her forehead. Dakota noted her erratic pulse and diminished pupil response.

Neck wound and probable concussion. Internal injuries were also possible.

"Who the heck are you?" Nell blocked his way, looking angry and wary and relieved, all at the same time.

"I was climbing over on the far side of Blaven when I picked up a distress alert from the local SAR. I changed route, circled the corrie and came up to see if you needed help."

Nell bit her lip, studying him intently. "You're American."

"Navy." Dakota gave a wry smile. "This was supposed to be a little holiday until I'm redeployed out of Coronado. I wasn't counting on the weather going all to hell."

Nell seemed to relax slightly. "It does that a lot here. So you're a good climber? Can you help me get these kids down?"

"I'll do whatever I can. Say the word." Dakota frowned. "You're up here alone?"

"Yeah, I am. Look—it's a long story and I don't have time to fill in the gaps. I'm Nell MacInnes."

"Lieutenant Dakota Smith."

"Well, Lieutenant Smith, you can put Amanda Wilson inside this tent." As she pointed to her right, wet sheeting snow cut off every sign of the terrain. "All of you stay in your tents and keep your backs to the rock. No one moves. Hammond, get that flap closed."

Dakota checked his watch as the teens obeyed Nell's terse commands. She had chosen the camp site well, bunkered down under a ledge in the narrow rift between two cliff faces.

The teenagers looked cold and confused as Nell went from tent to tent, giving calm orders. "Remember, you are fit and you are smart. We *will* survive this. Lieutenant Smith out there is going to help us."

"But what about Amanda?" A younger boy cut in, his voice shrill with panic. "She hit her head. Is she going to be okay?"

"She'll pull through." Dakota's voice was firm as he set the wounded girl carefully in the tent Nell had pointed out. Despite his assurances, he knew the girl was far from safe. If she had internal injuries, she might not last the night without medical intervention.

Briefly, he considered packing the wounded girl into an improvised travois and pulling her down as soon as visibility returned. But that would leave Nell alone in deteriorating conditions—and protecting Nell was his mission priority.

FUBAR.

As he rose from the tent, the wind howled over the ridge. Nell staggered, tossed sideways, and Dakota caught her quickly, his arms locked around her waist.

He felt the strength of her slim body as she fought the wind, trying to stand. "Thanks," she rasped. "We'd better get inside."

Beneath her safety helmet her eyes were calm and dark, the color of racing gray water through the mountains near his home in northern California. As the two squeezed inside the tent next to the girl named Amanda, Dakota pulled a silver thermal blanket out of his backpack. "Looks like you could use this. The girl's shivering. She doesn't seem to be breathing very well either."

"Asthma." Nell spread the blanket over the girl's body and tucked it in. "Thanks again, Lieutenant—"

"Dakota will do fine."

"Don't suppose you've got a few other seasoned climbers with you who could help guide these kids down?"

"Afraid not. I'm traveling alone."

Nell glanced at him intently. "Not many people I know climb alone." She raised an eyebrow, waiting for his answer.

"If I wanted noise and crowds, I would have stayed in London," he said easily. "I prefer climbing alone."

She nodded. "I can understand that." She unclipped

a rope from her belt and wrapped it in neat coils, every movement smooth and precise.

She was definitely a professional, Dakota thought. He gave a small nod toward the motionless girl and the boy at the other side of the tent. "She needs care. The sooner the better."

"Tell me something I don't know," Nell muttered. She turned to the other frightened teen, made a little light banter, then leaned back toward Dakota. She studied his shoulders, his high-tech boots and climbing gear. "How good are you, Lieutenant?"

"Good enough." There was no empty boasting, just cool truth in the words.

"Then you can help me rope a safety line?"

Dakota shook his head. "Maybe you haven't looked outside. This storm is gaining steam. I heard that sixty-mile-an-hour gusts were clocked near Portee. With windchill factored in, we—"

"We're screwed," Nell said quietly. "I got that much already Right now as I see it, our only choice is to get these kids down as soon as possible. They're not dressed for a night of wet, freezing conditions." Short copper hair tumbled around her flushed cheeks as she leaned down to check Amanda Wilson's pulse.

Dakota had seen that hair before. He'd seen her excited and tired. But he'd never seen her so focused or so worried, as if these kids really mattered to her. Somehow it didn't fit with the thrill-seeker image captured in her file.

But what she was suggesting was one step short of crazy.

"You can't get them down in a whiteout. One wrong step and they plunge into freefall, and you'll go over with them." Dakota kept his voice low so the others wouldn't hear. "We'll have to stay put."

Nell looked down at the girl named Amanda, whose breathing was growing more labored. "I know a way. This ridge leads down to a back trail. If you help me, I can set a safety line in fifteen minutes. I can get them down one at a time after that."

"How?"

"I'll clip each one into a harness, secure them to the safety line and work back down to the mid-peak."

"You've got only an hour of light left, and that will be pushing it." Dakota stared out the tent flap at the gray slope. He didn't like the risks—not for Nell or the stranded kids. "Have you ever handled a rescue like this?"

"At least a dozen times. A lot of climbers get cocky and forget that the weather up here can change on a dime. But I can get these kids down to the SAR meeting point. Trust me, I know this area pretty well." Her mouth curved in a sudden smile, and Dakota blinked at the force of the determination. Did *anyone* say no to Nell MacInnes?

The danger didn't seem to bother her, and her choices seemed logical. A good leader took controlled risks as necessary.

Dakota couldn't help but admire her courage and her skill.

"I've got a radio for contact. I've also got this." Nell pulled a silver whistle from inside her parka. "The SAR people will be expecting an alert once I'm close to the bottom of the safety line. I'll hand off each teenager and then head back up." She smiled gamely and gave an experimental whistle. "But if we're going to do this, it has to be now."

Dakota had to admit that her plan made sense, especially since staying put offered a risk of exposure and hypothermia.

But habit was habit. A SEAL never trusted any plan he hadn't tested himself. Watching on the sidelines wasn't in a SEAL's job description.

He had to keep Nell safe.

But he couldn't let any of these kids die in the process.

He watched Nell slide her climbing rope through her fingers, testing each coil. The fibers were smooth with no frays, clearly well tended.

She tugged on fingerless climbing gloves, frowning. "Look, Lieutenant—"

"Dakota."

"We have to move, Dakota. In twenty minutes we really will be boxed in here. Do you want to save these kids or not?"

"I want to see *all* of you get down safely."

"Don't worry about me. Last year I took third at Chamonix. That's an open climb with professionals— both men and women."

"But you were probably climbing in good weather, fully roped and hydrated." He glanced back and lowered his voice. "These kids are frightened and near the end of their endurance."

"I'll get them down the ridge. My safety line will hold, trust me." Nell leaned closer, her voice falling. "Otherwise we could lose them up here in the cold."

Dakota listened to the howl of the wind beyond their narrow, protected ridge. It was a perilous point of safety, one that would vanish as the temperature fell and the poorly dressed group of kids faced hypothermia. With gale-force winds in a whiteout, the disoriented teens could crack at any minute, driven by panic to do something stupid.

He was trained to be flexible, and he did that now, assessing the choices and the risks. As wind roared over the ridge, Dakota made his decision.

He zipped up his parka. "Show me where you want to set this safety line."

CHAPTER TWO

NELL SHIVERED IN THE biting wind, painfully aware that every second they were losing light.

So far she had managed to guide five of the teens down, turning them over to the Scottish SAR people at the waist of the mountain. The sixth one was clipped in and ready to escort down.

But conditions were getting risky. In a few minutes all light would be gone.

She rechecked all the carabiners and anchors, then gave a reassuring smile to the gangly boy who was watching her in abject adoration. "You'll be fine, Jess. Just keep breathing and count your steps the way I told you. Stay cool and stay focused. I'll be on the rope right in front of you, so don't crowd me. Can you do all that?"

"I—yes." He tried to hide his fear. "Let's go."

Nell touched his face and held his gaze with the force of her own. "You're going to survive this, Jess. The others are down and you're next. Just do what I told you and you'll be fine."

"You—you're amazing." The boy gripped the safety line with both hands, but his gaze was locked on Nell.

"I thought we were all dead, but you walked out of the rain like some kind of angel."

"I'm glad I was around to help."

"What about Amanda? Is she going to make it through this?"

He was a nice kid, Nell thought. They all were. None of them were going to die, she vowed. Not while she had hands to knot a rope and lungs to breathe in icy air.

She checked that all the carabiner gates were fully closed and secure, then gave the boy a jaunty smile. "Now get yourself down to the inn and warm up. They'll have a fire and dry clothes ready. Drinks tonight in the pub are on me. Cokes, of course."

He smiled crookedly. "I'll be waiting. You couldn't keep me away."

Nell looked down into the swirling blanket of clouds and gave two short bursts on her whistle. Seconds later she heard the faint answering notes from the SAR people waiting at the end of the safety line, followed by the answering whistle from her climbing partner lower down the slope.

Then a gust of wind slammed over the cliff face and she forgot everything but keeping her footing as darkness closed in around them.

WHAT THE HELL was taking her so long?

Dakota stood at the top of the safety line and checked the luminous dial of his watch. Nell had been gone almost twenty minutes.

He fought an urge to follow the line in search of her, but he needed to go back to keep an eye on Amanda, who had roused once, asked for water, then slipped back into unconsciousness, struggling for breath.

Asthma and possible internal bleeding, with hypothermia a distinct risk. In addition, the British tour leader had nausea, sweating and crushing chest pains that radiated down his left arm, clear indicators of a heart attack. Dakota had given him a small aspirin to chew, followed by sublingual nitro, but the man didn't look good.

He couldn't afford to lose Nell in the storm, the SEAL thought grimly.

He stared down at the safety line, thinking about the night two weeks before when a Renaissance masterpiece worth thirty million dollars had disappeared from a locked vault....

Washington, D.C.
South Conservation Workroom of the National Gallery
Two weeks earlier

THE SECURITY LIGHTS BLINKED, a nonstop race of green against a high-tech control panel. The night guard, fresh from six years at the Metropolitan Museum in New York, reached for his log sheet to verify a completed security cycle.

Even then his eyes didn't leave the sleek security panel, where half a dozen cameras picked up deserted hallways and an empty loading dock. Two floors above, Rogers walked the offices, checking every door. At the end of the hall he used his passkey to call the elevator, then continued on his rounds.

The night was quiet and uneventful. Even the streets were calm, with no sirens for several hours. But the museum was on special security measures due to a new piece of art entered for appraisal. Only five people on the staff knew that the work was judged to be from the hand of Leonardo da Vinci, a Renaissance masterpiece that would command millions when it eventually went up for auction.

The air-conditioning clicked. The head guard, Everett Jonell, checked the control panel. Lights flickered briefly. The locked room with the new da Vinci blurred to gray.

Everett's hand went to the alarm.

Then the power came back on, with the hum of the HVAC restored. The row of monitors showed empty corridors. The door to the vault in south storeroom #3-A was locked as before.

Everett Jonell relaxed, leaning back in his chair. He felt sweat bead his forehead and shook his head. He'd be relieved when the art in storeroom #3-A was on its way and things settled back to normal. Until then, people would be edgy, under orders to report anything that seemed unusual.

On the black-and-white monitor, Jonell watched Rogers cross the big atrium and move toward the new sculpture wing. There was something off about the man. Two nights earlier Jonell had stopped at a small jazz club for a drink after work and he'd noticed Rogers getting out of a parked car across the street. The sleek black Mercedes M-Class sedan had seemed way above Rogers's pay grade, so Jonell had made a point of checking out the driver and noting the license plate.

He'd been surprised to see one of the senior curators emerge, a slender workaholic from Harvard who never went anywhere without her cell phone headset in place. There were no explicit rules forbidding social contact between security and academic staff, but you didn't see it happen just the same. Different worlds, different goals, Jonell thought. But the way the curator had plastered herself all over Rogers as they'd kissed long and intimately in the shadows across the street had Jonell scratching his head.

Maybe you never knew what made people tick. After twelve years in the Marines he'd seen a lot of things and figured he was a good judge of people. Rogers seemed like an okay guy, but it wasn't up to Jonell to judge.

He'd report what he'd seen to the head of museum personnel, just in case. Until the da Vinci in storeroom #3-A left the premises safely, they would all be under extra scrutiny and Jonell wasn't risking his job and a nice pension for anything. Not with a new grandbaby on the way and three more years until Medicare kicked in.

He frowned into the security monitor as he saw Rogers reach into his pocket and pull out a cell phone.

What was the man doing? He knew that personal cell phone use was forbidden during work hours for security. Now Jonell would have to write the man up, which involved reports in triplicate and copies to both union representatives.

Blast the man. Didn't he know that the video cameras would pick him up?

The monitors flickered again and the HVAC clicked off. Lightning crackled high overhead, the sound muffled by the museum's thick walls.

Jonell sat forward as all the monitors went dark. Cursing, he lunged for the security phone, but the line was dead. He grabbed the battery-powered walkie-talkie to put in a radio alert to the general switchboard, standard procedure, even though a backup generator would kick in any second.

The movement came from his left and he dropped the walkie talkie as a leather strap locked him to the chair, his hands caught behind his back. He struggled against cool fingers that gripped his neck.

"No, you can't—"

The needle prick came quickly, burning against the inside of his nose, which made no sense at all. The room blurred and he tried to speak as he heard the sound of the security panel door being unlocked. Someone was removing the surveillance board timer, he realized. Blurring fingers ejected the surveillance disk.

It had all been planned to the second, Jonell thought dimly. Planned by someone on the inside.

Was it Rogers? Another one of the new guards they had hired in the past month?

He moaned, caught by crushing pain at his chest. As his body went slack, Everett Jonell realized that he'd never see the new grandbaby or his wife or his proud daughter again. The sorrow was the last thing he felt.

Six minutes, fifteen seconds to go.

The figure at the security command post inserted a

new time stamp digitally at the security panel, typing in a string of computer code. Then he pocketed the old surveillance disk and inserted a new one, already formatted and complete with museum images calibrated to the current time stamp. Nothing had been left to chance.

Nudging his boss's lifeless body onto the floor, the figure finished his disk exchange and then checked the black-and-white images that appeared on the row of monitors.

All good to go.

He opened his cell phone, dialed a number and hung up after one ring.

Though the far monitor showed no activity, he knew that someone was carefully easing open the door of storeroom #3-A at that very moment.

He closed his eyes, savoring his memory of the exquisite chalk sketch of the most famous woman on the planet.

Thanks to his discreet program override, the monitor display would loop back with preset images and movements timed to coincide with normal museum patterns. After the thorough infrared assessments that had just been completed, no new tests on the art were scheduled for thirty-six hours. Only at that point would the theft be discovered.

By then, da Vinci's preparatory ink and chalk study for the Mona Lisa would be safely locked in a vault, ready for covert transport out of the U.S.

He checked his watch.

Three minutes, twenty-two seconds to go. Calmly

he lifted Jonell's fallen walkie-talkie and studied its face. Everything appeared to be in working order, he was happy to see.

His cell phone buzzed quietly, one burst and then no more.

All clear.

Target acquired and clues in place. Ready to exit the building. Everything was moving nicely ahead of schedule.

He thought briefly about the funds that would be wired to four of his offshore accounts by this time tomorrow. Maybe he'd buy that island in the Seychelles after all. It was remote enough and there was a fresh water source as well as a sizable bungalow with upgraded docks.

He shoved away the thought. There was still risky work to be done. In two minutes he would phone in an emergency call notifying the switchboard of Everett Jonell's collapse, sounding suitably shocked and upset. Once his regular shift was complete, he would drive to the short-term apartment that he leased in northern Maryland under one of his many other names. Once there he would collect the carefully wrapped piece of art. After the transfer was done, he would follow his normal schedule with no deviation.

He'd even attend Everett Jonell's funeral and offer deep and sincere condolences to his wife.

He'd stay in place after the theft was discovered, monitoring progress on the investigation inside the museum. In six months he would resign quietly, pleading health problems, and then vanish.

He glanced at his watch.

Showtime.

He took a deep breath, schooling his features to a frown. When he triggered the walkie-talkie alert, the alarm in his voice was deeply convincing.

"Command post one. Guard down. I repeat—*guard down!* Backup needed immediately."

He was kneeling over Jonell's lifeless body, looking pale and agitated, when the first security patrol car screamed up the museum's back service drive.

CHAPTER THREE

DAKOTA WATCHED A SMALL shape appear out of the windblown snow. Relief kicked in when he saw Nell wave one hand in a brief thumbs-up gesture.

She looked like hell, he thought. Her hair was flecked with frozen snow. She had mud on her gloves and a welt across one cheek.

"Amanda's stable," Dakota said, catching the anxious glance Nell sent to the first tent. "The group leader needs hospital care, but he's finally calm, which won't create such an oxygen debt. Go inside. You need to rest."

Nell looked exhausted as she crawled into the second tent, snow swirling up behind her. She pulled off her climbing gloves and flexed her hands. Her teeth began to chatter. "There's more snow on its way. I can feel the moisture. In icy conditions—"

Without a word Dakota unzipped his parka and pulled it around her shoulders.

She stiffened and tried to push away his hands. "What are you doing? I can't take this. What about *you*?"

"I'll be fine. I've got excellent cold tolerance. You need this more than I do right now."

She continued to protest, but Dakota cut her off.

"How did it go?" He held out a canteen with water, taken from his pack.

Nell took a drink, then handed back the canteen. "They'll be fine. A doctor was waiting at the inn." Her voice tightened. "The last trips down were pretty bad. The wind—" She closed her eyes, hunching over to cough sharply.

"Let it go, Nell." Dakota leaned over and zipped his parka around her trembling body. "You've done all you can. Once the weather clears, a chopper will be dispatched for Amanda and the group leader."

Nell nodded slowly, but her body remained tense. She didn't seem to notice when Dakota pulled a thermal blanket around her and tucked it into the rope wrapped around her waist.

"How do you let it go?" She shivered, ran a hand across her cheek and stared at a line of dried blood covering her palm. "The last boy, Jess, panicked and he was going to let go of the rope. If he had, I would have lost him. No doubt about it. And it was so *close*."

Dakota heard the horror that she had tried to hide beneath anger. "Nell, you did everything right. Let it go."

"I *can't*. Not until everyone is safe."

He was acutely aware of her scent and the sounds of her breathing as he pulled her slowly toward his chest. He told himself the gesture was entirely impersonal, meant to drive off her panic and uncertainty.

She'd just completed one of the riskiest rescues ever undertaken, but even strong people had limits, and Nell

MacInnes was at hers now. Dakota didn't wait for more arguments, didn't try to reason or explain. He pulled her against his chest, sliding her thighs around his waist. His hands moved under her jacket, massaging her back and shoulders for warmth and circulation.

He was keenly aware of her hair, pressed against his cheek. In different circumstances he might have turned his head to taste the smooth line of her throat and test the full curve of her mouth with his lips.

Very bad idea. Here and now there was no place for emotion or desire. She was his mission.

Their eyes met. She shivered and studied his face as if she'd seen something there that she couldn't understand.

She looked down and seemed to realize how her legs were wrapped around his waist.

With a low gasp, she tried to pull away.

Dakota held her right where she was. "Don't fight me, Nell. We need to stay warm. Now close your eyes and rest. I'll keep an eye on things."

"Why should I trust you?" she whispered.

"Because right here, right now, I'm all you've got," Dakota said gruffly. As he wrapped the thermal foil blanket around them, the wind howled out in the darkness.

OKAY, THE MAN was tough and he thought on his feet. Calm under pressure, he had a way of moving in and taking charge before you realized what was happening.

But Nell wasn't a skittish child and she didn't take orders from strangers.

She yawned. Even as she struggled to keep her eyes

open, she couldn't ignore the hard lines of Dakota Smith's thighs. The man had a great body, and the warm strength of his arms was like a dangerous drug.

She felt the hammer of his heart beneath her cheek, felt the rise and fall of his broad chest. Even his scent teased her, a blend of salty air, sweat and heather.

As he stretched slightly, Nell felt his thighs tighten against her, and his arms shifted to hold her steady. Though they were thigh to thigh, chest to chest, he didn't brush her breasts or make suggestive comments.

Life seemed small and very fragile as they waited out the storm's fury. Idly Nell rubbed her elbow, which had begun to ache. Might as well try to sleep until the storm ended, since they were going nowhere.

She closed her eyes, feeling her hips slide over his thighs. The man had excellent thighs, too.

Maybe sleep wasn't going to be so easy.

"So what do you do when you're not on a climbing vacation?" she muttered. Anything to distract her from the feel of his lean, sculpted muscles.

"My job keeps me busy."

"Before we went down, Jess told me that you're amazing. I've never seen a kid in such an advanced state of hero worship. This is probably a walk in the park for you, Lieutenant."

"I never take any threat for granted," he said roughly. "That includes weather and people."

Was there an edge in his voice? Nell opened one eye, but in the darkness she couldn't read his expression.

His arm cradled her head. His chest was warm and he seemed calm, but absolutely distant.

Probably she'd been wrong about the edge in his voice.

Quietly, he slid free. "Time to check on Amanda."

"HOW IS SHE?" Nell was feeling a little blurry when he returned. Actually a *lot* blurry. A wave of dizziness hit her. She had forgotten the adrenaline spikes of rescue work—and the inevitable crash.

"Her pulse is stronger. Right now I'll take small favors. The cardiac patient is holding on, too." With economical movements, Dakota sat down and drew her against him, covering them both.

She tried to focus, but the growl of the wind was distracting. "So what made you decide to be a hero, Lieutenant?"

"I just happened to be around when you needed me. It's nothing heroic."

Nell studied his face as he switched on a small penlight. "When did you start your climb? I never saw you before today." She angled her head, trying to read the expression in his eyes. The man didn't reveal anything, she thought irritably.

"I arrived yesterday. I've been on the move."

It made sense. As he pulled her closer, the soothing warmth of his body made her relax.

The man would make a fantastic climbing partner, she decided.

The penlight flashed off. Rough fingers opened on her hair. "What are you thinking about?"

"I figure you have great deltoids," Nell said sleepily. "That's always the first thing I look for in a man."

"You look for his deltoids?" He sounded amused.

"Absolute first thing." Nell yawned. "Always look for the deltoids. Best way to judge climbing strength. How long can you hang, hands only, unassisted?"

"Seventy-one minutes." His breath was warm against her ear. "More or less."

Even in a growing haze of cold and exhaustion, Nell was impressed. "*No way*. Not for over an hour." Nobody could do that. At least nobody that *she* knew.

"I could be lying," he said calmly.

Nell didn't think so. He didn't strike her as the type for casual boasts. In fact, *nothing* about the man seemed casual. "What exactly do you *do* in the navy?"

"This and that. Nothing you'd be interested in." His hands slid slowly into her hair. Nell felt the strands spill over his fingers.

At every movement, she was stunned to feel little jolts of desire. The heat grew where their bodies were joined.

Crazy. They were camped on the edge of a cliff and he was a complete stranger.

But the heat didn't go away. His hands kept moving, slow and thoughtful, until Nell thought she'd scream.

Or curl up against his chest and sigh in noisy pleasure.

She frowned. She knew better than to relax or trust a stranger even if the gentle motion of his hands *was* hypnotic. "The tents are taking a beating. I need to go check to see if they—"

"Already done. The lines you rigged are solid. Nice work."

"Two of my best ropes are out there," she said sleepily. "I've got trail mix and three protein bars in my left pocket," she added. "Take them if you need to."

"I'll be fine. Go to sleep, Nell."

She wasn't used to being taken care of. It had been years since her father—

Don't go there.

The past was a sinkhole filled with bad memories. And this man was still a stranger. She wiggled, trying to find a position that wasn't starkly intimate, with their shoulders touching and their thighs locked together for warmth. Finally she gave up.

It was just one night, after all. She'd never see this man and his powerful body again. There was no chance for mingled laughter or shared secrets.

And that was *exactly* the way Nell wanted it.

She twisted, shoving away his hands as she closed her eyes. "Just don't get any ideas while I'm asleep," she said huskily. "That cliff wall is only a few feet away. You wouldn't like the drop."

She thought she heard his quiet laugh before she drifted off with the howl of the wind in her ears.

NELL FELT the wind in her hair.

Hands sweaty, she was chalking up before her last climb of the day. The sun lay hot and heavy on her shoulders in a band of liquid gold. Body straining, muscles in the flow while Yosemite spread out like a Technicolor postcard.

Beautiful.

Then the sudden hiss of falling rope. A violent jerk

as a cam broke free, slamming her into a wall of granite, breaking her nose and cheekbone, blood gushing onto her neck.

The sound of her own scream jerked her upright in the icy darkness.

"Nell, wake up."

Lines broken. Carabiners blown. Falling, falling...

"Hey, wake up." Hard hands locked around her shoulders.

She fought blindly, her nails raking warm skin.

Panic. Falling...

"Stop fighting, Nell. It's Dakota. You're just dreaming. Something about Yosemite, but it's over now. Calm down and breathe."

Breathe.

Nell forced her muscles to loosen.

Just another dream. Always about falling, somewhere alone in the darkness...

She took a deep breath and shoved a damp clump of hair from her eyes. "Okay, back among the living—more or less. Thanks for the wake-up call. What time is it anyway?"

"Almost five. Should be light soon. You okay now?"

Nell straightened the small light clipped to her belt. "Great," she said through clenched teeth.

"You keep that light with you all the time?"

"When I'm next to a three-thousand-foot drop, I do. In case you didn't notice, that first step can be really unpleasant." Nell slanted her small light through the tent. "How is she?"

"No change. Stable and warm."

"Westlake, our fearless tour leader?"

"Asleep, last time I checked."

Nell frowned. "What about you? Don't *you* ever rest?"

"I closed my eyes for a few minutes. It's all I need." His hands smoothed the thermal blanket around her shoulders. "Do you always ask this many questions?"

"Yeah, I do. Call it terminal curiosity."

Amanda Wilson tossed in her sleep, and Dakota leaned down to check her pulse.

At his touch the teenager twisted, muttering hoarsely. "Mummy, you left the window open again. It's so c-cold…" Then her eyes opened and she coughed, staring blankly up at Dakota. "My arm hurts." She craned her head anxiously from side to side. "Where are the others?"

"Back at the hotel. We'll get you there shortly." Dakota raised the tube of her hydration pack. "How about you drink a little water?"

"How long have we been up here?"

"Most of the night." After Dakota helped Amanda drink, he pulled the silver blanket back in place around her. "But the weather looks to be clearing. Just think of it this way. You're going to have a great story to tell all your friends."

The girl's lip quavered. "I want to g-go home."

"We'll get you there," Nell said firmly. "We're going to make it through this."

Amanda took a labored breath. "Is that what you do?"

"Sometimes life gets messy and complicated, but I

don't look down and I don't look back." Nell's voice was flat.

She sensed that Dakota was studying her. "Something wrong?"

"I didn't say anything."

"You were *thinking* plenty loud, Navy."

Across the tent Amanda giggled. "She's got you there. You do seem kind of—intense. I guess that's a navy thing."

Dakota moved to help her drink some more water. "What, can't a man enjoy the company of two gorgeous women in peace?"

The teenager wheezed out a laugh. "Very funny."

Over the howl of the wind, motors droned closer. Nell could see the dim pattern of light around the flap of the tent. "They'll have to land below the ridge. Someone needs to guide the rescue team up." Nell pushed to her knees and grabbed her climbing gear.

"Sure you're up to it?" Dakota asked quietly.

Nell shoved a coiled rope over her shoulder. "No offense, but I think I'm the best guy for the job."

His expression was unreadable as he reached out and brushed one finger along the corner of her lips. It was almost as if he was memorizing her smile, Nell thought.

Then his expression hardened. "I hate to admit that you're right. Watch your six out there."

"SHE'S REALLY GREAT, isn't she?" Amanda was watching the spot where Nell had disappeared. "I don't think anything in the world frightens her. I wish I was that way."

Dakota listened to the chopper approach. "You never can tell what makes people tick. I think Nell enjoys the thrill of being in danger. Besides, you're pretty brave yourself. You took a real beating."

The teenager shrugged. "Not like you two. So why don't you *like* her? I mean, you smile at her, but it never quite reaches your eyes."

The girl was a little too observant, Dakota thought irritably. "Nothing wrong with Nell MacInnes. I like her fine." He just didn't *trust* her.

"How's Ian doing? Is he…" Her voice trailed away.

"He's still alive." Barely, Dakota thought. "That's a helicopter coming in out there. With luck, you'll be down at the hotel in ten minutes. How do you feel?"

The girl swallowed hard. "Like I might throw up."

"I'll let you in on a secret." Dakota slanted her a quick smile. "Happens to the best of us."

The tent flap rose and Nell appeared, snow on her cheeks. "A team is headed up to hitch you into a sling, Amanda. Ready to go?"

"I guess so. You'll both go down with me, right?"

Dakota zipped up his pack. "You bet."

"Do you need any help in here?" Nell's climbing helmet was hanging over her shoulder and she was half turned to the light, looking relieved that the ordeal was nearly over.

"Not a bit. I'll help Amanda outside and then go see if I can help them with Westlake."

Nell stuck out one hand. "Nice to meet you, Navy. You can climb with me anytime."

Dakota gripped her hand and studied her face,

looking for traces of cunning or arrogance, but there was only excitement and a hint of a smile.

"I hear the girls are placing bets down at the inn."

"What kind of bets?"

"Whether or not your butt is as incredible as they all think it is." She gave a wicked smile. "I'm guessing it is."

Dakota's brow rose. "I thought you were into deltoids."

Amanda gave up trying to hide her laughter. "Where *are* the deltoids?"

"Right here." Nell reached out and tapped Dakota's upper arms. "Something tells me these are pretty spectacular. Too bad I'm never going to find out."

"I'll show you mine, if you show me yours. Just name the time and the place," Dakota said huskily.

Nell's smiled faded. "I don't think so. Something tells me it would cost a lot more than I'm prepared to pay."

"How much are you prepared to pay?"

She studied him a long time. "I'm not sure. Whatever it is, you'd probably cost more. Watch yourself on the big walls, Lieutenant." She tossed a coiled rope over her shoulder and headed out into the cold gray light of dawn.

Dakota was still watching her as the snow swirled up and the rescue team appeared on the ridge below them.

CHAPTER FOUR

THIRTY MINUTES LATER the storm clouds had moved inland and Amanda Wilson and Ian Westlake had been transferred to a medical flight bound for Edinburgh. Now the rescue team was relaxing, glad to have a successful end to their dawn ascent.

Meanwhile, Dakota's Foxfire contact was waiting in a military helicopter on the far side of the loch. Izzy Teague was roughly six foot five and could have passed for Denzel Washington, but his grave eyes made him look older than his years. One of the government's finest security operatives, the man could assess photographs or triangulate cell phone positions faster than most people could breathe.

The chopper was quiet. Restless, Dakota drummed on the window, waiting for the pilot to return.

"Something wrong?" Teague opened his medical bag and pulled out a small metal case.

"Not a thing."

"Yeah? Then why are you scowling?"

Dakota shrugged.

"How's your hand?"

"Fine." Dakota didn't look up, intent on stowing his

gear. He especially refused to look around in hopes of seeing Nell.

Teague glared at him. "Fine? You've got two lacerations that need sutures."

"Nothing that can't wait."

Izzy stared at him thoughtfully, then glanced down and made quick notes on the sleek laptop that was never far away. "How did that climbing gear work out?"

"The shoes get high marks. Solid traction and balance. The gloves were useless. No possible way to handle a weapon in them."

"I'll pass the word to Ryker and his science boys." Izzy gave a cocky smile. "Back to the drawing board on the gear." When Dakota didn't answer, Izzy raised an eyebrow. "Something eating you, Smith?"

"I'd like to get moving, that's all. Has my surveillance mission changed?" he asked quietly.

"First things first." Izzy's eyes narrowed as he held out a digital keypad. When he triggered a button, a row of lights flashed red-orange. "Before we leave, Ryker wants a medical update. Log in for *Madonna* and record your response times."

Madonna, as both men knew, was the code name for Dakota's unique visual skills, part of the biomedical program based at a top-secret government lab in New Mexico. Thanks to his extensive training and ongoing enhancements, the SEAL could see far beyond the normal spectrum into infrared, ultraviolet and thermal ranges. His skills offered unique applications for military surveillance in high-risk, fast-extraction situations.

But excellent was never good enough for the head of the Foxfire program. A cold, untrusting bureaucrat, Lloyd Ryker demanded constant updates on all his assets.

"*Madonna* is doing just fine." Coolly Dakota logged on to the handheld unit and ripped through the tests, shifting easily from light source to light source. Like every man handpicked for the elite Foxfire team, Dakota liked difficult challenges, and he always played to win.

Izzy watched the lights flash, scoring Dakota's speed. "Want to tell me about Nell MacInnes?"

"Not much to tell. She saved those kids, no doubt about it." Dakota started to add a character assessment but decided against it. Saying more would amount to empty speculation.

"Did she say anything useful? Any comments about her father or her future plans?"

"We didn't get around to trading life stories," Dakota said flatly. "There was a gale up on the summit, if you recall. And now maybe you'll let me concentrate here."

For some reason the questions about Nell irritated Dakota. When he was done with the test, he handed the unit back to Izzy.

Across the snowy field, Nell was talking animatedly to a man in a bright green parka and high-tech climbing gloves. "Is that her partner?"

Izzy nodded. "He helped coordinate the rescue ascent. I understand he's climbed with Nell for almost twelve years."

Dakota watched the tall climber squeeze Nell's shoulder. "Are they sleeping together?"

"He's married with two kids."

"Which means nothing," Dakota said curtly. "Married men can screw around as much as single men. Maybe more."

Nell laughed at something her partner said, and for some reason that irritated Dakota, too.

"My research says no. The relationship is strictly about climbing."

"Any sign that he's involved in the theft?"

"I've got him on the radar just in case. He's had no large bank deposits that would indicate unusual payments." Izzy closed the digital unit and stowed it in a secure case.

"Neither did Nell." Dakota rubbed his shoulder idly. "Maybe he's being careful."

"I'll handle him. Right now I want you to calm down and rest."

"I'm not—"

"Of course you are. You've been wound up tight ever since you got down. I checked out Amanda Wilson and gave her one of the field hydration lines before she was flown out. You could use one too."

"I'm fine, Teague."

"Can it." Izzy slipped a syringe expertly into Dakota's arm. "There's a serious nutrient boost in that line. Shut up and let it take effect." Dakota muttered something gruff that made Izzy laugh. "I doubt that's physically possible, my friend, and I don't intend to find out."

As the liquid dripped into his arm, Dakota's gaze slid restlessly over the lower glen. He couldn't seem to stop thinking about Nell. What made her tick and how many secrets was she hiding? Both questions were suddenly very important.

Izzy followed Dakota's gaze. "What's eating at you?"

"Nell. She doesn't add up, Izzy, and I don't like things that don't add up." He took one last look across the loch, where Nell was laughing with her partner, piling ropes in a canvas bag.

The woman had guts to spare and a quick, clever brain. If things had been different he would have enjoyed a little recreational climbing with her. They could start on a cove in Thailand near the South China Sea.

A beach where clothing was optional sounded good.

The thought of Nell in a tiny string bikini—and no top—made muscles tighten all over Dakota's body. He let the 3-D fantasy smolder.

And then he put the thought away.

Never gonna happen, pal. She's the target and you're too smart to forget that.

Staying focused on the moment was the best way to stay alive.

Dakota's rules.

He glanced down at the sealed security file Izzy was holding out. "New developments?"

"An international terrorist group just took credit for the da Vinci theft via the Internet. Ryker wants you fully briefed within the hour. The mission just got elevated to a level-four priority."

Dakota watched the loch glitter silver beneath them as the chopper pilot returned, squinting into the wind. "What group?"

"The October Twelfth Brigade. They've been on our watch list for almost two years now."

"That's the same group who claimed credit for the theft of the Rembrandt last year?"

"One and the same. The painting never resurfaced, and we assume it was sold clandestinely." Izzy's eyes hardened. "I don't need to tell you the money will be used in very unpleasant ways."

"How much money?"

"The da Vinci could bring somewhere in the area of thirty million dollars."

Dakota said something low and vicious.

"My sentiments exactly. Meanwhile, no more surveillance. Our new orders are to locate that piece of art and make certain it does not leave U.S. soil at any cost." He pointed to the file in Dakota's hand. "Read it. We have new information from a prison source that Jordan MacInnes is involved. You're to use Nell to locate the painting. Use her in any way that's necessary," Izzy said coldly. "Is that clear?"

"I TOLD YOU already. I'm fine."

Despite Nell's protests, a young paramedic was scrubbing her hands with Betadine. When he pushed up her sleeve, she was surprised to see cuts and bruises covering her wrists. In all the chaos, she hadn't noticed.

"Bad night up there, I'm thinking. Nasty patch of weather you had." The paramedic glanced out at the remaining clouds that drifted across the dark summit of Blaven. "At least no one was killed."

"The cold was the worst part." Nell's teeth chattered a little. She was feeling dizzy, which irritated her. Fighting exhaustion, she rubbed her face with her free hand. "Where did my partner go?"

"He's helping to sort out the last kids. They're phoning their parents now."

"I should go help—"

"You'll stay right where you are. Your friend is managing fine."

Nell had trained with Eric and climbed with him on three continents. They had shared dangerous conditions, then traded stories when they came down. And after that Eric went home to his beautiful, understanding wife and two kids back in Idaho.

End of story.

There was no other man in Nell's life.

Nell looked up as she heard the roar of a motor.

"One of the choppers is pulling out." The paramedic glanced through the ambulance's rear window. "They seemed in quite a rush, according to my crew. Your American climber was aboard."

Nell shifted, trying to look out the window, seeing Dakota's outline inside the helicopter. So he was gone. No farewells or an exchange of phone numbers, just a swift, silent departure.

Which was for the best, wasn't it? There had been something too physical and intense about Dakota Smith.

"Did you need to speak with him? You look upset."

Nell stared out at the dark peaks trapped in heavy clouds. "No. He's just someone I met up on the mountain."

She felt an odd punch at her chest as the dark chopper lifted off.

He could have said goodbye.

He could have found time for that.

Well, she didn't care one way or another.

"I hear you've climbed at Chamonix."

Nell nodded, trying to ignore the chopper as it droned past. She didn't let men into her life, not ever.

No trust.

No leaning.

MacInnes rules.

"I thought I recognized your name. You took third prize, didn't you?"

Nell nodded, barely listening. In the gray light the chopper's black body grew smaller.

"It makes you feel alive," the paramedic said quietly. "Nothing can touch you up there. You'd know that feeling, I guess."

Nell knew exactly what he meant. Her art restoration work kept her busy, but her climbing kept her sane. She had to admit that Dakota Smith would have made one heck of a climbing partner. Maybe he could have been something more.

Instantly she forced away the thought.

"By the way, did you get the messages?"

"Messages?"

"Your father has been trying to reach you. The manager of the inn asked us to tell you that he had called six times. He said it was urgent that you phone him as soon as you returned."

"Did he say *why*?"

"I'm afraid not. But I'm almost done here. Then I'll drive you down to the inn."

Nell felt an odd prickle at her neck. Her father wouldn't have phoned her here unless it was something very serious. "You're sure he called six times?"

"That's what I was told."

Out over the Sea of Hebrides the big black helicopter thundered south and was swallowed up by the fog.

CHAPTER FIVE

Jackson Square Art District
San Francisco

JORDAN MACINNES SAT in a pair of worn leather slippers and watched night claim the San Francisco skyline. Home, he thought. Such as it was.

He closed his eyes, angry that he had bothered Nell with his urgent calls to Scotland. It was only natural that he needed to be certain she was safe, but he wished he hadn't bothered her with his worries. He'd served his seventeen years in prison and he knew how to protect his back. He'd also taken steps to protect Nell now that the shadows around him were closing in.

They'd never release him now. He'd finally accepted that and factored it into his final plans.

The phone rang beside his chair. He forced a smile when he heard his daughter's worried voice. "Nell? Of course I'm fine. Why aren't you asleep? Worrying about me? Now that's a waste of precious time. No, I'm not having any health problems." Jordan winced a little at the lie, but there would be a time and a place for explanations. "I shouldn't have called you like that, Nell. Sorry if I scared you."

But deep inside, the quiet man sitting in the darkness knew all the risks before him. He understood the kind of people he was dealing with, people who wouldn't hesitate to kill if they were crossed. As long as he did exactly what they wanted, he would be safe.

Even more important, Nell would be safe, too. He'd seen to her protection as his first priority.

As the bridge lights shimmered over the bay, Jordan MacInnes cross-examined his daughter about her Scottish climb and her upcoming conservation projects, keeping any uneasiness from his voice. But he kept thinking about the calls that came at odd hours of the night. Calls with rough, whispered warnings, a reminder that his life was always under scrutiny now. Everywhere he went, he was watched. And it was all because of his years of success—followed by one failed robbery that should have been the perfect crime. Every detail had been precisely planned for almost two years and no expense had been spared in buying insider information. But no one had expected an extra guard to key in and drop off a clean uniform off-shift at three in the morning. As a result, the guard had tripped over a set of glass cutters on the museum's stairs. Falling headfirst, he'd plunged over a banister and dropped two levels, his neck broken instantly.

A terrible accident, and the only mistake Jordan had ever made in his burglary career of almost two decades. Of course criminals always said that, didn't they?

He forced a smile into his voice. "I'm listening,

Nell. Of course I heard you. Stop worrying about the Tintoretto. No one has better hands than you do. I saw you clean that last Caravaggio, remember? The dealer was delighted."

With every calm word, he hid the bitter truth from his daughter. He'd sweated out every week of his prison sentence, determined to put the past behind him, but now he was being pulled right back into that world of shadows.

He couldn't let Nell be pulled in with him.

He stretched his right arm carefully, feeling a sudden throb at his elbow. With every weather shift the ache returned. The beating he'd received the night of his arrest eighteen years before hadn't helped. Nor had the later beatings he'd received from guards and fellow inmates during his years in prison.

Jordan blocked out the grim memories. All that mattered was the *now*.

The lean, white-haired man cupped his right elbow, wincing as fresh pain radiated out from the bone. The weather was definitely changing again.

He remembered how Nell had warned him to be prepared, that the world would look and sound different after his release. How right she had been. Wise and quiet and stubborn, his daughter was the only thing that mattered to him. He had failed her miserably by breaking the law and failed her yet again by being clumsy enough to get caught afterward.

Most of all he had failed her by indirectly causing the accident that had left a museum guard dead.

As Jordan MacInnes stared out at the Oakland Bay

Bridge, he felt his fear return. Finishing his prison sentence should have brought a measure of peace and a chance at happiness. But you never walked away from your past. He saw that all too clearly now.

Nell deserved a father she could rely on, a man she could be proud of. In the years he had left, Jordan MacInnes was determined to be both those things, even if it killed him.

"What did you say, honey?" When his daughter repeated her question, he frowned. "Watch that Chinese vermilion. Mercuric sulfide is toxic in minute amounts, no matter how careful you are." Nell knew all about toxic material safety, of course, but a father couldn't stop worrying.

Jordan was reaching for one of his old books on Renaissance pigments when he heard a click on the line. Another call was coming in. Another whispered warning.

He scanned the number.

Blocked.

Damned cowards.

But he was ready for them now. He trusted only three people in the world, and two of them knew about his dangerous plan. Even if he failed, Nell would be protected from the shadow world and those who refused to let him go.

"Lunch tomorrow? That sounds fine, Nell. I want to hear all about Scotland. You haven't said more than a few words about the climbs you and Eric made, and that's not like you."

Jordan MacInnes was almost certain he wouldn't be at that lunch, but he didn't want to alarm Nell. She would be told all she needed to know in due course. His old friend would see to that.

The white-haired thief with the aristocratic face stared out at the darkness, sensing the danger waiting in the shadows.

There was no turning back. Now his death might be the only gift he had left for Nell.

CHAPTER SIX

THE WIND OFF THE BAY was freezing.

Nell shivered as she rubbed her arms, glancing up at the fog that covered the Oakland Bay Bridge. For some reason the advancing white curtain reminded her of a gate opening slowly, swallowing all light and motion.

Nell forced away her uneasiness. Her windows were all closed, her doors locked. Her workroom alarm was set, which made her absolutely safe.

Of course you are. You always set your alarm when you work late. Stop dithering and finish the painting.

She had been uneasy since her return from Scotland the week before, and to her great irritation she hadn't been able to get Lieutenant Dakota Smith out of her mind, even during long days of intense restoration work.

Now that project was almost done. Looking down at Tintoretto's jewellike study of Saint George fighting a dragon, Nell didn't want to let go. Living in the mind of a genius could be extremely addictive.

But now the exquisite restoration was complete. She studied the area near the dragon's head and then put down her fine Russian red sable brush.

Done.

There was nothing more to add, no detail that would intrude to place *her* vision over Tintoretto's. No art restorer allowed personal technique to challenge the integrity of the original image.

The moment Nell was finished, exhaustion struck. The restoration process required fanatical focus and patience. When you were hunched over a sixteenth-century masterpiece, you couldn't afford even one slip of the hand. So you never let down your guard. Not ever.

And that also happened to be one of Nell's unshakable life rules, right up there under *don't trust* and *don't lean.* If most people would consider that cynical, it was too damned bad.

Life had not exactly been a kind teacher.

She rubbed her face. After long hours of meticulous brushwork cleaning the canvas, her eyes burned, her fingers ached, and her shoulders felt as if they'd been impaled by razors.

One more reason that Nell was looking forward to walking home after closing her workshop. San Francisco's cool, salty air always helped her loosen up and put the work behind her.

After that, she would call her father to check in. If she was lucky, she might get the truth about his urgent calls to her in Scotland. For the moment, he was sticking to his story of sudden chest pains that had made him panic and call her from the emergency room.

Nell didn't buy it—she knew her father well enough to know that he cared little about his own health. He was worrying about something else. She just didn't know what.

She locked her workshop door and triggered the alarms for active monitoring, jogging in place to warm up. So far she'd been lucky, with no robberies or thefts of any sort, but she made it a point not to take chances. Her alarm system was the best you could buy. Even her father had approved of it.

She stretched from side to side, savoring the silence of the street while mist curled past in pale tendrils. The cool air felt good on her face as she settled into a stride up Geary Street.

A few blocks later she noticed him, a lone figure in black. He'd been half a block behind her for almost five minutes now, which didn't do much for the coincidence theory.

Nell picked up her pace. Geary Street was deserted, its boutiques and wine bars closed for the night. There *could* be a good reason for a man to be following her; she just couldn't think what it was.

At least she had her pepper spray.

Nell sprinted across the street and cut down an alley that led to an all-night coffee shop with poetry readings fuelled by unlimited caffeine. Right now she wanted bright lights and warm bodies.

She was one block from the shop's beckoning lights when she heard the snap of gravel behind her. A hand snaked around her neck, groping for her throat.

She reacted before panic could set in, spraying him and then tucking her chin as she snapped forward and sent the man flying over her head. Blood geysered as he hit the dirty concrete and moaned brokenly.

Nell kept on moving toward the end of the alley.

Maybe the creep would think twice before hitting on another woman walking alone at night.

Or not—given that more figures had appeared from behind a parked car. She sprinted to the wall at the far side of the street.

One of her pursuers pulled something long and narrow from his pocket.

A big cardboard box rustled near her feet. Nell recognized the homeless man who looked out of the torn box that was his current home. She had made a practice of leaving him a sandwich or a jar of his favorite honey maple almonds on her night walks.

His grimy face creased in a smile. "How ya doin', Legs?"

"I've been better," she muttered.

Her first attacker was back on his feet now. The two men crossed the street, headed toward Nell.

"What are you doing?" The old man stood up unsteadily, one hand on the graffiti-covered wall. "Leave her alone, you shits."

The closer man, a Caucasian with gang tattoos on one arm, gave two vicious kicks of his steel-toed boot and crumpled the old man onto the pavement.

Nell reacted in fury, kicking his legs out from under him. When he toppled, she twisted sharply to the left and swung a piece of discarded plumber's pipe toward the other man's face. He was big, but Nell was quicker and she knew these streets and alleys well from her frequent walks home. Jumping onto a cement wall, she struck hard at the side of the man's head, catching him unaware.

Creep number two hit the alley, gurgling as his face slammed into the greasy pavement.

That had to hurt.

Something rolled across the ground near her feet. Nell realized it was a syringe. Had it been meant for her?

She felt her hands start to shake. She tried to think, digging in her pocket for her cell phone to call 911.

Off to her left, the homeless man gave a groan and spit out two decayed teeth. When he saw the attackers out cold, he gave Nell a crooked smile. "Hell, Legs, where were you when I needed you back in January '68? My boys and me coulda used you when we stormed the crap out of Hue."

"A little before my time." She helped the old man to his feet, dug in her dropped handbag and held out some bills. "Dessert's on me tonight. Watch yourself out here."

"Count on it. Got my Purple Heart to protect me." He pulled out a medal from beneath his stained jacket, the ribbon caught around his gnarled fingers.

One of the nation's highest honors, the medal was the only thing of value left to a forgotten hero. Talk about crappy unfair.

"Thanks for the ducats, Legs."

"Anytime."

Nell was dialing 911 when she saw two men slide out of a gray van parked across the street. Under a broken streetlight she noticed that the closer man had a small pistol level at his leg.

She fought a sickening sense of fear. This was no simple robbery. They had come here for *her.* But why?

Were they after the Tintoretto? Maybe another piece of art in her workshop?

The old man in the torn jacket pushed Nell toward the far end of the alley. "R-run, honey. They got—"

A sudden crack of gunfire cut him off. Nell saw blood splash over his pile of boxes. He groaned and then a bullet screamed past her ear.

Nell pushed past her fear, struggling to keep her mind sharp and focused. Above all, she knew that fear was her worst enemy. Her father's friends had taught her that, along with an array of carefully selected judo and kickboxing moves. She had never forgotten any of those lessons.

But she was running on caffeine fumes now, exhausted from a twelve-hour day, and there was no telling how many more of the creeps were waiting in nearby cars.

Nell scanned the shadows and then grabbed two heavy lids from a row of garbage cans. She threw the lids at her pursuers, then ducked behind a VW bus with four flat tires. Bullets drilled the garbage can lids and cracked the windows of the VW. Falling glass rained down around her.

Nell's heart pounded as she peered through the broken windows, looking for fresh cover.

A low voice called out of the darkness. "Stay where you are, Nell. We don't want to hurt you."

They knew her *name*?

Fighting panic, she threw a third garbage can lid behind her, then crawled along the foot of the wall, staying low until she reached a smaller street behind a dilapidated warehouse.

A bright beam of halogen lights cut through the darkness, blinding her.

"All we want to do is talk, Nell. Your father will explain everything to you."

Her father? Surely he didn't *know* these people.

Fighting a sense of horror, Nell crawled on in the darkness. Could her father be involved with men like these? He'd sworn that he was done with stealing and she'd believed him.

A bullet whined over her head, hitting a big white Dumpster at the far end of the alley. Nell tried to remember how far it was from the Dumpster to the nearest cross street.

Ten feet and she'd be eating lead.

"Last warning, Nell."

She kept inching backward. Her foot struck an empty can, the sound echoing down the narrow alley.

A bullet hit the wall near her shoulder. Cement fragments tore at her cheek and she tasted blood on her lip.

They were cutting her off.

She saw a sudden movement at the end of the alley, beyond the Dumpster. She froze, boxed in completely now. There were too many of them.

"Nell, over here." The voice from the darkness seemed familiar. "Turn around."

She blinked, trying to place the voice. A client? No, not that. Scotland.

Dakota?

"Keep moving six more feet. I've got your back covered."

CHAPTER SEVEN

NELL BACKED UP slowly, straining to breathe, straining to make sense of why this man had suddenly reappeared in her life. "How did you find—"

"No time for that. Just keep moving." He sounded very calm, not remotely surprised to see men with guns following Nell and circling warily.

In one smooth movement, he pulled her toward him and then shot out the halogen light. Behind them, bullets cracked on cement, the noise deafening in the confined alley. Rough fingers gripped Nell's arm and then she was yanked back behind the protective metal walls of the Dumpster, out of range of the gunfire.

Where were the police when you needed them? Hadn't anyone reported the disturbance?

"Three feet behind you, Nell. *Focus.* Reach up and you'll feel the top of a metal fire escape ladder. Pull yourself up and move. Don't look back and don't stop, no matter what happens down here."

Nell didn't even consider arguing. She was already grabbing for the ladder. "What about you?" she said breathlessly.

"I've got unfinished business here." His voice was cold. *"Move."*

Nell didn't hesitate. With one jump, her hand closed around the middle rung of the fire escape and she swung her legs up.

But when she reached the third rung, a retaining brace pulled free, dumping her and twelve feet of rusted metal right back in the middle of the alley.

"Go out the alley behind me," Dakota snapped. "My car is the black Explorer at the crosswalk. Here's the key."

He shoved something into her hand. "Drive home, lock your door and stay there."

Footsteps hammered toward the far end of the alley, cutting off that route of escape.

"Forget it." He sounded irritated. "Stay right behind me, but keep clear of my right hand."

His shooting hand.

But Nell wasn't about to slow him down against what looked like increasingly bad odds. With both ends of the alley blocked, that left only *up*.

She ran past the fire escape and grabbed a heavy rain gutter. A bullet ripped over her right shoulder. Pain burned through her neck as the round gouged a piece of brick out of the wall.

Ignoring her pain, Nell pulled her way hand over hand up the gutter until she reached the roof. To her right, a limestone wall rose to the neighboring apartment building.

Another bullet tore through the air beneath her, nicking her calf. Certain that he could handle himself better alone, she grabbed the end of a heavy gutter and climbed onto a second-story patio.

She had to get to Dakota's car and call the police.

She heard the first wail of distant sirens as she hit the adjoining wall at a run, channeled her momentum up into a vertical walk, then swung her arm to the wooden flagpole near the roof. Rocking hard, she jammed one ankle into the eaves.

Standard moves for a free climber.

Except for the bullets, she thought grimly. But the rounds appeared to be high, going over her head, and she had the feeling the attack was meant to be a kidnapping, not murder.

The same wasn't true for her homeless friend...

Or for Dakota.

The thought stole her breath, freezing her in place. Her fingers were bleeding, both elbows rubbed raw. Panting, she forced herself to move, pulling herself up over the eaves and onto the roof. Below her the gunfire cleared. When she peered down into the darkness, no one was there. The alley was empty.

Her fingers locked on Dakota's car keys, shoved deep in her pocket. She didn't have a clue who these people were, or how they knew her name, or why they had mentioned her father.

Currently, she had half a dozen art projects in the process of restoration, but none of them was exceptionally valuable. Private dealers all over the city had more valuable art in their back rooms awaiting sale. So she didn't think the attack was for simple theft.

She sprinted down the opposite fire escape to

Dakota's black Explorer and jammed in the key, relieved when the big motor growled to life.

They had mentioned her father. This had to involve him.

The thought left her sick at heart. In his criminal career Jordan MacInnes had made dozens of resolute, life-and-death friends. Unfortunately, he'd made just as many enemies, competitors with no scruples and very long memories. Had one of them targeted him now?

Nell checked the street, but there was no sign of Dakota or her attackers. As she drove slowly north, she passed two police cruisers with sirens flashing headed the way she'd just come. She briefly considered pulling over and flagging them down.

And tell them what? *My father, who happens to be an ex-con, may be in some kind of trouble and I may be a target, too.*

Yeah, like that would work.

Especially since any hint of contact with other criminals would send her father right back to prison for parole violation.

As a compromise, Nell placed a shaky 911 call to report a wounded homeless man in the alley. After leaving the exact address, she hung up before they could ask for her name or number. They might be able to trace her cell phone, but it was a risk she had to take for her friend's sake.

Driving through the dark streets, Nell fought a wave of exhaustion. She didn't feel safe, even at the door to her apartment, where she stood frozen, listening for any sign of intruders. But there was no sound except the low whir of her refrigerator. Her locks had not been touched.

Was she really safe?

The past hour was a blur, and she gave up trying to process it. Instead she dropped her purse and jacket and headed for the bathroom. The sight of her face in the mirror stopped her cold. She had the beginning of a black eye, cuts on both arms, and a long welt down her right cheek. Her condition would have been far worse if the SEAL hadn't appeared out of the darkness to protect her. Nell still couldn't figure out how he'd found her—or why. Only one person would have that answer.

Her hands were shaking as she dialed her father. After six unsuccessful tries, she tossed the phone down on her bed. Nothing made sense.

Her clock read 3:04 a.m.

Impossible to believe that in sixty-eight minutes her life had collapsed in on itself like a black hole, dropping her straight into a nightmare.

Meanwhile, she had cuts to attend to. Quickly, she bandaged her arms, then washed her face. One of the bullets had grazed her calf, and she cleaned that next. She'd had enough falls while climbing that the shallow wound didn't panic her.

Finally done, she looked around her silent apartment, trying to plan her next move. The logical choice was to find her father and pray that he had a solid explanation. If not, she would have to go to the police.

Cool air drifted across her face. Out of the corner of her eye Nell saw the curtains drift out above her kitchen window. She swung around so fast that she dropped a box of bandages.

A shadow crossed the kitchen.

Dakota was back, and he looked mad as hell.

CHAPTER EIGHT

"YOU'RE...SAFE." NELL heard her voice crack. She felt cornered as he studied her in taut silence. "Allan, the homeless man on the street—did you see if he was okay?"

"An ambulance picked him up. He was loudly demanding food and a hot bath when they left. I take that for a yes."

Nell felt a wave of relief, but it didn't last long. Dakota looked hard and distant, like a complete stranger.

An *angry* stranger.

He stalked closer, eyes narrowed on her face. His powerful shoulders were outlined by a black turtleneck, his legs encased in dark jeans. This was definitely a man you didn't want to mess with, Nell thought.

But he owed her some answers, and she was going to get them. "Why are you here?"

"You tell me."

Nell crossed her arms and fought the urge to back up. "I don't know what you mean." Why did the man seem to fill her living room?

"I doubt that."

Nell ignored the challenge in his voice. "You're certain that my friend was conscious when the ambulance came?"

"Positive. Now why don't you stop worrying about him, and start worrying about what just happened to *you*. Those men in the alley weren't playing around, Nell. Neither am I."

"Did you—are they—alive?"

"One took a round in the chest." Dakota's voice was clipped. "He's gone. Two others got banged up. They're in custody now, and I'll be interested in what they have to say. The rest ran when the cruisers got close. Why don't you give me your version?"

Nell cradled her bandaged arm. "I don't have a version. You're not making any sense. And how do you know where I live?"

"My question first. What were you doing in that alley?"

She stood rigidly. "Walking home from work. Then *boom*—those men appeared." Her voice wavered. "And if you hadn't arrived when you did, I probably wouldn't be here."

The cool look in his eyes told her he agreed. "Nice move on the rain gutter. But if you'd lost your hold, I'd be scraping you off the pavement right now." Frowning, he lifted one of her bandaged hands. "It was reckless and unnecessary."

"But I *didn't* lose my hold, and it gave you time to deal with them without me slowing you down. So it was hardly unnecessary." She pulled away, angry at him and angry that her life was slipping out of control. She needed to think, but she couldn't, not with Dakota studying her as if she was some kind of one-celled lab specimen. "If you won't tell me why you're here, you'd better leave."

He did some muttering, then stalked toward her kitchen, ignoring her completely.

"What are you doing?"

"Getting some water. It's been a trying night."

"I said, I want you to leave or I'll—"

"Take one." A water bottle flew in her direction. Nell caught it by instinct.

"Go get packed."

"Packed for what? Why should I?"

"We're leaving. Together. In ten minutes."

Oh, sure she was.

He stared at the luminous dial of his watch and pushed a button that changed one of the sets of numbers.

Nell had never seen a watch do *that* before. The fiber of his turtleneck seemed strange too. Heavier than cotton, it looked smooth and tensile; it also appeared to shed water. Nell stared at the drops that dotted his sleeve.

Dotted, but didn't sink in.

She watched more letters scroll over the face of his watch. "Who *are* you?"

"Someone you'll have to trust," he said flatly. "Whether you like it or not."

"I *don't* like it, Navy. And I'm going nowhere with you." She didn't bother to explain that trust wasn't part of her vocabulary.

But she wanted answers about the thugs who had

followed her into the alley and what her father had to do with them. Clearly, this man knew what was going on. It was equally clear that he assumed she knew too. "Look, let's talk."

"Later." He walked past her down the hall toward her closet. "Where's your suitcase?"

When he saw that she hadn't moved, he took a long drink from his water bottle and pulled a file from the backpack angled against her antique coffee table. "Okay, I'll spell it out. I need you to do a job." He spoke curtly, as if he wasn't happy about the prospect. "It's all there in the file. You can read it on the way."

"This is a joke, right? I barely know you, and I have a full schedule of restoration commissions for the next six months. Even if I didn't, why would I consider—"

"Because you don't have any choice. And because those men in the alley won't be the last ones who come looking for you. Most of all, because this is the only way you can help your father."

HE WAS EITHER GOING to strangle her or pin her against the wall and tear off all her clothes, Dakota thought grimly. Right now the odds were running about fifty-fifty.

He never lost his calm, never broke a sweat. Not during a mission and definitely not with a woman. But for some reason Nell MacInnes punched through his detachment and hit raw nerves he didn't know he possessed. She hadn't fallen apart in the alley, and she'd surprised him when she'd climbed up that rain gutter, all edgy grace and fearlessness.

Her move up on the roof had scared the hell out of him. He knew she was an excellent climber, but the fool could have lost her grip and landed on her head. End of story.

And now he was stuck with her.

Dakota cut off a curse. Things were starting to get complicated and he hated complicated. If he had a choice, he'd let Izzy handle Nell while he took over the backup surveillance, but asking for a reassignment would be admitting failure, which was not a word in his vocabulary.

He could handle one smart woman with a bad attitude.

What he couldn't handle was the way this whole mission was starting to feel wrong. Everyone from the FBI to the head of Foxfire assumed that Nell's father was back at work, orchestrating a complex theft within days of his release from prison. They also believed that his daughter was involved. The local FBI team had made that much crystal clear in their reports.

It just didn't feel right.

He had watched Nell cross an icy ridge in Scotland, showing quick judgment and courage. She had herded the teens and gotten them to safety at considerable risk to herself. No whining, and no backing down. She was many things—prickly, stubborn and a little reckless, but Dakota wasn't convinced that she was a thief.

Not because she wasn't smart enough. Not because she didn't have the skills. It was her personality that didn't fit the pattern. Doing undercover work, you learned to read people fast, and Dakota had pegged

Nell for a loner, while a complicated job like the museum theft required a big, well-knit crew, long weeks of coordination and close communication as well as dependence on one another.

Not Nell's style at all, he thought.

But Jordan MacInnes was a different story. The man was smart enough and manipulative enough. According to his file, he had highly placed criminal connections scattered over every continent. The art fraud experts in the FBI were convinced that MacInnes was back at work with a vengeance, and Dakota could buy that. But his stubborn, gutsy daughter?

He watched Nell pace the room, her face wary but intent. She wasn't beautiful, he thought. She didn't have perfect features or the kind of cool sexuality that would make a man turn to watch her in a crowd.

But for all that he couldn't seem to take his eyes off her.

When they'd huddled together inside the tent, with her legs wrapped around his waist, he'd wanted to do a whole lot more than talk. He couldn't get the memory of her body out of his mind. He woke up dreaming of how she'd feel when he drove her over the edge to a blinding climax. Starkly erotic fantasies involving her had already cost him more sleep than he cared to admit.

The SEAL shook his head. He had to forget how her body had felt on that snowy cliff. Sex with Nell MacInnes wasn't happening in this or any other lifetime. She was his target to assess, the key to the location of thirty million dollars worth of missing art.

She was *work*, nothing more.

Since the museum break-in, Dakota had been fully briefed about her habits. He knew her usual route home, the names of all her friends and her favorite foods, along with everything else of importance in her life. He would use all those details to assess her response and ensure that she followed orders. This blood-stirring response to her body would change nothing.

Her cell phone rang on the table, and she reached out to answer it, but Dakota cut her off. His hand circled her wrist. "Let it ring."

He felt her stiffen, her cell phone dropping to the big leather sofa. "You can't make me—"

"I just did. I will keep on doing it, too. Right up until my mission is complete."

Her face paled in the glow of the overhead light. "Do you always treat people this way?"

"Only when it's necessary."

The phone stopped ringing. He saw her glance down, reading the caller ID. Dakota didn't bother checking, because he knew Izzy was already in place nearby, monitoring her phone and e-mails.

She still hadn't opened the file.

"Are you afraid to read it?"

"Tell me instead."

Dakota crossed his arms. "I'll talk while you pack."

"No, *now*." She sat down on the sofa beside her phone, but made no move to reach for it. "Exactly *what* is this urgent job that I need to do?" she said tightly.

Dakota prowled the room, choosing his words carefully. "Last month a newly discovered, unpublished and unrecorded piece of art was brought to the

National Gallery for assessment. Two weeks later it was stolen."

"What period and provenance?" Nell sat up a little straighter, frowning. "And how did they get in?"

He watched her face closely but saw only questions. There was no guilt or calculation. He moved closer, reading the heat spots of her body using his enhanced vision. Normal flow at pulse points. Normal respiration heat patterns. She wasn't trying to block him.

Which proved nothing.

Dakota narrowed his focus. His orders were to see how much she knew. His Foxfire training gave him the ability to assess changes in eye response, pulse rate and skin temperature. All those factors would indicate whether she was involved in the theft or not.

"It was an English landscape painting," he said. "Very old, very rare."

As he spoke, he watched Nell's face. There was no sudden flare of heat. No spikes in pulse or pupil dilation at his lie. Not satisfied, he eased into the deeper skills he'd been taught as a Foxfire agent, reading her emotions through thermal shifts and eye response. But Dakota picked up only curiosity and confusion.

She didn't know about a theft at the National Gallery. And that first piece of evidence made him doubt everything else he'd been told by Ryker and their FBI contacts. How much else was wrong with this mission?

"So a painting was stolen. I don't understand why you need me?"

Dakota crossed his arms. "Because we already know who took it and we have to steal it back."

"I don't *steal* things, Lieutenant."

"But your father does."

"Did." Nell glared at the unopened file on her table. "Not anymore."

He sipped some water, watching her face, checking her. It was time for the detail that would hurt her most.

"We know this piece art was stolen from a locked room in one of the most secure institutions in the world." He waited a heartbeat, watching her face. "The thief or thieves were exceptionally skilled and left nothing behind but a single fingerprint. The print belonged to the president of the United States."

Nell's hands clenched.

"Obviously, we do not consider the president to be a suspect. Given the thief's m.o.—"

"No," she whispered. She shot to her feet. "You're wrong."

"I'm not wrong, Nell. You know what that mark means. Your father always left a single carefully trans ferred presidential fingerprint behind when he stole a piece of art. It was his signature."

"My *father* did not do this." Her voice tightened. "I know that was his pattern, but half of the law enforcement personnel in this country knew it, too. It's hardly a secret now. Any thief could have done this." Color flared in her face, and Dakota picked up shock and anger. The anger came in waves, registered in a sudden thermal flare at her face and neck, signs that could not be hidden from him. No, Nell definitely hadn't known about this detail of the theft, either. She was fully convinced of her father's innocence.

"*Get out*. You've wasted enough of my time."

"Those are the facts, Nell. Why don't we call your father and ask him about those men in the alley. Let's see what he says."

"You weren't on vacation in Scotland," she said slowly. "That was a lie. You were *following* me, weren't you?"

When Dakota started to counter with a question, Nell cut him off. "I told you to get out." She gestured furiously toward the door. "I don't have time for more lies and accusations. I've lived with too many in my life."

"Your father's in trouble, Nell. The only way to help him is by telling me the truth. All of it."

"I don't—"

Outside in the hall the elevator chimed softly and footsteps crossed the corridor. Nell's doorbell rang twice. She turned, frowning at the clock.

Dakota took her arm and shook his head, one finger covering her lips.

The doorbell rang again.

"F.B.I. Ms. MacInnes, open the door."

Dakota felt her flinch as if she'd been hit. "Did *you* call them?" she whispered.

He shook his head and pulled out his cell phone.

"Ms. MacInnes, please answer the door. We know you're in there. The doorman saw you come home."

Dakota's hands tightened on her arm. "Ask them for names and badge numbers," he whispered.

Nell looked at him as if he was crazy. "You think it's someone else out there?"

"I told you there would be other men coming."

Nell swallowed hard and then asked for their ID numbers. Dakota quietly relayed the information to Izzy via cell phone, then nodded. "They check out. You'd better see them. I'd suggest you tell them no more than necessary and leave out what happened in the alley unless they ask directly. Leave me out, too."

A muscle worked at her jaw as she watched him grab his file and backpack and move quietly into the bedroom, closing the door partway.

The doorbell rang again. Dakota found a position where he could see the middle of the room and the couch and then he waited, still and silent.

The FBI was supposed to be updating Izzy on all developments, but government agencies were well-known to play power games. Dakota's rule was to trust no one until you had solid proof or clear orders to do otherwise.

He watched Nell open the door warily.

"Nell MacInnes?"

"Yes."

"I'm Agent Fuller and this is Agent Kolowitz. May we come in?"

"Do I have a choice?" Nell said coldly.

"We could come back with a warrant and twenty other agents and trash your apartment."

"There's no need. I've got nothing to hide." Nell held open the door, reading the woman's badge. "Agent Amy Fuller. I'll remember that name."

Agent Fuller was a thin woman with sharp gray eyes. She scanned the apartment, then tossed a sealed envelope onto Nell's coffee table while her partner, short and heavily muscled, sat down on the sofa.

Nell stared at his holstered gun, visible beneath his jacket. "What do you want?"

"Tell us what you know about the da Vinci," the female agent said curtly.

Nell frowned. "The one in the Louvre? The ones in the Uffizi? Which da Vinci do you mean, Agent Fuller?"

The woman's face reddened. "Patience was never my strong point, Ms. MacInnes. Either you cooperate now or I'll have your ass locked up in a cell so you don't see daylight for five years. Do we understand each other?"

"Perfectly."

The agent opened a small notebook. "Do you know a man named Vincent de Vito?"

"He's an old friend of my father's."

"Vincent de Vito of San Francisco—alias Vincent Mosconi, alias Vito Corso."

"I wouldn't know about any aliases."

"But he works with your father, using his criminal contacts."

"I wouldn't know about any criminal contacts. He is just a friend."

"That must be very convenient, having a known organized crime figure on tap for a favor. Did he help you and your father set up the theft from the National Gallery last month?"

Nell's expression turned stony. "I've never heard a more outrageous and ungrounded set of lies. Does speculation pass for field research these days at the FBI? If so, Agent Fuller, I can see why we haven't won the war on terrorism yet."

"We're losing nothing." The federal agent tossed a set of photos on the coffee table. "Take a look at those surveillance photos, Ms. MacInnes. They show your father and Vinnie de Vito having dinner at the Golden Szechuan restaurant in Berkeley last week."

Nell shrugged. "They make an excellent hot-and-sour soup. Highest scores in Zagat's, I understand."

"They didn't go there for the soup, *Bambi*." Agent Fuller smiled thinly. "They went for the strategy session. Perhaps you'll recognize who is sitting at the table to their right."

Nell looked down. Dakota watched her face intently, noting the shifting thermal waves that colored her cheeks and neck, red and mottled yellow.

Discomfort.

Anger

Uncertainty.

"Go on, Ms. MacInnes. Tell me what you see in the pictures."

"I don't know him."

The agent tossed more pictures on the table. "Yussef Zayed. He's currently at the top of our terror watch lists."

"A coincidence." Nell's voice was a whisper. "It... must be." She didn't understand and she didn't like it, Dakota thought.

"Don't waste our time. With all banking transactions closely monitored post-9/11, art and antiquities theft provides an excellent means to funnel money to terrorist organizations. To terror organizations like the ones run by Zayed, Ms. MacInnes. We've seen it in Italy. We've seen it in Iraq, and now we're seeing it right here in the United States."

"The U.S. has never shown any incidence of terrorist involvement in art theft," Nell said angrily. "Most art thefts are for financial gain, often with specific pieces chosen in advance for illicit buyers abroad. Any professional watching the art market knows that. You're barking up the wrong tree with this."

"Wrong answer. If you remain uncooperative, I'll haul you to Washington in cuffs and we'll finish this talk in a cell and be sure the word gets out." The agent smiled faintly. "Goodbye reputation. Goodbye fine art restoration career."

Dakota's hands clenched. Now *he* didn't like what he was hearing. And why hadn't Foxfire been briefed about the Zayed connection with Jordan MacInnes?

Nell's face was pale, but she stood very straight. In Dakota's careful assessment, she showed no signs of excessive heart rate or stress triggered by guilt. "Those photos don't show a conversation taking place. It's just men having good Chinese food. Everything else you've said is speculation."

"If that's the way you want it." Agent Fuller pulled out a pair of handcuffs. "Nell MacInnes, I am holding you as a material witness in a federal terrorist investigation and—"

Before she could cuff Nell, Dakota strode into the room. In one sharp movement he sent the cuffs flying onto the floor. "Talk time is over, Agent Fuller." He raised an eyebrow as two 9 mm handguns leveled on his chest.

"Trust me, you really *don't* want to do that."

CHAPTER NINE

"STEP BACK," Agent Fuller ordered coldly. "Then drop your cell phone on the floor."

Dakota let the phone he was holding fall onto Nell's carpet. "Before you land in more serious trouble, I suggest you call my superior at the DOD."

The woman frowned at him. "Hands in the air where I can see them. *Both* of you."

"Calm down. No one is going for a gun. I'm here conducting an investigation, as you'll find out if you call the Department of Defense." He rapped out a number with a 202 area code.

The other agent studied Dakota, then glanced at Amy Fuller. "Do you think we should—"

"I'll handle this," she snapped. "Get his ID from his wallet."

Dakota didn't move as the man searched his pockets.

"Nothing here. No wallet, no keys, no money. The man's clean."

Agent Fuller's gaze never left Dakota's face as she pulled out her cell phone, dialed the number Dakota had given and waited for a connection. "Agent Fuller, FBI. I have a man here who claims—"

She stopped, frowning as she listened to someone at the other end. "My badge number? Who am I speaking to?"

She went quiet again. Her eyes turned dark as she listened.

Ten seconds later she snapped her phone shut, motioned to her partner to take the photos and envelope from the coffee table and then turned without a word, letting the door slam shut behind her when she left.

"Good riddance, whoever you were." Nell took a long breath. "So you're not in the navy. You're with the Department of Defense."

"No reason I can't be with both," Dakota said coolly.

"I don't want to know anything more. All I want is for you to leave."

"I can't do that."

She spun and lunged for her phone, but Dakota's hand held her where she was. "Making me leave won't change anything. You and your father are in serious trouble, Nell."

She stared down at his fingers, locked around her wrist. "You're hurting me, Lieutenant."

He loosened his grip, frowning. "Sit down. We need to talk."

"And what if I say no? Will those FBI agents return? Or will your police friends take care of me the way they handled my father the night he was arrested? Will they break my nose and smash a few ribs to make a point? I saw them do it," she said hoarsely. "Even though he didn't resist arrest, they still beat him. But no one listened to me then and no one will listen to me now."

That part hadn't been in her file. Dakota made a mental note to ask Izzy about the details of her father's arrest. Meanwhile, he was starting to understand her general lack of trust.

"The stolen art was a da Vinci, they said." She stood very still. "The story you told me was another lie. You'll never leave my father alone. He'll always be the one you people suspect first."

"You're wasting precious time, Nell. Do you want your father back behind bars? He won't last another ten years there, not with the cancer they discovered last year."

He watched her face whiten, watched her sway as if he'd kicked her.

"Cancer?" she whispered.

She hadn't known that detail either. Her father must have kept it from her.

"He was diagnosed in prison. I'm sorry, Nell." Dakota watched her work through the possibilities, all of them bleak. If her father went back to prison he would probably die there. On the outside, with the best medical care possible and support from his friends and family, he would have a much greater chance of survival and a better quality of life.

Dakota didn't particularly like the choice he had forced on her, but there was no time for subtlety; they needed a thief to catch a thief before the da Vinci was spirited out of the country. Only Nell could persuade her father to give himself up—and turn in the people who provided access to international terrorist networks.

Clearly, she didn't like the choices he was giving her.

Dakota watched her fingers at the sleeve of her white shirt. *Fold.*

Unfold.

She turned, staring blindly at the wall of photographs from mountain ascents in France and Germany and Scotland, hanging beside the framed gloves she'd worn on her winning climb at Chamonix.

Fold.

Unfold.

"What's your answer, Nell?"

She rubbed her bandaged arm slowly. All her stubborn energy seemed to have drained away.

"I'm going to pack. Then you can tell me where we're going…and what I have to do for you."

CHAPTER TEN

NELL WALKED blindly into her bedroom, lost in a blur of shock and pain.

She pulled sweatshirts and outdoor clothes from her closet without really seeing them. She couldn't believe that her father was involved in the theft of the da Vinci. He'd given her his word, swearing on her mother's photo and the Bible itself, assuring Nell that his old life of theft was finished forever.

And she *believed* him. He wouldn't break his solemn vow to her.

Glancing through the doorway, she saw Dakota talking quietly on a cell phone, probably tracking her father or requesting updates about the stolen art, but thoughts of intrigue and theft faded before the rest of his bleak news.

Her father was dying.

Why hadn't he given her a single hint? Didn't he realize that you didn't *spare* the ones you loved? You shared and confided and wept when you had to, and then you asked for their strength when you needed it. She knew that her father had tried to protect her and now it was time to protect him.

Nell closed her eyes, battling hot tears. She would do whatever it took to keep him from going back to prison. She would vanish and search until she found the real thief, because she didn't trust the FBI or Dakota Smith or anyone else the government sent. This search would be hers and hers alone.

But where would she start?

When her cell phone vibrated outside on the coffee table, she ignored it. It might be her climbing partner, who had stayed behind in Scotland, but the only call she wanted to take was from her father, and she couldn't talk to him while the SEAL was nearby.

Listening to the rising wind, Nell sorted through everything Dakota had told her. Proving her father's innocence would not be easy. An informed enemy had revived her father's signature mark of a presidential print left behind at every robbery. That detail had been kept from the press and the public up to the present, though it would be available to law enforcement insiders, along with those in her father's tightly knit circle.

That left a wide pool of candidates.

Closing her eyes, she forced herself to relax, muscle by muscle, the way she did before an important climb.

Think, don't react.

When she looked up, she saw her home phone at an angle on her dresser. She shoved the handset into her pocket and grabbed a pile of clothes from her dresser. Dakota glanced through the open door, then looked down, pulling out a small notebook and a pen.

When he turned away, Nell hit her speed dial. She had only seconds to find some answers.

JORDAN MACINNES couldn't sleep again.

He nudged aside the plain cotton curtains and glanced out at the dark street. There had been no more calls, no more threats, but he knew it was simply a matter of time before they came for him.

Too many enemies.

Too many secrets.

Uneasiness seeped into his bones like December wind through a broken window, and after a life spent skirting danger, MacInnes never ignored his intuition. He glanced at the clock, wondering if it was too late to call Nicholas Draycott in England.

A moment later his phone rang. He lifted the receiver, half-listening to the first drops of rain on his window.

No caller ID available.

"Hello?"

"Just listen. I can't talk long." His daughter's voice was low and tense.

"Ne—"

"No time." Nell sounded out of breath. "The FBI was just here about the National Gallery theft. Did you *do* it?"

She couldn't know about the stolen da Vinci. Only one of his oldest friends knew, besides his contact in England.

"Did you steal the art?" she hissed.

Jordan MacInnes gripped the phone. "No, love. That I did not." A simple answer for something that had become dangerously deep and complicated, but a phone call was no place to make difficult explanations.

There were still things she needed to know in case the worst happened, and he didn't make it through the next week. "Just listen. Write down this number and keep it safe. Show it to no one. I don't know its full importance yet, but I have grave suspicions." He rattled off five numbers. "Memorize them."

"But I need to know why men came after me tonight. They said they wanted to talk to you."

Jordan's breath caught. They'd been far faster than he'd expected. "Listen to me, Nell. You need to leave. Don't take a bag, don't make a call, just *go*. I should have told you sooner, but they promised me—" Panic cut like a knife. It was never supposed to touch Nell. They had promised him *this* above all else.

But only a fool believed in promises, Jordan thought. "Call Nicholas in England, then go climb a mountain. Fly to Thailand or Tibet, anyplace remote, where they can't find you."

"Where *who* can't find me?"

"Later. You need to move, Nell. Go now."

"It's too late to run. They…were outside waiting for me tonight," she whispered. "And then the FBI came a few minutes ago. You should have told me." The words were heavy with despair. "You should have told me about *everything*, including the cancer."

Pain blocked Jordan's throat. He had hoped to keep his illness from Nell until the end. There was no point in adding to her pain when he'd caused her too much already. "I couldn't tell you. I'm sorry, Nell. Call Nicholas, please. Don't trust *anyone* else. Nicholas will explain." Jordan frowned. He heard a sharp gasp, then a rustling sound.

"Hello? *Hello,* Nell, are you—"

The line went dead.

He stared at the phone clutched in his hand. His cell phone was charging on a nearby table as he pulled on a raincoat.

No taking the cell phone. They could follow you with a cell phone, so he'd been told. They could track you anywhere, and they could listen in even when you thought your phone was off. His most trusted friend had told him about this new technology over coffee two days earlier. What had happened to the world when even inanimate objects could betray you?

No more time. He had to act. If they came after Nell again—

The man who had stolen two Rembrandts and three van Goghs in his life bit back a wave of anger and cleared his mind to a cold, flawless focus. He had given Nell the things she would need to know, things she could share with Nicholas Draycott. As soon as possible, he would find out the rest of the number.

Now he had to determine what in hell had gone wrong and how word had leaked out, despite all their planning.

So many secrets.

He moved outside and quietly locked his door. The elevator at the end of the hall was clanging as it approached, but he walked on toward the narrow stairs beyond the incinerator. The small elevator hissed to a halt at his floor.

By the time two men with tattooed hands got out, weapons bulging under their jackets, Jordan MacInnes was long gone.

"WHO DID YOU CALL?"

Nell swung around so sharply that her bandaged hand struck the corner of her dresser. She stifled a sound of pain. "I called my father. You'll probably track the call anyway. I wanted answers from him."

"Did you get any?"

"All that matters is what I *feel*," she said angrily. "I know he didn't do it. That's all I need right now. I'll prove the rest...somehow." She looked away, swinging her travel bag over her shoulder. "Let's go."

Dakota caught her arm. "Take it easy." He retaped the edge of the gauze strip that had pulled free, then studied her bandaged arm. "You don't do anything the easy way, do you?"

The silence was very loud, the only noise the faint ticking of an antique clock on her desk.

"The easy way?" She looked around the room, frowning at the framed art conservation diplomas on the wall and the dramatic mountain photographs she'd taken on distant climbs.

Dakota saw emotion churn through her haunted eyes. Gathering weight, they pulled her down, made her shoulders sag. She swayed slightly, one hand to the wall.

And then she walked toward the door, her fear shoved down deep.

That small act of courage hit him more than any amount of anger or threats. An unusual woman, he thought.

Something shimmered in her eyes and then vanished. Tears? *Regrets?*

What if it was? Never let it get personal.

Dakota knew the Foxfire rules by heart. He lived by them, worked by them. He was experienced enough to know that the rules kept him and the rest of his team alive. And if the rules required sacrificing any kind of personal life or private commitment, that was fine with him.

Without a word, he held out Nell's suede jacket. As he helped her slide it in place, Dakota planted a small, translucent square of plastic just behind her ear where it would be impossible for her to see. He kept his hand on her arm as she locked her door and crossed to his Explorer parked at the opposite corner.

The city was coming awake to a miserable day of sullen rain, workers hunched over umbrellas and cars churning through deep puddles. Nell turned up the collar of her coat and slid into the passenger seat, saying nothing.

As she sat, she could have been a million miles away. At least she'd stopped fighting him. Small victories, he thought grimly.

Meanwhile, Izzy was waiting.

A truck raced past, spiking a wall of water across the windshield and cutting off his visibility. As he hit the brakes, Nell shoved open the passenger door and jumped out into the rain.

CHAPTER ELEVEN

NELL WAS A BLOCK from the school crossing when the first police car two-wheeled around the corner, spitting gravel. Two more black-and-whites raced by at the next intersection.

Looking for her?

Hunched beneath the long plastic poncho she'd stuffed in her travel bag, she sprinted between a row of SUVs with parents waiting to drop off their kids at school.

She heard the screech of horns behind her and figured it was Dakota, trying to find a place to stop in the middle of the road, but she didn't look back, twisting north toward an alley that led away from the main streets.

She had to talk to Nicholas Draycott, her father's English friend. Then she needed a place to vanish.

She panted as she ran, brushing rain from her face. Once she knew who was behind the theft, she'd contact Dakota and pass on the information. But that would take place only after she had a written guarantee of her father's protection in exchange for her cooperation.

The scream of sirens two blocks away warned Nell

that she couldn't underestimate Dakota Smith and the people he worked with. She glanced at her watch, sprinted through a row of backyards, down a smaller alley and headed toward the closest Bart stop.

"WHERE IS SHE NOW?" Lloyd Ryker felt sweat slip under his collar.

"Sutter near Kearny, sir. I let her go as you instructed if she ran." Judging by the background noise, Dakota was on foot, phone to his ear.

"What about the chip?" Ryker snapped.

"In place and operational. Izzy is monitoring her now. I've got her in sight."

"Keep me up to date. I want to know every word she says—to her father, to her priest, and to everyone else." Ryker slammed down his phone and sat back in the chair.

Damn the da Vinci and damn the museum's inept security. If the staff had done their job properly, this nightmare wouldn't have landed in his lap.

Because of the terrorist connection, his unit had been brought in to check out any security flags. Given the suspicion of insider involvement, Teague had been running museum staff dossiers for a week, but so far they had no clear suspects. Meanwhile, every passing second brought the stolen art closer to the network of illegal art dealers working hand in glove with a well-financed terrorist group whose activities had sharply escalated in the past year.

And now Ryker had been forced to involve a civilian.

A *female* civilian.

In three prior Foxfire ops, females had been pulled in. When the dust had settled, each woman had managed to snare one of his top operatives, men he couldn't replace. Why couldn't people see the cold, hard truth the way he did? Marriage and espionage were a no-match. No matter how careful you were, emotions slowed you down and got you killed.

His Foxfire unit had been founded around that rule.

But Dakota was different, Ryker thought. Dakota was too professional to lower his guard, hormones or not.

At least he hoped so.

Scowling, Ryker picked up his office phone and punched in a number. "Ryker here," he growled. "Get me ten-minute updates on Teague and Smith. I want to know every step they take."

NELL DUCKED down an alley behind a rusting Dumpster and closed her eyes, breathing hard. Only twenty-four hours ago she'd been safe in her quiet workshop cleaning the last corner of *Saint George and the Dragon*, worrying about nothing more important than refilling her pigments and meeting the increase in her next commercial lease. Her life hadn't lacked challenges, but they had been manageable and contained.

Until now.

Now she was huddled beneath a torn plastic poncho, her hair a wreck and her life in shreds.

She heard a sound across the alley. Silently she wedged her body back into the space behind the

Dumpster, trying not to think about the rats or the layers of unnamed garbage surrounding her.

But she couldn't stay here for long. She had to keep moving. Dakota wouldn't be far behind.

ACROSS THE STREET in a dusty white van, Izzy Teague slid his headphones into place and touched a sleek metal track pad.

A red light flashed on the street map that came up on his laptop screen. The surveillance op had been ordered at the highest levels, and Ryker and his superiors were taking no chances on a screwup.

Right on Market.

She was on the move again. Probably headed to the Bart stop at Montgomery Street.

He zoomed in on the screen and checked every possible form of transportation in and out of the area. Nell MacInnes didn't have a car nearby, so her choices were limited unless she hailed a cab.

He frowned at her sudden change in direction. She'd stopped at a bookstore near Market that had just opened. She was going inside.

A small digital clock clicked out passing seconds at the bottom of his laptop screen. The missing art had to be located and recovered before it vanished into the shadow world where international crime merged with political terrorism. That wasn't going to happen on Izzy's watch.

He tapped a button. "Smith, you have her?"

"I'm headed around to the back. Is she still inside?"

"I'm picking up conversations and the sound of a phone ringing. She's in there somewhere."

"Stay on the front door. I'll give her two minutes to make contact with her father again. Then I'm going in."

"Copy." Izzy listened to the sound of muffled conversations and laughter. He heard the creak of a chair sliding out. The bookshop had a café, according to his quick online research.

A blue button lit up his screen.

Call in progress.

The phone number belonged to her father, but no one answered. Seconds later a new call was initiated, but the number wasn't one that Izzy recognized.

He tapped in a query and frowned.

Sussex, England?

Izzy knew that Nell made frequent trips to England to meet clients and acquire pigments and paper. During those trips, she used a GSM cell phone, which was enabled for European calls. Quickly he tapped the phone number into his commercial database.

No luck.

Frowning, he keyed into the huge, secure system that was housed in Maryland. As the cursor blinked, he drummed his fingers impatiently, glancing up to monitor the bookstore's front door. Who in the hell was Nell MacInness calling in Sussex, England?

A voice came over the line, cool and polite and decidedly aristocratic. "May I help you?"

The hell of it was, something about the voice was familiar. Izzy waited, suddenly uneasy. Where had he heard that aristocratic pronunciation before?

"Thank God. It's Nell." She sounded tired and at the edge of panic, breathing hard. "I've got to see you."

DAKOTA STOOD to the left of the bookstore's rear entrance, watching a tired employee toss trash and empty book boxes into the garbage.

He didn't think about Nell's face when she'd learned of her father's illness. He shoved the thought of her despair out of his mind.

Not your problem, pal. Do the job. Nail her contacts and haul her gorgeous ass out to the airport, as ordered.

Then forget her.

At least try to forget her, he thought grimly.

Dakota fingered his ear wire. "Teague, what's happening?"

"She's inside. She's making a call. Hold on…."

NELL SAT STIFFLY in a worn leather armchair at the back of the small café. Wet and frightened, she tried to remember the time difference between the West Coast and England.

Nicholas Draycott was one of her father's oldest friends. The two had loved to argue about pigment and painting styles and brushwork. Nell had listened to their conversations for hours whenever Nicholas visited her father, and it was during one of those heated, rambling arguments that she had decided to make restoration her career.

Then her world had shattered when her father had gone to prison. Even then the Englishman had called Nell with encouragement and advice, cheering her on through her studies and her final art internships in Europe. After that, Nell had occasionally advised him on the care and preservation of the vast collection of art at his magnificent estate in Sussex. She had never visited Draycott Abbey, but from photos and her father's descriptions she almost felt she knew the great old house.

Nell prayed the viscount could help. She gripped the phone, keeping her voice low. "It's about my father. I have to talk to you."

The phone shifted and Nell heard a chair scrape back. "Can you hold on for a moment?"

She heard footsteps and then the sound of a door closing. "Nell, is this about the gas chromatography tests you wanted for the Constable landscapes? If so, they—"

"It's about my father, Nicholas. It's a mess—he's in some kind of trouble. Things are crazy here, and I—I need your help. He told me to contact you immediately."

"Jordan told you this? When?"

"Twenty minutes ago. There are people following me. My father told me I was in danger and I should leave everything to go someplace safe. But where is safe? I—I don't know who to trust, Nicholas." She caught a breath and forced herself to stay calm. "Some people from the FBI came to my apartment tonight and the government has a man following me. I need to know what my father is caught up in."

Silence stretched out. "Nicholas?"

No answer.

Outside the store, cars crawled past, swallowed up by the rain. Nell wondered if her life had turned into one of those cars, crawling through rain and wind, barely staying ahead of a storm that was about to swallow her completely.

She pushed away the rest of a dry croissant, her appetite gone. "Nicholas, are you still there?"

"I'm here, Nell. Look, I'm in San Francisco right now, finishing some business. I was heading to the airport, but I'll swing by. Tell me where you are."

Nell felt the hairs stir at the back of her neck. A coincidence? Who could she trust? Was even this man an enemy?

"I...when did you arrive in San Francisco?"

"Sorry I didn't call you. It was an unexpected trip with a tight turnaround. Nell, listen to me. I'm sure there's a simple answer to your problem. We can go see your father and sort all this out together. How would that be?"

Like a miracle, she thought. Except her father wasn't answering his phone. "Can you come soon, Nicholas? These people are following me."

"Where are you now?"

Nell gave him the address, watching every customer who passed by her table. So far there had been no sign of the SEAL or anyone who looked like police, but she was certain her luck wouldn't last.

"Fine. I'll be there within twenty minutes. Stay put, Nell. Do not go outside and speak to no one." The politeness had shifted into something steely. "Between us, we will find our way to the bottom of this, I promise."

The line went dead.

SHE ORDERED another cup of tea, thumbed blindly through two glossy art magazines and called her father four times.

No answer.

Sliding down in her chair, she watched the clock, expecting Dakota to loom down one of the aisles at any moment, but no one bothered her.

Exactly eighteen minutes after Nicholas Draycott had ended her call, she looked up to see his lean, handsome features. He had an old Burberry trench coat folded over his arm, and water glinted in his dark hair.

"Thank heavens, I was afraid you'd left." Nicholas looked at her in concern as he slid into the chair beside her. "Are you okay, Nell? Your arm is bandaged." He leaned forward, frowning. "Is that a cut on your face?"

"Nothing serious. Just…climbing stuff. But I'm tired and confused. Have you heard from my father lately? There's something going on, but he isn't making any sense."

"What has he told you?"

Nell shrugged. "Something about numbers and promises." She frowned at an employee carrying a tray with pastries for a nearby customer.

The twelfth viscount Draycott drummed his fingers on the arm of his chair. Nell realized several people in the café were studying him discreetly, wondering if he was someone important. "Your father gave you a number? Did he say why, Nell?"

A movement to her left, down an aisle with children's books, caught her eye. She flinched.

Dakota Smith walked silently down the aisle and

sank into the seat beside her. Another man, the mirror image of Denzel Washington, emerged from the opposite aisle.

"No," Nell whispered.

"Who are *you*?" The Englishman fixed his cold stare on Dakota. When the Denzel Washington look-alike sat down beside him, Nicholas drew a sharp breath. "Don't tell me you're part of this, Teague."

Nicholas *knew* this man?

"You have a hell of a lot of explaining to do, Draycott," the man called Teague said curtly. "Let's go outside and get started."

Nell closed her eyes, hit by weariness and panic.

Trust no one.

She'd remembered her rule too late.

CHAPTER TWELVE

RAIN HAMMERED at the windshield as the black SUV cut through the sluggish traffic.

So far none of the three men were talking to Nell. Nicholas had spoken quietly on his cell phone for the past five minutes, but Nell had only caught one word in five.

She watched her father's friend put away his phone. When he turned around, his face was grim. "She's not involved. I want that absolutely clear."

Neither Dakota nor his friend responded.

"What agency do you represent?"

The man called Teague flashed a badge that only Nicholas Draycott could see. Apparently it was enough to satisfy the Englishman.

"I see. In that case your people messed up. That's why Nell's father contacted me. He knew what was going to happen because he was approached before he left prison."

"Approached by who?" Dakota's gaze didn't leave the road.

"An inmate who wanted help to sell a major piece of stolen art. He wanted Jordan's contacts. When

Jordan refused, the man threatened him. He threatened to hurt Nell, too."

Nell looked out at the rain, breathing hard. Now she understood. They had tried to pull her father back in, and he'd gone to the only person he could trust, his old friend from British intelligence. "So my father is working with you undercover?"

Draycott nodded. "Only one person over here knows what Jordan's doing. We had to keep the loop closed."

"Why?" Things had changed again, and Nell was struggling to keep up. "If my father agreed to help, why weren't the officials here notified?" Then the answer came to her, awful in its implications. "Someone here is involved. That's the only possible reason."

The brave, stubborn fool, she thought. *He did it for me. To protect me the only way he could.*

"What exactly did your father tell you, Nell?" Nicholas asked quietly.

"He told me I could be in danger. He told me to leave and go away. Somewhere remote, like a mountain in Thailand."

"What was the number he gave you?"

Nell hesitated. She trusted Nicholas, but she wasn't sure about the other two. For all she knew, either one of them could be the traitor.

"You can trust them, Nell. I've worked with Teague before."

"I don't trust anyone right now. First I was chased down an alley. Then *he* tried to kidnap me." She glared at Dakota. "For all I know, he's the one you're looking for."

Dakota turned, his eyes cutting to the Englishman.

"If you knew what MacInnes was doing—assuming this story is true—why didn't you have protection in place for him? And for his daughter?"

"We did. Jordan had several old…associates watching Nell. Something must have gone wrong."

"Where is he now?" Nell leaned anxiously toward Nicholas Draycott. "Can you call him and tell him to cut this undercover mission short?"

Her father's friend shook his head slowly. "I can't, Nell. It's gone too far."

Nell heard the chime of her cell phone from somewhere in the front of the car, but she clearly remembered leaving the phone in her apartment.

Dakota glanced back. "Answer it." Nell realized he was holding out her cell phone.

Stiff with anger, she answered the call. "Yes?"

"Don't talk." Her father's voice was edgy with adrenaline. "Here's the second number. Memorize it."

"Done," Nell said.

"Good. Did you reach our friend?"

"He's here with me now."

"Trust him, Nell. He'll take care of you. I'm leaving. I have to help them, but I'll make contact as soon as—"

She heard the sudden sound of a door slamming. A car motor whined. Then there was only static.

She gripped the phone, imagining her father's danger. The phone shook in her fingers.

The man called Izzy Teague slid her phone out of her hand and into his pocket, then pulled a plastic box from beneath the seat. "Your arm is bleeding. Why don't I have a look? You banged yourself up last night, I understand."

Nell barely realized that he was examining her arm. She winced as he pulled up the old bandage.

"Your father? What did he say, Nell?" Nicholas Draycott looked worried.

"He said he's leaving and that he has to help them." Nell took a sharp breath. "They'll kill him if they find out what he's done."

Draycott leaned over to touch her shoulder. "If anyone can pull this off, it's Jordan. Right now I'm far more worried about you. I want you to come to Draycott Abbey. It's the one place I know you'll be safe."

"What about my father? What if *he* needs help, Nicholas? Who's going to help him?"

DAKOTA WAS FITTING new pieces into the puzzle. They were going to need Nell's help to reach her father, wherever he was. To ensure her help, it was important that she know what she was up against.

"Give her the file," he said flatly, glancing back at Izzy. "The complete one this time. She's entitled to the whole picture."

Izzy frowned. "But Ryker—"

"Stuff Ryker. See what she can pick up from the documents. Show her the photos of the museum guards and all the dealers who have been interviewed. Maybe she knows one of them."

Izzy hesitated, rubbing his neck. "Ryker's going to chew bricks when he finds out." He stared out at the rain and then shrugged. "You're right. She knows this world. She might spot something that we've missed." He looked down at the sound of low humming. "How did we live before cell phones?" His eyes narrowed as he checked the screen. "That's my liaison at the FBI. What am I supposed to tell him?"

"Nothing." Dakota took a sharp right turn, and the control tower of the airport loomed out of the rain. "Let Ryker handle it." He snapped a look at Nicholas Draycott. "You have safe transport for her? Things are going to get hot back here."

Draycott nodded. "That has been arranged."

The viscount looked cool and professional, but Dakota wasn't paid to take chances. "You'll have to keep her off the radar, you know that. But she'll need constant access in case her father calls."

The Englishman smiled briefly. "We'll manage our part. Meanwhile, I suggest that you start working on those numbers. They must have great importance for Jordan."

"Already running possibilities," Izzy cut in. "I'm eliminating international phone exchanges and map coordinates. I tried the prison database but nothing there matched. Next we'll try offshore banking accounts."

Nell paled. "You know the numbers? Were you monitoring my phone?"

None of the men answered.

A plane thundered by, wings dark as it climbed up through the driving rain. Beyond the security fences, more planes lined up for takeoff, filled with bustle and normalcy.

Some of that normalcy was an illusion. People never realized the constant threats to the nation's security,

Dakota thought. And that was only right. If a threat made it onto the front page of the *New York Times*, then he and his team had messed up.

"It could be some kind of art database," Nell said slowly. "Maybe a number from a list of stolen pieces. Or possibly it's a museum acquisition number. I can check those for you, not just here, but around the world."

"I could do that too—but you'll do it faster. Let Ryker chew bricks." Izzy nodded at Draycott. "Looks like you two have a plane to catch."

Draycott Abbey
Sussex, England

WIND PLAYED over the English roses, filling the air with perfume. The moon drifted behind racing clouds and silver light fell on weathered gray walls.

In the clear night air the old abbey seemed to dream, alive with forgotten legends and painful secrets, its beauty earned at fearsome cost.

A figure moved in the shadows of the Long Gallery. Light swirled along the gaunt aristocratic face, brushing the fine lace at his cuffs. He was out of place in these shadows, out of place in the bustle and clamor of the twenty-first century, a world too loud.

Too fast.

Too…real.

His eyes dark with memories, the guardian ghost of Draycott Abbey crossed the silent rooms, past the paintings of kings and heroes and sad-eyed patriots.

When he stopped, it was to stare up at his own portrait, painted by the hand of Sir Joshua Reynolds, with the abbey captured in golden sunlight behind him. Now there was an artist, Adrian Draycott thought crossly. No posing and braying, only a brush that spoke, unerring in its color and grace.

But this noisy world was a different place from the one he'd known in life. Then he had been lord and master; now he was nothing. Anger swirled up, filling the darkness with the weight of sad memories.

Without warning the air churned. He felt the sudden weight of danger, as he had so many times before.

A gray shape ghosted from the shadows, tail high, amber eyes agleam. The cat's cry was low and restless.

"I agree, old friend. It begins again. If I mistake not, there will be meddling and pain before we see an end to it. *Maledetto*," he whispered, the word cold on his tongue. "Fools. Their greed knows no end."

The cat wove between Adrian's booted feet, head raised while the air shimmered between them. For an instant light seemed to swirl in lazy patterns over the hard-faced portrait on the wall.

Adrian studied his likeness critically. "It was a night of high play, and all of us in our cups. That must be the reason that Cavendish staked such art—and lost it in one roll. Poor bastard." The eighth Viscount Draycott stared out over the moat, over the wooded hills, remembering a night of recklessness and loss centuries before. He had done all he could to protect that night's treasure. The diary was still hidden.

But the art was gone....

Somewhere out over the dark hills, a clock chimed twelve times and then once more, a low, phantom sound that made passing travelers cross themselves and hasten their step.

In a swirl of lace and velvet the abbey's ghost strode off through the moonlight. "The wine cellar first, I think. And after that the library, Gideon. The same path I walked that night. Perhaps the danger is already here."

The great gray cat flicked his tail, jumping onto the sill of an open window. Light shimmered over the room with its priceless paintings and antiques.

And then in the space of a heartbeat, the ghost and his oldest companion were gone. Only the curtains moved in a breeze that was suddenly cold.

CHAPTER THIRTEEN

"RYKER WILL GO nuclear when he hears about this." Izzy watched Nicholas Draycott's chartered plane move into position for takeoff. "Especially the part about the FBI holding back the Zayed connection."

"He'll live," Dakota muttered. "It didn't play right for me. The father, absolutely. The daughter…" He shook his head. "Not the type. Too independent to work with a team and too smart to think they could pull it off alone. At least now we have a trail to follow. By the way, who *is* this Draycott person?"

"Impeccable British family as old as time. In point of fact, he's the twelfth Viscount Draycott."

Dakota didn't look remotely impressed.

"Don't worry, the man's got a solid military background. Ex–Special Air Service, with years of field-work. He spent a good deal of time in Southeast Asia until he was captured and tortured. I can find a dozen highly placed references to his reliability. In fact, I just got done sending the list to Ryker." He raised a brow. "Any other concerns about Draycott?"

"Not for the moment."

"Hard case, aren't you?" Izzy punched up an address

on the Explorer's GPS. "How about we go pay a visit to that warehouse in Oakland? I'm thinking Ryker's contact at the shipping company might be onto something."

"Sounds good to me. I'm in the mood for some B and E."

Izzy nodded at the plane taxiing down the runway. "Her old man's got guts, I'll tell you that."

"I only hope his guts hold out. He's going to need them if the October Twelfth people realize he's sold them out. How about the number MacInnes gave Nell? It could be a private courier service with a nine-digit tracking number."

"I've traced all the big commercial carriers, but zip. It will take me longer to access the smaller ones. One more reason to go see the warehouse in Oakland. Their company could use nine digits." Izzy gave a little two-finger salute to the air as Nell's plane gathered speed and lifted off into the rain. "Smooth sailing. Say hello to the abbey ghost for me."

Dakota's gaze cut across to Izzy. "What?"

"Just a legend. Even the smallest cottage has to have a betrayal or beheading in its past. You know how the Brits are about their history. And Draycott Abbey is a heck of a lot more than a little cottage, trust me."

MORE RAIN, Dakota thought, working his way through the crush of morning rush hour traffic. Wasn't it ever sunny here in the Republic of California anymore?

His boyhood memories were all about sun and sky and the flash of water spilling through the bottom of steep canyons. Growing up on the rugged coast north of Mendocino, he'd climbed most of the mountains near his house. With only a distracted uncle for family, he'd been given the run of the coast. Often as not, his schoolbooks were ditched in a bush near the bus stop while he went in search of his own form of education, tramping the high forests or scavenging on the beach.

By the time he was ten, he'd lost both of his parents. They had died within a year of each other, one from leukemia and the other in a late-night collision caused by a drunk driver from Malibu. Dakota hadn't spoken for three months, confused at first, then angry at being left alone. But eventually he'd settled in with his uncle, an ex-army sniper. He found his feet in the solitude and the foggy forests that could be as dangerous as they were beautiful. His uncle had taught him to track deer, shoot a rifle and orient by the stars. By the time he was fifteen, Dakota could live for a month in the mountains with nothing but a knife and a canteen. All in all, it had been excellent groundwork for his SEAL training.

Dakota hadn't been back to California since his uncle had died six years before, and he didn't care to dig up old memories now. There was no point. One thing he'd never disagreed about with Ryker: emotions could get you killed faster than an Uzi burst.

Ditch the emotion.

Focus on the mission.

But the fog and rain outside his window kept bringing flashes of memory from a past that had once been full of the joy of wonder and discovery. He seemed to hear the comforting boom of his father's laughter as he taught Dakota how to tie a trout lure and the grace of his mother's hands as she worked on the one-of-a-kind art quilts that had kept the family in cash between his father's disappearances doing work that was never defined for agencies that were never named.

With the eyes of an adult, Dakota now knew that his father had been part of the shadow world of espionage, taking short-term assignments that wouldn't keep him away from his family for long. From his memories, the money must have been tight, too. Despite popular belief, intelligence work didn't make you a millionaire. Not unless you sold out. Dakota had done some searching after he joined Foxfire, and his hunch had been confirmed. But he hadn't probed deeper. Best to let the cold truths lie, while he remembered more important details, like the flash of emotion and warm colors of what family had once meant to him.

All of which explained why Dakota Smith understood Jordan MacInnes's devotion to his daughter better than most people. Any good father would do just the same, sacrificing himself without hesitation to save the people he loved. He understood Nell's fierce need to protect in turn.

Family complexities were a serious obstacle, to be avoided at all costs, but Dakota remembered how deep the pull of family could be embedded in the soul and why no other loyalties held so much risk.

"You listening to me, Smith?"

"Of course I'm listening," Dakota lied.

"Ryker's on the phone. He wants an update on that warehouse layout within the hour."

"We'll be there in twenty minutes. Get your camera ready." Dakota's gaze cut across to Izzy. "What did he say about the plan that Draycott cooked up?"

Izzy covered the phone. "Don't ask."

HOLT BROTHERS SHIPPING, LLC, sat in a messy sprawl at the edge of Oakland's construction district. Lit even in daylight by tall halogen lights that cast sullen circles against the rain, the warehouse looked as if it had seen better days. A derelict truck on two wheels rusted in one back corner, while a load of recycled newspapers lay moldering in the rain.

Dakota nudged the Explorer off the access road and cut the motor. "Looks busy. Lots of forklifts working that pile of construction materials. We're not going to be able to walk in without being noticed."

"Ryker's contact violated his parole, got caught with a firearm. He was willing to trade information if it kept him from a ride back to Folsom. He told Oakland PD that his boss has a safe in the office and new security locks were added. He's seen art being packaged up, going in and out. He ID'd a van Gogh that's been off the books for almost eight years."

"Where was it headed?"

"An unnamed buyer in Asia."

Dakota watched men in plastic ponchos push carts between half a dozen scattered buildings. "So they're definitely dealing."

"I'd say so. One problem. When the Oakland police brought in the FBI, our guy closed up like a clam. Said he wouldn't talk to anyone. We're talking real panic."

Dakota tapped two fingers on the wheel. "Like he knew there was someone on the inside."

"Looks that way to Ryker. Whatever the boss wants to protect is locked inside the safe." Izzy pointed across the road. "Right there in that gray building. Ryker figures the art could be held in there, along with details of other transactions."

"Let's see what kind of security we're dealing with." Dakota pulled out a pair of Zeiss 10x42 FLT high-range binoculars and studied the layout of the buildings. "Power source to the right. Access via the rear door. No visibility from the street. What about night security?"

"Four men, three shifts."

Dakota zoomed in on the back door of the building, scanning the wall with the newest exterior wiring. "When do they close down for the day?"

"Six-thirty, but there could be day crew around until eight or so."

"Good halogen light and a decent alarm, but nothing I can't manage. I say we pick our spot and come back at midnight. Until then, it would help to know the model of this safe I need to crack."

Izzy reached into the back seat, pulled out a clipboard and a hat that read *National Law Enforcement Officers Memorial Fund.* "Give me ten minutes."

IZZY WAS SMILING when he came back, his clipboard under his arm and rain dotting his shoulders. "It's solid, all right. Some nice Japanese digital technology, but nothing we can't override." He set a small camera on the dash and hooked it up via cable to his laptop. "Here's what we've got. Steel wall-mounted model with a digital keypad. I'm thinking thermal imaging is the easiest way to see what keys have recently been pressed. I just finished a security white paper for Ryker on the subject, as it happens."

Dakota smiled faintly. "You want thermal, that can be arranged."

Midnight

THE GUARD SHUFFLED past the shadow where Dakota was crouched, motionless. Satisfied that the yard was quiet, the guard crossed to a truck and slid behind the seat, reaching for a silver Thermos.

Silently Dakota overrode the alarm, jimmied the rear door and studied the digital keypad, reading high-heat signatures on five keys. Now he had to determine the order.

Not so difficult. Higher heat, most recent contact.

Eighteen seconds later the safe hissed open. Dakota stared at a row of nine cell phones wrapped in plastic. No art. No cash. No stolen passports.

Just unopened cell phones.

He fingered his mouth mic. "Teague, no art. Only cell phones. They look brand-new."

"Slip one out. I'm going to need it. What's the brand?"

"Nokia."

Dakota heard Izzy tap at a keyboard. "Okay, get back pronto. We're going to tap into the SIM card and find the smart key."

Dakota shook his head. So what if they had a cell

phone? The clock was ticking. Where in the hell was the missing art?

Out in the yard the guard stretched, then tossed an empty snack bag into a garbage can and headed toward the office. Dakota opened the door and worked his way silently along the back fence. The guard had vanished by the time he climbed the fence and dropped lightly to the ground near his parked SUV.

"Let's see what we've got." Izzy pulled out a smart-card reader and several cables, which he attached to his laptop. "This could take a while. I've got to challenge until I get the right response."

Dakota leaned back in his seat. "Wake me when you redesign the wheel, Einstein."

HE SHOULD HAVE SLEPT.

His eyes were closed, his breathing slow and relaxed, but he couldn't sleep. Nell's face kept drifting through his mind, her body moving into the rain. Irritated, Dakota looked the other way.

The image appeared again.

He had to smile a little, remembering the crazy way she'd climbed the rain gutter and then walk-jumped onto the roof.

"Teague, you ever hear of something called parkour?"

Izzy was staring at his computer screen. "French sport. A discipline of dexterity to vault or bypass obstacles. Very cool to watch. Don't tell me you're taking it up, because it's not your style."

Dakota stretched, watching rain streak the windows.

"Nell's style. I watched her do that in the alley. I didn't believe it even when I was seeing it."

"Some woman."

Dakota's mind drifted again, carrying memories of a snowy ridge and the heat of their entwined bodies while the Scottish gale raged outside the tent. But somehow the dream shifted to a white sand beach with soft wind and a woman who wore nothing but sunlight and a smile.

Her face looked exactly like Nell's.

NELL SAT RESTLESSLY, covered by a blanket as the chartered jet droned east. Whenever her mind locked up, caught in frightening scenarios about her father, she forced her thoughts back to explanations for the numbers he had given her. So far the process had left her exhausted, with no useful answers.

Finally she gave up. As her eyes closed, she saw a man with wary eyes and callused hands that could be surprisingly gentle.

It didn't matter. She'd never see him again anyway. Better to think about finding a way to save her father.

Nell yawned. She wondered if Draycott Abbey was as lush and magical as her father had described to her. There had been a strange legend, which she had almost forgotten. Something about a clock…and a brooding ghost.

Ridiculous.

Nell drifted into dreams.

And then, strangely, there were roses around her.

Peach and cream and crimson, with perfume that spilled magic through a quiet spring night in a place that felt oddly like home....

"WAKE UP, Dakota. We're in."

Dakota sat up instantly. He'd been dreaming. Something about colors and night.

A perfume that might have come from roses.

Weird.

But most dreams worked by rules you couldn't define or understand.

Dakota forced the ragged images away. "I wasn't asleep," he lied. "And exactly *what* are we in?"

Outside in the darkness the warehouse enclosure was deserted.

Izzy gave a cocky smile as he unplugged the thin cables and tossed them into his bag. "We're inside the phone's SIM card. I've got what I need. I'll wipe off the unit and you can slip it back into the safe, to all appearances untouched. Trust me, we just hit pay dirt."

CHAPTER FOURTEEN

NELL FOUGHT EXHAUSTION, listening to the low drone of the airplane motors. The words of the museum reports blurred and then refocused as she struggled to accept the details she had just read.

> *The work appears to be a preliminary sketch of the* Mona Lisa, *of white chalk, ink and black charcoal executed on cream linen rag paper.*
>
> *Surface includes nine smaller sheets of paper adhered together. Considerable fragility and signs of acidification of all sheets. Slight water damage at the upper left corner and tearing of the paper at center bottom.*
>
> *On initial examination, details of paper conform to period composition. Restoration...*

The dry description went on for page after page, inadequate to express the sheer power of such a discovery. A sketch by da Vinci, with what appeared to be an overdrawing by Michelangelo, if stylistic evidence was to be believed, bringing two of the world's greatest artists—and keenest competitors—together in one work.

Nell closed her eyes.

When word of the discovery leaked out, the art world would be thrown into hysteria. And of course word would leak out. Nothing this immense could be covered up for long, even if the museum delayed their official release to the press.

But was the fragile sketch, captured in a large-format photograph before her, authentic? So far the museum's head curator, Lydia Reynolds, had performed only initial noninvasive tests, like infrared and ultraviolet X-ray scans and energy dispersive X-ray fluorescence. The test results were collated and tacked neatly inside the folder. All supported the historical dating and appropriate styles of the two artists.

From the photo, Nell could see that the design showed the strength and detail that were Leonardo's trademarks. The colors were faded, but Nell could see that the placement of the figure was different from the finished painting. In this sketch *La Gioconda* faced the viewer head-on, with none of the seductive over-the-shoulder posture that was part of her enduring charm. Only faint outlines suggested the pose of the final painting, but these outlines were made in a different style completely. These the curator had assessed as possibly in the style of Michelangelo's work.

The paper dating also appeared appropriate, as were the chalk and pigments, although no invasive sampling had yet been undertaken.

Michelangelo and da Vinci together. The idea was staggering.

But Nell's biggest question still loomed: was it *real?*

Or was it a product of the apprentices whom Leonardo used extensively during his far-flung projects? Worse yet, was it a careful copy, either by a near contemporary or by some later forger who had stockpiled authentic period materials?

Impossible to say without more information, more tests, but sampling would be unlikely, given the nearly incalculable value of the piece.

Nell's head began to ache as she stared at the haunting photograph of the world's most famous face. She could imagine the excitement of the curator. Nell had met Lydia Reynolds twice and knew her reputation for succeeding at any cost. But there were still too many questions. What was the history of the second set of markings, once bold lines now nearly ghostlike, executed in silver chalk along the figure's face and shoulders? In the photograph, they were so light that Nell had almost missed them.

Nicholas Draycott crossed the cabin. "Any luck?"

Nell rubbed her neck as the viscount held out a cup of tea. "I'm only on page five of the curator's report from the National Gallery. She seems thorough enough. All the tests made at the time are recorded, although she didn't have time—or approval—to complete many. I would like to speak with the two museum conservators she called in, to check their impressions."

"I expect that can be arranged." Nicholas nodded toward the photo. "Amazing, isn't it?"

"Beyond amazing. Michelangelo and da Vinci."

The viscount's eyes narrowed. "Is it real?"

"That's never a snap judgment. Even with materials

and style consistent with the artists, tests are required every step of the way." Nell ran her fingers restlessly through her hair. "We can't plug in one or two numbers and wait for the final printout. Art doesn't work that way. We deal in black and white, but in every shade of gray, too. You play with all those in-between shades, weighing possibilities, sorting and sifting until you find the style, habits and passions that make every piece of great art unique. Is it authentic? That's always the final question. The curator, Lydia Reynolds, was inclined to believe so according to these files, but without a dozen more tests, she couldn't begin to make a final assessment. It takes weeks, even months of exacting work, and even then three experts will walk away with three different conclusions. X never marks the spot," she said wryly.

"Ah. Indiana Jones. I'd have to agree with you there, since I've never found anything to be what or where I expected it at the abbey. Records have been misplaced, books are damaged, and art….is stolen." His eyes hardened. "You do not know the whole story."

"What story?"

"My father told me that one of Leonardo's greatest charcoal drawings had been won at cards during a night of reckless play at the abbey. With the drawing came a notebook from Leonardo's own hand, detailing his final plans for the design."

"This art is *yours?*" Nell's breath caught. "*You* took it to the National Gallery?"

"No, the piece was never found in our collection. All I had was the word of my father, based on old family accounts. He insisted that the sketch was lost during the life of the eighth viscount, sometime in the late eighteenth century."

"Lost? You mean sold or stolen?"

"Stolen. Adrian, my ancestor, left a list of all those he considered suspects. As far as I knew, the piece was never found. Naturally, when your father contacted me, I was dumbfounded."

"So…we're talking about your family legacy, Nicholas."

"It would be impossible to prove without more documents." The viscount shrugged. "I doubt I will bother to pursue it. I'm not a greedy man. I have art to savor for the rest of my life, and this piece might cost more than it's worth."

"Cost in what way?"

He stared out the window into the darkness, looking uncomfortable. "According to my father, the sketch was…cursed. Go ahead and laugh if you like. I know that I did when I first heard the tale."

"I won't laugh. If a person believed that the art was cursed, then it might affect them exactly that way."

"*Maledetto*," Nicholas said softly. " 'Cursed in hand and tongue.' That was what the notebook of Leonardo said. He believed that his thieving young apprentice stole the piece and sold it to his chief enemy, Michelangelo. But Leonardo was never able to prove it."

"Have you looked for the notebook?"

"Whenever we remodeled or had structural repairs, the notebook was the first thing on my mind, but we never found a trace. My ancestor, the eighth viscount, had a sad life. Married very late, he had a rakehell son who gambled away a good deal of the family fortune. Maybe there was a curse after all," he mused. "One way or another, I'd like the issue settled. This will be my chance." His expression hardened. "If you had to make a decision right now, with no more tests, only with your heart—would you say that piece is real?"

Nell stared at the subtle curves of the woman's shoulders and the elusively sensual curve of her smile. She wanted to believe it was by Leonardo's hand, but wanting wasn't enough. The tests would turn up details that no vision could provide.

And yet the answer would not rest in charts and graphs.

The artist was everything. In the end, the whole complicated array of canvas and pigments fell away and only the artist's soul remained. The artist held the answer, but only if you looked into his heart.

Distant or vain. Violent or generous.

Nell had learned that at her father's knee, then learned it again in high school as she moved, stony faced, through mockery, harassment and despair. As a conservator she knew that you went to the person first, back to the habits and biases and hundreds of small eccentricities that made an artist stand out from the pack. Those details grounded any decision about restorations, maintaining the artist's original vision.

Nell was searching for those tiny eccentricities now, thumbing through chemical analyses, pigment layers and X-ray reports, looking for something that caught her eye. And her instincts were sharp. She would know the clues when she saw them.

"Is this piece of paper the work of Leonardo? An impossible question, Nicholas. But if I had to say now…" She smiled slowly. "Yes. That face with its cool eyes. Complex and emotional. Not simple, not even nice." She felt a wave of awe. "Here we see the slightest shadow of eyebrows, and her posture is different, but only the master could create a mix of emotions like that in a face that is unforgettable."

For a long time Nicholas didn't speak. "Then we'd better find a way to get it back," he said. "And your father along with it."

"There's something else. Did he tell you that he was sick, Nicholas?"

"Sick?"

The surprise in his voice told Nell the answer, and she felt a moment of guilt for revealing her father's secrets. But Nicholas had to know the rest of the story. "He's got cancer. He didn't tell me, didn't say a word. Izzy and Dakota knew, probably from the prison records. It's…bad."

The Englishman made a low sound and gripped her hands tightly. "Lord, what a thing to happen now, just when he's got his life back. But there are procedures that can be done, Nell. New techniques, new medicines."

"Not if he's in prison, there aren't. And unless we find out who is behind this theft, prison is where he'll go." Nell closed her eyes, feeling the grip of regret, feeling anger mixed with bitter hopelessness. "I want him back, Nicholas. I want a little time with my father…."

Before he dies.

She forced down the words. Hopelessness would get her nowhere. Straightening, she studied the sketch, slipping beneath that fragile surface to probe all its secrets. "I'll do whatever I have to do, Nicholas. Understand that. Whatever happens, don't cut me out the way my father did."

"Understood." Nicholas drank the last of his tea, then nodded. "I'll do all within my power to keep you informed. But I may not have the final say. I have a feeling that Dakota Smith and Izzy Teague will be taking over very soon. Whether we like it or not."

"SAY IT IN ENGLISH, Teague." Ryker sounded more irritated than usual, which was saying something. "Cut the *SIM card* and *algorithm* talk. I know it's about memory in a cell phone. Just tell me what it all means and how it's going to help us find the da Vinci."

"The phone has two numbers stored in memory and nothing else. None of the nine phones have ever been used. I checked the account, which was opened by a construction consortium in Macau that handles luxury residential projects and high-end gambling resorts throughout Asia. The business, East West Properties, has been family-owned for three generations."

"So it's a dead end," Ryker growled.

"Not quite. I tracked the company's other cell phone traffic. Turns out, they have a brand-new subsidiary in D.C. Forty-one cell calls were made from Macau to their D.C. offices during the night the painting was discovered stolen. The calls were made to two different cell phones."

"Get me a log of every call made that night. And I

want to know every U.S. company they've ever done business with."

"Already on its way to your in-box," Izzy murmured.

"No sign of any art concealed at the Oakland warehouse?"

"None. There was no extra security on any of the outbuildings that would indicate valuables in storage, only at the office. The office safe held only the nine unused cell phones. My guess is that whatever comes in is shipped out immediately. With building supplies in constant transit, a few random boxes wouldn't be difficult to hide. They'd probably have used a more secure location than this one though."

"What about a connection with the October Twelfth people? Have the men from the alley given up any information yet?"

"That's a problem. An hour ago one of them tried to slash his wrists with a tin can lid. Luckily an officer caught him before he bled out."

"So they're running scared?"

"I'd say that, sir. The other man swears that the job was anonymous, with their partial cash payment left at an abandoned warehouse in San Jose. They were supposed to drive around with Nell until they got a call and someone would meet them."

"No names, no numbers?"

"I'm afraid not. Not completely. But when I ran their names, I picked up a connection with criminal investigation six years ago in Macau. One of the men was working for East West Properties at the time. Another *ping* for our favorite company."

"What have you got on the owners?"

"The president, Luis Gonsalves, is a big-time art collector. *Macau News* ranks him as the number-two buyer in Asia, yet his collection has never been photographed, studied or published. None of the major insurance companies handle coverage for his art, either."

"Hardly surprising. If you stockpile *stolen* art, you can't exactly go to Lloyd's of London for coverage, can you? What else?" Ryker asked impatiently. "Does Gonsalves have any known terrorist connections?"

"There have been several investigations by the Macau police, sir. Nothing stuck. This Gonsalves looks like a careful man. Either he's clean—or he's kept his distance from anything that would be damaging."

"Stay with it. I'll have our tech people work it from this end, too. Whatever you do, none of this goes outside us. I don't care if the director himself calls you. Be polite, be accessible, but relay all questions to me."

"Understood, sir."

"I'm packing you two out tonight. You're to be in D.C. by dawn. I want every detail about the people connected with those cell phone calls the night the theft was reported."

"Rog—"

Ryker hung up before Izzy could finish.

Dakota was watching him. "Where to next?"

"We've got orders to be in D.C. by dawn."

Dakota put the SUV in gear. "Join the navy, see the world."

Washington, D.C.

THEY MET in a green van parked below the Lincoln Memorial. Rogers looked nervous, constantly checking over his shoulder even though the streets were deserted.

"It's getting hot. They've been running everyone's personnel files and doing background checks."

"Nothing we didn't expect. Relax, Rogers. Sit tight until the storm passes. You're going to be a very rich man in a few months, remember?"

The guard managed a thin smile. "About time, too. I'm getting too old for this kind of work."

"After this, you won't need to work again." His contact flipped on the windshield wipers as a soft rain began to shroud the Potomac. "The replacement tapes have held up so far?"

"Perfectly. I don't know how you did it, but every pixel checks out."

The curiosity in the guard's voice was irritating. "I leave nothing to chance. That's all you need to know on that subject."

Rogers watched the rain. "Lydia is getting worried. I'm not sure she's up to this."

"You found her, Rogers. If she is no longer trustworthy…" The driver let the phrase trail off.

"I can keep her in line," the guard said firmly. "She'll be quiet. I just thought you should know." He cleared his throat. "She wants more money, too."

The driver didn't move. "Out of the question. I think you need to explain to her how this works."

The guard shrugged. "I tried. She's spooked."

"In that case I'll call her myself." The head of the October 12th Brigade traced a line in the fine dust on the dashboard. "Where is she now?"

"At the museum. Cocktails with several big collectors. She should be finished around nine."

"I will take care of all the details for her. Money, a new passport, whatever she requires. I want no problems."

"I knew you could handle it. I told her that."

"You told her about *me*?" The question was very soft, but the sudden tension in the air made Rogers turn sharply.

"Not your name or any details. Nothing like that. Nothing about the…organization, of course. She's not a believer. All she cares about is her job and her latest bank balance. I said that she'd be taken care of, and no one would ever know she was involved."

"I see. You are a very valuable member of our group. Have I told you that lately, Rogers?"

The guard shook his head and turned back to watch the rain that hammered against the steps beyond Lincoln's feet. "I saw it when they brought it in. So much life packed into a small sheet of paper. How did he do that?"

"Every artist has asked that question. Some call it madness, some call it genius. The beauty and skill are irrelevant, however." The driver didn't look up. "Good night, Rogers. I will be in touch soon."

The guard nodded and pulled up the hood on his cheap plastic poncho, then stepped out, hunched against the sheeting water.

The driver of the van frowned and punched a number on the new cell phone. "He's headed south. Blue plastic poncho and a black gym bag. Do it now."

Down the broad drive a black laundry truck pulled out of a service road, headlights off. When it accelerated sharply, the man in the poncho turned and began to run, arms flapping. Rain muffled the thump of contact. The scream was abruptly cut off as the truck's heavy wheels crushed Rogers's throat and chest.

The driver of the parked van watched to be sure there was no more movement from the body sprawled on the wet pavement. After a lingering glance at the Lincoln Memorial, blurred by rain, the figure at the wheel turned south, keying in another number.

"I need to talk to him now. Get me his home number on the boat. Of course it's *important*, you fool."

CHAPTER FIFTEEN

DAKOTA STARED out at the quiet streets of Fisherman's Wharf, dark and silent in the fog. "How does someone set up a sale like this, Teague? You need good people and a secure location, something remote, off law enforcement radar."

"Remote but accessible," Teague corrected. "They'll require account transfers up front for all bidders. Millions just to secure a spot, so I'm told. Everyone gets a look at the art and then the bidding starts."

"So they'll have to be present to bid?"

"That or a trusted representative. Would you drop thirty-two million based on a few pretty photographs?" Izzy laughed grimly. "No, they'll be present, count on it. They'll have an expert on hand, too, someone they all trust to declare the art authentic." He looked down at his computer screen. "Here's what I've got on the phones. They were purchased two months ago in Kuala Lumpur. They've got some interesting new illegal encryption technology installed. Looks like someone doesn't want to have any conversations monitored." Izzy shook his head. "But why *nine* cell phones, and none of them activated? That's starting to bug the hell out of me."

TWELVE MILES away on the northern edge of San Francisco Bay, a short man with jet-black hair raised a bottle of expensive single-malt whisky. "A drink, Jordan?"

Fog swirled around the elegant houseboat docked in Sausalito's quaint harbor. "Of course. To celebrate our mutual success." Jordan MacInnes gave a smile of considerable charm, raising his hands to the fire. "My apologies, Martim, for taking so long to return your calls."

"No apologies needed. Your hesitation was expected." Martim Gonsalves splashed an inch of amber spirits in two etched glasses. "The men I sent were clumsy and acted far beyond my orders. They frightened you and frightened your daughter, and I offer my sincere apologies." He gave a thin smile. "They have been dealt with."

Jordan took a seat. "The contacts I gave you in Europe were useful, I hope?"

"Without question. We have six confirmed bidders so far, with completed bank transfers. Your contacts in Asia and Argentina are still considering." The younger man sat down in a handcrafted leather chair and studied the fire. "Do you know that my father still remembers you from years ago in Paris? Even now your name carries a great deal of weight among many of his acquaintances."

And that's why I can never be free of my past, Nell's father thought bitterly. "So the location for the auction has been set?"

"I prefer to wait." Martim Gonsalves set his glass on the table, frowning. "A small precaution."

"Perhaps I can advise you on the choice." Jordan raised his glass to the light. Only someone sitting very close would have seen the tremor in his fingers. "Something with impeccable amenities and...agreeably absent hosts."

Gonsalves laughed. "Thank you, but I have my own sources."

Jordan leaned forward and coughed sharply. His face paled.

The pain again. Now it ate through his stomach. How long did he have?

"Jordan, are you sick?"

"Me? Not a day in my life. I had an argument with my daughter, that's all. Didn't sleep well after that. The little fool doesn't like what I do or how I do it. Always complaining, just like a woman." He sipped his whisky, trying to hide the pain that was growing sharper. "What about the art, Martim? I would prefer to examine the piece before we leave. There are bound to be questions before the auction."

His elegant host smiled politely. "I am afraid that will not be possible. I have matters to complete before we leave in two hours."

Jordan kept his cool smile in place, raising his glass to his host. "In that case, all I need to do is relax."

His shoulders tensed as Martim walked across the room to his desk. "And now, Jordan, I'll need the cell phone in your jacket. No point in risking a leak. You'll be given a new phone after the auction is completed."

Jordan stared into the cold, predatory eyes of his host and shrugged. "Of course." He stood up and stretched carelessly. "After all, my work is nearly done, and you're paying me very, very well."

He tried not to think about Nell or wonder if she was safe.

Pain gnawed at his joints. He bruised easily now, and it was growing harder to hide the purple marks. But he held out his cell phone with a jaunty smile. "I'll consider it my vacation."

Gonsalves nodded to his bodyguard, sitting in shadows by the window. "You won't mind if we verify you have no other phones?"

"Be my guest."

MacInnes felt sweat brush his neck as the stocky bodyguard approached. Rain hammered at the deck. Across the bay, the lights of San Francisco flickered, visible but a million miles away.

Ignoring his pain, MacInnes raised his arms and allowed the bodyguard to search him thoroughly. When the man muttered approval, MacInnes sat down again.

The second phone, which he had shoved between the cushions of the sofa, slid back inside his boot.

WHILE JORDAN MACINNES WAS escorted to a secure cabin at the back of the yacht, Martim Gonsalves sat alone, staring at the fake fire in the fake marble fireplace. Ignoring the expensive drink near his hand, he picked up the cell phone taken from the American and flipped through its call history.

The call log was empty.

A resourceful man. MacInnes could not be trusted, of course. With thirty million dollars at stake, *no one* could be trusted. Gonsalves thought about the fragile piece of art hidden in a climate-controlled storage unit outside Baltimore. In two hours it would be taken aboard one of their specially outfitted freighters. Once at sea, it would be transferred to a larger ship, locked in a cabin guarded by ten handpicked men who had never before met each other. The exact destination would be relayed to the captain after the da Vinci was safely transferred.

The theft had gone smoothly enough, discounting the deaths of the museum guards. Once again the October 12th Brigade prevailed.

The thought made Martim smile faintly. Fortunately, the Americans were easily drawn into paranoia about terrorists on their soil. While their FBI busily chased suspects, his contacts had worked undisturbed for months. Now the job of the October 12th Brigade was nearly done. One day they would simply stop claiming credit for new crimes, and the FBI would crow about another threat being neutralized.

He swirled his whisky, staring into the fire. Once the auction was complete, the funds would be wired to his private account in Brazil. Then he would finally be free of his father's constant scrutiny. As a boy he had never been smart enough or tough enough, but all that was about to change. One day his criminal enterprise would dwarf his father's.

All of it was due to the skills of the dangerous and elusive October 12th Brigade. Raising a toast to the false fire, Martim laughed softly. *"Saude,"* he whispered.

"CAR COMING. Watch those trees to your left." Crouched beneath a tree, Izzy scanned the fallow fields below them with Zeiss binoculars. They had been parked out of sight for six hours already, waiting for activity near the scattered industrial buildings where the calls had come on the night of the National Gallery theft. Up the hill heavy foliage covered their Jeep, but provided a narrow view of a dozen buildings locked behind a twelve-foot fence with brand-new security cameras.

An hour before sunset a brown Ford van cruised to the electronic gate. The driver leaned out and swiped a keycard, giving Dakota a glimpse of a stocky figure in sunglasses and a second man in the passenger seat. Immediately upon exiting, the Ford picked up speed, fishtailing over the pitted road.

A second van pulled out of the compound, headed in the same direction.

"Run the plates, Izzy." Dakota rattled off the Virginia license plate numbers as the two vans raced south, then turned onto an unmarked dirt road.

In two minutes Izzy had an ID. "Both of them are licensed to Holt Brothers Shipping, LLC. We sit here all afternoon and no one goes in or out, but suddenly we get two vans heading south hell for leather."

"Let's find out what's got them so excited," Dakota muttered. The two men sprinted up the slope to their mud-spattered Jeep and eased through the trees to the dirt road.

Dakota stayed out of sight behind the dense foliage along a small stream.

"They're headed straight south." Izzy moved his

binoculars. "Looks like some kind of a dock down there." He pointed across the weed-covered fields. "The first van's stopped. Someone getting out." The second van turned sharply and backed up to the edge of the river.

Dakota slowed, dropping below the curve of the hill to stay out of view of the two parked vehicles. Below them the vans were silent. No one got out. No one got in. The area was deserted, one small dock on one small waterway amid a maze of estuaries of the Potomac River, flowing out into Chesapeake Bay.

Dakota pulled off the road and cut the motor.

As shadows gathered into twilight, he pulled out night-vision binoculars. "Maybe we should go back to the compound."

"Give it a little longer."

"A hunch? I didn't think you tech guys believed in hunches. But then again, I'm just the brawn here."

Both men knew it wasn't true. Dakota's insights were as honed as Izzy's. But the joke was an old one between the Foxfire operatives and their cool counterpart.

Izzy muttered something nasty without looking up.

"Any developments on the numbers MacInnes gave his daughter?" Dakota rubbed his neck. "What about a social security number?"

"Already checked. That number was never active. I've scanned phone databases for every major carrier, but *nada* there, too. We're working on offshore accounts, but that will be slow going. All in all, it's starting to piss me off."

"Don't like to lose, Teague?"

"Oh, I haven't lost. I'm going to crack this, count on it."

Down by the dock, the dark gathered.

Neither van moved.

"HOLD ON. We've finally got some activity." Izzy focused his night-vision binoculars over a line of boulders. "Van in front just turned around. Right front door opening."

Dakota crouched on the ground beside Izzy, staring at the dock. "I make three men," he whispered.

The driver, a stocky man with a buzz cut, was talking on a cell phone. Two other men, both wearing brown coveralls, stood a few feet away. By their sharp gestures, it was clear that they were arguing about something.

Dakota pulled on a black vest, then slid a receiver over his ear. "I'm going down."

The tactical vest held a Sig Sauer P226 pistol and two combat knives. With the weapons secured, Dakota quickly streaked black and olive camouflage face paint over his cheeks, chin and hands.

Then he vanished into the darkness.

By the time he reached the edge of the creek, the moon was rising. Hidden in the marsh grass, he edged through the dark water toward the dock. As the cell phone conversation continued, he heard occasional words that were too low to understand.

The driver moved past the vans and stood at the end of the dock, watching the water while he spoke quietly.

The other two men leaned against the van's front fender, their argument growing more heated. None of them saw Dakota circle past and inch through the trees.

Abruptly a door snapped open and someone emerged from the van near the dock. A woman's voice cut through the night, angry and querulous.

"You said he'd be here with the passport. Where is he?"

"Probably caught in traffic." The calm male voice coming from the dock was American. "Have you finished copying all the files?"

"Only two more to go. My laptop is nearly out of memory." She lit a cigarette and Dakota saw her face, its narrow forehead and thin mouth caught in the sudden yellow flare of a match. He recognized her from the briefing as one of the senior curators at the National Gallery. Now he knew the inside link, but where was the stolen art?

His fingers slid to his Sig as he crept closer.

"What else do you *need* me for? I've already wrapped the package. It's gone. There's nothing else—"

Inside the van a light flickered.

"Finally." She tossed down the cigarette and ran a hand through her hair. "The files are all transferred. All the tests I ran are there along with complete photos." She glanced down at the luminous dial of a small sleek watch and cursed. "Where *is* he, damn it? You said he'd be here an hour ago. I *need* that passport to—"

Four fast bullets coughed from a suppressed pistol at close range, and the woman spun sideways, thrown against the back of the van. She tried to talk, but only gurgling sounds came from the entry wounds at her throat and chest. Her body jerked twice and then crumpled to the ground.

As Dakota moved in, the man with the cell phone leaned down and sent two bullets into the fallen woman's forehead.

In the sudden silence, Dakota smelled cordite and perfume and the dank odor of stagnant water. His hand closed into a fist. He fought the urge to cut down every man in the clearing.

But it wouldn't bring the woman back. It wouldn't help him find the missing art. It would ruin the only new leads they had.

Dakota forced his fingers to relax, forced the Sig down until it wasn't aimed at the killer's head as the man prodded the body with one foot and then gestured to the others.

"Get her into the back, but stay away from the computer. We're done here."

Dakota touched his lip microphone. "You seeing this, Teague?" he whispered.

"I'm on it with video. She's definitely dead?"

"No question, after those last two shots."

"I'm calling it in to Ryker. The FBI will be all over this. He'll have to report it."

"You want me to nab our friend with the buzz cut for a nice, long chat before the FBI makes an appearance?"

"Nice idea, but we need him on the move. Get back here pronto." Izzy's voice hardened. "He's going to lead us straight up the food chain."

FIVE MINUTES later the head of Foxfire received a call from Izzy. "I've got the FBI on the phone. They want to talk with my superior."

"Put them through," Ryker snapped. When he answered the call that Izzy patched through, he gave no identification nor department affiliation.

"Yes."

"Agent Amy Fuller calling for Lloyd Ryker."

"You found him. How can I help you, Agent Fuller?"

"You're a hard man to reach, Mr. Ryker."

Ryker ignored the comment.

"I thought you'd want to know that one of the National Gallery guards was killed last night in what appears to be a hit-and-run accident near the Lincoln Memorial. We received the information a few minutes ago."

Ryker frowned at the paperwork stacked in a neat pile at the edge of his desk. There was nothing else in the room. No family photos, no travel mementos, no coffee mugs with inspiring mottos. "Any witnesses?"

"None have come forward. We've got people checking the area on foot. We've also requested surveillance feed from the National Park Service. We may get lucky and pull an image from the video."

Ryker said nothing. They both knew the likelihood of that happening was razor-thin to laughable. "Have you checked the guard's banking records for large deposits?"

"We should have the information in the next two hours. Rogers—the guard—didn't live beyond his means and he drove a ten-year-old pickup, but he might have had money tucked away somewhere. Of course if the money was banked offshore it could be difficult to locate."

"I appreciate your call, Agent Fuller. I'd like hard copies of anything you turn up."

"Where should I send them?"

Ryker gave her a fax number.

"And exactly where is that, Mr. Ryker? As far as I can see, you work for a department with no name, in a location that has no address on jobs with no description."

Ryker smiled thinly. He didn't dispute the comment. It was in fact, highly accurate. The Foxfire unit appeared on no government rosters, he'd made damned sure of that. "Need-to-know, Agent Fuller. And I'll be watching for that fax."

He hung up as she was gathering breath for an angry response.

Women in nuclear submarines.

Women in the FBI.

Next thing you knew, there'd be a woman presiding over the sacred duties of the Oval Office.

The thought was incomprehensible to Lloyd Ryker. With luck it wouldn't happen during his lifetime. Scowling, he glanced at his watch, then punched a button on the sleek silver office phone, reconnecting with Izzy.

"Agent Fuller just notified me that one of the National Gallery security staff was killed in a hit-and-run last night. I'll send through the report as soon as it arrives."

"That makes two dead, sir. A senior curator was just

shot during our surveillance. The vans came from the Holt Brothers facility on the outskirts of D.C. We tracked them to an isolated marsh near the Potomac, where the shooting took place." Quickly, Teague relayed the rest of the details.

"Description of the computer files?" Ryker said curtly.

"She mentioned photos and tests. She also said she'd helped them 'wrap the package' and that it was gone. I'd say that has to refer to the da Vinci."

"You're trailing these vans now?"

"Looks like they're headed back to the warehouse facility."

"Don't give them any hint they're being followed. I'll put someone on the dead woman's phone and credit card records. I want to know everyone she spoke to and visited over the last six months. We'll check for any receipts from a vacation home or storage facility where she might have stashed the art."

"Unlikely, sir. She said the package was gone and indicated her work was done."

Ryker steepled his fingers. "I want that da Vinci and the people who stole it, Teague. Pick up the pace. And get me this information before any *other* agencies have their nose to the wind."

CHAPTER SIXTEEN

London

CAR HORNS BLARED.

Tires screeched.

Nicholas Draycott seemed oblivious to London's pollution and snarling traffic as he slid Nell's bag into the back of a red Mini Cooper. "How nice to get back to the quiet bustle of England," he murmured.

His well-placed government contacts had expedited their passage through customs and immigration. What would have taken two hours had been finished in a few minutes.

After she slid into the car, Nell made certain that her cell phone had a clear signal, in case her father called. Waiting calmly for that call was the hardest thing she had ever done.

Nicholas pulled into the traffic, ignoring the angry blare of horns behind him. "When we get to the abbey, I'll run those museum acquisition files you gave me. I'm sure that Izzy and Dakota Smith are also working on the numbers from their end. Why don't you try to sleep until we reach the abbey?"

Nell shook her head. Her eyes ached from too many hours of traveling, but anxiety about her father left her too jumpy to relax. The cuts and bruises from the night of her attack didn't help, a constant reminder of the danger that might have followed her even here.

She managed a smile for Nicholas. "I'll be fine. But there's something I need to know. How long have you and my father been working on this under-cover plan?"

"For nearly eight months. Once he was contacted in prison, your father managed to get word to me through a journalist who was finishing an article on prison reform." Nicholas slanted her a thoughtful look. "He didn't tell you because he didn't want you to worry, Nell. I hope you can understand that."

"I might understand, but I still don't like it. In case I didn't say it before, thank you," she added quietly. "If not for you, he would have tried to handle this alone."

Nicholas kept glancing in the rearview mirror, and Nell realized he was checking to see if they were being followed. "Is someone back there?"

"Not that I can see. If there is, I'll ditch them. And don't thank me yet, my dear. We're far from out of the woods."

"Have you heard anything from Dakota and Izzy Teague?"

"No messages yet." The viscount sailed through a roundabout with steely confidence, feathering past a silver Audi and a grocery truck. His face looked tense.

"Is something wrong, Nicholas?"

"Of course not."

Nell could have sworn his fingers tightened on the wheel, just for a moment. There was something that he hadn't told her. "Nicholas, I—"

"Get some rest," he said gruffly. "I'll wake you when we're at the abbey."

SOUTH OF MAIDSTONE the hedgerows slid into a green blur. Old stone cottages flashed by, and every bend in the road held years of rich history. The Normans had walked here. Before that Saxon, Celt and Roman had marched along long-forgotten roads.

But the history that gripped Nell now had begun months before, the day her father hatched a desperate plan that might get him killed. As the miles slipped past, her eyes closed, and with sleep came restless dreams like dark companions, moving in ragged bursts of noise and shadow. Somewhere in those dreams her father walked down a hall full of da Vinci masterpieces lit by a dying fire.

Nell reached out to him. "I can't lose you now," she whispered. "Stay safe."

He didn't hear, didn't turn and the shadows swallowed him, building to a greater darkness. But this new darkness was alive. Fluid with ghostlike shapes, it moved at the corner of Nell's vision.

"NELL? WE'RE HERE."

The hiss of brakes cut through the shadows. Nell sat up abruptly, rubbing her eyes in the streaming sunlight.

And then she was swept into beauty, into a green curve of trees towering over silver water. Swans cut through the mirrored reflection of high walls as the Mini Cooper grumbled up a curving driveway.

The abbey rose before her, all twisting spires and arrogant grace. She took a sharp breath as she saw the roses.

White, pink and cream, they climbed in a riot of color over the abbey's ancient gray walls.

"So many colors in one spot. And the fragrance—" She leaned closer to the open window, half-drunk with the scent that drifted on the wind.

"We've always been known for roses," Nicholas said with quiet pride. "They are blooming late this year. They do that sometimes. An expert told me it has something to do with the walls facing south." For the first time since Nell had seen him in California, some of the tension left his face. "It's odd living in a relic packed with so much history, but I miss every inch when I'm gone. Welcome to Draycott Abbey, my dear. I'm glad to see that the swans are out for you."

Twin shapes shimmered on the quiet moat. Nell felt overwhelmed by the majesty and contentment of the place.

She rubbed a hand over her face. "As amazing as Draycott Abbey is, I think I'd better stay somewhere in town, Nicholas. I don't want to put you or your family at risk."

"Of course you'll stay here," the viscount said gruffly. "You'll appreciate the art more than any guest in a decade. Besides, you couldn't leave if you wanted to. I'm afraid I had to declare that you would remain here at the abbey in my keeping, as that was the only way to bend a few rules at the airport. We have one week before your arrival will be officially noted, just to throw off anyone inclined to ask."

Nicholas was right, of course. People would be watching for her. This way was safest. Nell frowned at the moat, complete with swans and a weir below ancient, gnarled oak trees. Suddenly she felt the weight of the place and the care and attention of centuries of ancestors who had kept the house safe.

Someone always paid a price to keep things safe.

She turned to look at Nicholas. "Tell me this. What if you had to choose between this beautiful place and its legacy…or the life of someone you love? I know it's a strange question, but something about this glorious house makes me wonder."

"There would be no question. The people I love are my world and all my joy. Without them, this house and everything else would be ashes."

The absolute certainty in his voice made Nell wonder if he'd ever had to make that kind of choice. She knew that his wife was a well-known American scholar specializing in the art of Whistler. Nell had heard Kacey Draycott speak once in Boston, and the talk had been all the more fascinating because Kacey had discovered an unknown Whistler painting right here at the abbey.

"I don't like this, Nicholas. I can't let your wife and daughter be put in danger."

"They are staying in London all week for a textile workshop, arranged with my daughter's school. To tell you the truth, I think the two have forgotten I'm alive."

His smile faded as he glanced at his watch. "But now I've got a dozen calls to make. Marston will give you the quick tour, and I'll do a more thorough job tonight."

"Marston?"

"Our butler. The man has been here forever. He probably knows more about the abbey than I do. Ask him for whatever you need, Nell. He always complains that we don't have enough guests, so he may smother you with attention. Be warned."

"I'm not a guest, Nicholas." Nell had to fight a treacherous dream of belonging here, in a place of such beauty. But she was here to save her father. She couldn't forget that.

No trust.

No leaning.

She stared out at the sweeping green lawns, steeling herself against their beauty, blocking out all but the task ahead of her. "Did you send for those files I wanted?"

"They should be waiting in my e-mail. But you've seen the test results already. Why do you need the conservator's handwritten notes?"

"I don't know yet. I may not know until it's right in front of me." She smiled crookedly. "It's just an instinct, Nicholas. Remember, X never, ever marks the spot. Indiana Jones was dead right about that."

TRUE TO HIS WORD, Nicholas disappeared almost immediately upon their arrival, but his butler was entirely versant in the abbey's history. "I will direct you to your room in the gatehouse, Ms. MacInnes. And we have met before, though it has been years. It was in London.

I recall that your father was selling a piece of art to the viscount—a very fine drawing from a notebook of Leonardo da Vinci, as I recall."

"My memories are a little blurry. Sorry, Marston."

"No reason to apologize. You were only nine at the time, but a very mature nine. You asked me what a butler did and if there were opportunities for advancement."

Nell coughed in embarrassment. Had she really said that?

"I told you that in the right circumstances there was no better job. I stand by my comment today."

Nell glanced down and hid a smile. Marston's lime-green running shoes made a strange contrast to his beautifully tailored but severe black suit. Clearly this was not your average English servant.

"I will serve tea on the south lawn in twenty minutes, if that is convenient."

"Please don't go to any trouble. I'm only here to work, Marston."

He shot her an imperious glance. "You are a guest, one who *chooses* to work," he corrected. "In twenty minutes. On the south lawn."

There would be no arguing with the man, Nell realized, wondering if he ordered the viscount about in this way. After a little thought, she decided it was highly likely.

As they walked through the shadowed rooms, Marston straightened an occasional picture or antique Chinese porcelain, and the beauty of the old house struck her anew.

"I've prepared the front suite for you in the gatehouse, Ms. MacInnes. Family legends hold that Elizabeth I slept there on one of her many royal circuits." He coughed slightly. "The story has never been proved, I am sorry to say."

She was going to sleep in the same room that Elizabeth had slept in? Maybe even in the same bed? "I really don't think it's necessary—"

"It is the viscount's pleasure." The butler's arctic tone cut off further discussion.

They walked down a corridor filled with portraits of imposing aristocrats and an exceptionally fine set of Anasazi burial bowls displayed in climate-controlled cases. Inside the gatehouse, the smell of roses filled the air with spice and cloves from blooms scattered in crystal vases and silver holders.

Marston cast a critical eye over the bedroom. "I'm told these roses were a passion of the first viscount, who carried dozens of plants back from the Holy Land and the Crusades. A grander day, but his story was far from happy." Sunlight gleamed on yellow silk curtains and blue toile wallpaper. "Your room, Ms. MacInnes. I hope you will be comfortable here."

Comfortable? Words failed Nell.

When she turned around, Marston was gone. The heavy curtains drifted in an unseen wind.

Tea in twenty minutes on the south lawn.

Nell ran a hand through her hair. What had happened to her simple, orderly life?

Something nudged her feet, and she saw a gray cat sitting on the carpet. While Nell washed and changed, the cat claimed a spot in the middle of the big bed.

Keen amber eyes stared at her, unblinking. With a low, imperious meow the cat jumped to the floor. At the door he turned, waiting for her to follow, the message of impatience unmistakable.

"So you rule the roost and I'm supposed to follow?" Another meow. "In that case, lead on."

When she opened the door, the cat raced across the courtyard. Nell had to hurry to catch up.

NICHOLAS DRAYCOTT STUDIED the big wooden globe next to his desk, frowning. "No, Mr. Ryker, I must *insist* that you maintain the terms Jordan MacInnes set. None of your government agencies are to be informed of this plan. At least one person on the inside—and possibly more—was involved. Jordan tried to learn who, but gave up when his prison contact became suspicious. Nell has already made a list of possibilities for the numbers he gave her. In addition, I have just received the latest conservator's notes from the National Gallery. I'm sorry, what did you say?"

Nicholas Draycott's face hardened as he listened to Lloyd Ryker's description of the senior curator's death. "She was transferring files? So she was definitely involved in the theft."

The Englishman turned away, watching sunlight play over the moat. For once the house's beauty did not raise his spirits. "Yes, I've heard of East West Properties. I've met Luis Gonsalves once or twice at auctions." Nicholas didn't mention that he had once bid against the wealthy businessman for a Tang Dynasty ceramic funerary horse, but the bidding had quickly spiraled far beyond Nicholas's limit. His impression that night was that Luis Gonsalves enjoyed spending money while people watched; even more, he enjoyed winning while people watched. "The father is a very determined man. The son? I've never met him, but I can make discreet inquiries." Draycott frowned as his cell phone began to vibrate, dancing over the mahogany desktop. "Excuse me. My cell phone is ringing, and I give this number out to very few people."

The British royal family and three heads of state were among those people.

Nicholas picked up the phone. The calling number was unfamiliar, but there was no mistaking the voice of his old friend.

Nell's father.

CHAPTER SEVENTEEN

"I REPEAT. There was nothing you should have done differently."

Dakota stripped off his gloves and tossed them into the back seat. "Tell that to the parents who just lost their daughter."

"Your orders were clear. *Do not alert the target.* You complied with those orders," Izzy said curtly.

"And now the woman's dead. If I'd taken them out first, she'd still be alive to question."

"Do the math, Smith. We now have a concrete link between Gonsalves's company, a murder and the museum theft. The October Twelfth Brigade is hidden in there somewhere. It's time to focus on the chain and work the details."

Dakota scowled down at his metal case filled with high-tech firepower. All the expensive, shiny equipment in the world wouldn't bring the woman back. Dakota knew he was going to see her face in his nightmares.

But Teague was right. Ryker's orders had been unequivocal. Dakota was going to have to live with the memory of Lydia Reynolds's crumpled body.

Civilians always meant trouble during an op. They headed straight into danger, a disaster just waiting to happen. When things went hot and the civilians were shot, all a soldier could do was move on.

And try to bury the guilt.

Soldiers knew the risks they took when they picked up a weapon. Killing another soldier was a cold, predictable part of war, but civilians were a curse, he thought grimly.

Nell MacInnes was a perfect example. Whenever she turned up, things took a nosedive straight to hell. It wasn't her fault that she'd been pulled into her father's dangerous scheme, but her presence only complicated things.

Sure, she'd been fast and decisive on the peak in Scotland. Dakota remembered the calm way she had maneuvered the panicky teens down to safety in near-zero visibility. Not many people—men or women— could have done that.

And he still didn't like it. He especially didn't like how he couldn't get the memory of her sleek body or her smoky laughter out of his head. Bottom line? Civilians meant unacceptable complications. Getting mixed up with one during a mission could get you killed fast.

"What do we have on Lydia Reynolds, Izzy?"

"I've got someone running her employment history and credit card usage. Seems that she had a habit of slipping off to Atlantic City every few months."

"Love interest?"

"Gambling interest," Izzy said flatly. "I'm thinking that she owed money to the wrong people, which made her a target for more wrong people. One thing probably led to another. I called a friend in Atlantic City while you were on your way back from the dock. He told me that Lydia Reynolds was recently posted on every casino's no-admit list because her losses were getting worse. If they wanted an insider, she would be easy to turn."

"She won't be doing any gambling now," Dakota said harshly.

The van pulled off onto a smaller dirt road. Izzy opened his cell phone and dialed Ryker. When he hung up, he was smiling for the first time in three hours. "Score one for the home team. Once Gonsalves moved up on our list of probables, I put a tech team in place. They've been running aerial and satellite photos of all the family properties. One compound is on an island in the Caymans, one estate is in Ireland and two sites are in Scotland. I've been watching traffic patterns and food deliveries on the assumption that they'll need to prepare before people assemble for the auction and bingo, and I've just established a pattern. We're looking at a castle Gonsalves owns on a small island north of Skye."

"Castle as in turrets and parapets?"

"The genuine article, built in the twelfth century and expanded by Edward II. Full renovations were made just last year. Their people started stocking provisions two days ago and today two dozen of his private security force blew in from Macau."

"*Bada bing.*" Dakota frowned at the van racing under the dark trees. "What about them? They can't just walk away."

"I've got a videotape for future legal action. My people will handle them from now on. Ryker wants you in England tonight."

"You're sure this castle in Skye will have the art?"

Izzy nodded. "You're going in. Ryker's been given a green light on forced-entry scenarios at Gonsalves's estate." Izzy rubbed his neck, frowning.

"What else? Teague? Your pulse just spiked and I'm reading heat fluctuation in your hands. Something else is going on."

"You're to meet Nell in England. Given that there is no time to locate and transport an outside expert, Ryker wants her to go over the estate photos and provide whatever technical instruction you need."

Dakota's head snapped around. "I *don't* work with civilians. Ryker of all people knows how dangerous that kind of situation can be."

"I don't like it very much either, but that castle has sheer walls and constant armed surveillance. You're going to need all Nell's help to get in and out without tipping off Gonsalves. Ryker said to suck it up and get moving."

Dakota glared at his gear bag. The hell of it was, he could see that Nell's knowledge, training and climbing ability made her the perfect fit for a successful mission. She was a prize package with vital expertise in two areas—climbing and art.

He didn't want it to be true, but it was.

"Damn," he said softly.

"My thoughts exactly." Teague looked away. "Let's get moving."

NICHOLAS DRAYCOTT LISTENED to static hiss over the phone line.

The American spoke quickly. "Is she there? Is she safe?"

"She's here with me, don't worry." The English-man's voice tightened. "I just got word that one of the curators was killed."

Jordan MacInnes expelled a harsh breath. "They had someone important inside at the museum. I never could find out who. There may be more than one. Remember that."

"Understood."

Out of the corner of his eye Nicholas saw Nell emerge from the gatehouse. With a sweater pulled around her shoulders, she paced the front courtyard, deep in thought. Then she crossed to the front door, frowning.

Worrying about her father, no doubt.

Static broke over the line. "Look, I don't have much time. The package has been transferred to a freighter. I'm being watched closely and all I've been able to find out is that the destination is somewhere in the U.K., on an island. Check the known residences of Martim or Luis Gonsalves, as well as any corporate properties that they own or lease." Jordan talked fast, his voice strained. "Martim said there's a fishing operation nearby, but I don't know where. He's paranoid—locks everything up at night, even his phones and computers, then turns off all power. He hasn't told his pilot where we're going yet, but I know he plans to auction the package off within the next three days. Did you get that? Three more days."

Jordan MacInnes's voice fell. "Keep her safe, my friend. Whatever happens, whatever things you hear, promise me that."

There was a note of finality in the words that made Nicholas frown. "You have my word."

"Last thing before I go," MacInnes said breathlessly. "I've verified that Gonsalves has a contact inside the government. Those numbers belong to the contact's offshore banking account. You'll have to track down the name. If I ask any more questions, they'll get suspicious." The line went dead.

Nicholas Draycott stared at the phone for a very long time. If there was a contact inside the government, his old friend was in gravest danger. Jordan had always been too intelligent—and too complicated—for a simple thief, part of the reason that Nicholas had liked the man so much. Few people knew that Jordan had made it a practice to steal only from criminals or from institutions that dealt in illicit art. That he had occasionally provided timely warning of thefts planned by others was another fact that few people besides Nicholas knew.

Now they had a date to work with, but they had to know the location of the island. No one would find it faster than Izzy Teague. Draycott stared at a framed map of England and Scotland, then picked up the phone.

NELL FOLLOWED the gray cat up the staircase past a dozen imposing paintings. She counted one Sargent, one van Gogh and a small but exquisite Picasso. At the top of the stairs, the cat disappeared into a room with vaulted ceilings and mullioned windows along one wall.

He ghosted through the dim room and stopped at the far wall, then stared up at Nell, as if awaiting her reaction.

"Okay, I'm impressed. I admit it. Great art."

The cat didn't move. Nell rubbed her eyes and studied the blank wall. Nothing there.

She put her hands on her hips.

Jet lag. High stress. There was no other way to explain why she was standing in a room full of shadows having a one-sided conversation with a cat.

Nell could have sworn the keen amber eyes blinked with irritation. "Okay, I give up. All I see is a blank spot on a big wall." As she spoke, cold air swept through the long gallery, brushing her hair back over her shoulders.

Except all the windows were closed and locked.

The sound of footsteps startled her. She turned to find Nicholas Draycott crossing the hall.

"Is something wrong, Nell?"

"Your cat seemed so intent that I followed him up here. He kept staring at that space on the far wall."

Nicholas Draycott didn't move. "What cat?"

"The gray one. You must have had him a very long time, because he seems to know every corner of this house."

The viscount frowned at her. "A large gray cat with amber eyes?"

Nell nodded. Why was he staring at her so oddly? "He darted away before you came. Very intelligent. What is his name?"

Nicholas's gaze ran the length of the gallery and settled on the portrait of an imperious ancestor in lace and black velvet. "We never knew that."

They had never given their family pet a name? That was odd. "I'm sorry if I disturbed you by coming up here, Nicholas. Maybe the cat is—"

"You won't find him, trust me. He comes and goes at his own pleasure. Actually, it's been quite a long time since I've...seen him." The Englishman stared at the bare wall where Nell had last seen the cat. "It used to be right there." Draycott's fingers traced the old plaster carefully.

Nell frowned at him. "What?"

"The da Vinci sketch, the same piece that was stolen from the National Gallery," he explained.

"Here?"

Draycott nodded. "It was hidden in a secret niche behind this wall. Before it was stolen," he added quietly. "And that cat you saw is part of Draycott legend. He was often seen with one of my ancestors, a brooding, difficult man according to all reports." The viscount stared at the blank space where the da Vinci had once been hidden. "I have seen the cat only a few times, Nell. Each time great danger was involved."

"This is a joke."

"Hardly. I searched for that cat during most of my boyhood just as I have searched for details of the da Vinci's loss during most of my adult life. Yet you, within an hour of your arrival, unerringly walk to the last spot where the piece was seen."

Nell didn't move. She believed in facts, not hallucinations. The simple explanation was always right.

"Then the cat must have been a stray. Probably I imagined that he walked to that wall. It is a scientific fact that light can be misleading in a house like this. Old mullioned windows are uneven and cast odd shadows, making distances hard to judge." She glared at the wall, glared at the beautiful room, refusing to be misled by legends and her imagination. "Maybe I just thought I saw a cat."

It was a lie of course. She would never forget those keen amber eyes.

MARSTON POURED tea on the south lawn, his face impassive. The quintessence of propriety, he straightened a vase with newly cut roses and then left.

Nicholas stared at his untouched tea. "I'm afraid I have to go back to London shortly."

Nell heard tension in his voice. "Something's happened, hasn't it?"

After a moment he nodded. "Your father called me a few minutes ago, Nell."

She took a deep breath, forcing herself to stay calm. "How did he sound?"

"Frightened but probably enjoying himself just a little, the old fool." The viscount watched a pair of swans drift beneath a sweeping oak. "He always said it would be hard to give up the life he led because the danger and excitement made him feel important."

Nell stiffened. Was she more like her father than she'd realized? Climbing brought her the same feeling of risk and importance, along with the addictive adrenaline rushes. "What else did he say?"

"The numbers relate to an offshore bank account. There was no time for more details."

"Because they're watching him and he couldn't talk." Nell rubbed her arms, feeling cold. "Can you track the accounts by country? Isn't there a bank routing code as part of a full account number?"

"I'm having it checked out." Draycott leaned back slowly. "Do you know someone named Lydia Reynolds?"

"She's the curator at the National Gallery, the one who handled the tests on the da Vinci. I've met her several times. Her reports were in the file you gave me."

"What did you think of them?"

Nell hesitated. "Some of the results looked wrong. Since it was slight, I wanted to be sure before I said anything. Two of the X-rays showed perfectly acceptable linen content in the paper, consistent with the materials of da Vinci's known work, several other X-rays suggested much lower than normal linen content. It seemed odd to me, but hardly conclusive," Nell said slowly. "It suggested—only suggested—that there might be two pieces of art being tested."

Nicholas's eyes narrowed. "How would that be done?"

"Not easily. Once a piece is logged in, there is a consistent chain of documentation for everyone who handles it. Especially on a piece of this value, no one could remove it without approval and written notation."

"So what happened?"

Nell worked through the possibilities. "It could be that the initial tests began with the real piece, establishing the probable date and use of authentic materials. Then more complex tests were done, the kind of tests that always show contestable results. The uncertainty is something every scholar lives with. Only in the second phase someone may have substituted a forged piece of art with similar, but not the same materials."

"Why?"

"To give a thief time to remove the real piece safely from the museum. Only when the theft of the forgery took place did the pandemonium ensue." Nell shook her head. "But any expert going over these reports would have noticed the inconsistencies. It was just a matter of time."

"Exactly. A matter of time." Nicholas stood up, watching clouds darken the woods to the south. "They needed time to get the real art away, and Lydia Reynolds bought it for them. But none of the technicians would have noticed that the second piece was a forgery?"

"Not if she'd limited access to the piece. The quality of the art is not a technician's area of expertise. Assuming the copy was good, they would be busy with the chemistry, not the *look* of the thing. As a short-term tactic it would work." Nell drummed her fingers on the table. "But Nicholas, this curator might know where the painting is. If she was involved, you can ask her—"

"I'm afraid no one can ask her anything, Nell. She died several hours ago. These people are taking no chances on being found." He glanced at his watch. "Now I'm afraid I have more calls to make before I leave for London." He glanced at the darkening sky.

"You should go inside, too. There's nasty weather on the way, I understand. Storm before morning."

Wind shook the white tablecloth as Nell stood up. She felt cold, afraid for her father.

"Marston will provide whatever you need in my absence. He will also have my cell phone number if you need to reach me. I will try to be back by midday tomorrow."

THE AFTERNOON STRETCHED into the long shadows of evening. After picking at her dinner, Nell took a walk to fight off her growing restlessness. Back in San Francisco she practiced at a climbing gym and walked the hilly streets every day. Being cooped up made her feel like a captive.

Retreating to Nicholas's paneled library, she pored over her notes and narrowed the list of probable buyers for the da Vinci, double-checking the most recent auction databases. All the while she prayed for a call from her father.

But the call never came. Finally she pulled out an old manuscript on siege instruments written in da Vinci's curious mirror script, part of the abbey's singular collection.

Somewhere a clock chimed. A bird cried out shrilly in the darkness.

Nell barely heard.

CHAPTER EIGHTEEN

NELL SLEPT FITFULLY. The house seemed too quiet, the wind too loud. She awoke with a cramp in her neck. Through the big French doors overlooking the moat, she saw swans cut through silver water, their wake forming cryptic hieroglyphics.

She sat up, yawning. Time to get back to work. She had to recheck all the Asian databases for collectors who had bid on works by da Vinci.

Her father's life could depend on every clue she unearthed.

AN HOUR BEFORE DAWN she was still huddled in Nicholas's big leather chair, surrounded by research books and computer printouts.

With her laptop she had logged into every online research database, tracking recent auctions for da Vinci sketches. Stacked on the desk was a list of every private collector or institution that had acquired similar da Vinci pieces over the past three years. She could have gone back further, but she had a feeling the pattern she was looking for would be recent.

Unfortunately, her databases would only reveal one

part of that pattern. There would be others who had purchased illegal art, the kind that passed from hand to hand through underground networks in Rome, London and New York, never surfacing officially. Nell knew stolen art could vanish within hours and not be seen again for years—if at all.

This kind of collector bought from a need to possess, not to display. Transactions would be in cash and appear in no academic databases or auction catalogues.

Her father would know those names better than anyone, since that shadow world had once been his domain. Nell had never spoken to him about that world or its dangerous allure. As a child she hadn't understood his secrecy or late-night meetings, followed by sudden, unexplained travel.

As an adult she had been *afraid* to understand.

Now, standing by the window of Nicholas's study, watching wind toss the banked roses, Nell thought of all the things she should have asked and the dark, hard truths about her father that she ought to have faced long before. She wanted to believe with all her heart that his old life was over, that it would never touch her or her father again. But there was no point in pretending things were normal or ever had been normal.

Jordan MacInnes had been a very good thief, and she was a thief's daughter. Nell had evaded those hard facts, shoving her memories deep to escape their pain, working harder and longer than her colleagues to prove the past couldn't harm her. But it had. Now there could be no more refuge in lies.

As the wind prowled, whipping waves across the

moat, she pulled on her jacket. The violence of the night seemed to call her as she went outside to face the storm. The roses were ghostly in the moonlight, their perfume lost in the cold wind. A few beads of rain fell as she walked toward the gravel driveway.

She had felt like a guest for most of her life, moving from foster home to university and then on to months of advanced study throughout Europe. Always she had been an observer and a quiet traveler, without roots or deep contacts.

The distance in her life had never been painful to her. She loved the infinite challenge of her work and the focus it required. But now Nell wondered if she had used her travel as an excuse to hold people away. She had no relatives except her father. Even with her closest friends, she had always shunned anything that hinted at attachment or dependence.

No leaning.

No trust.

MacInnes rules.

How much joy and rich experience had those rules cost her, through years of rootlessness meant to ensure that she would never be abandoned again? She had never been to a therapist or a priest after her father's arrest. She had never joined discussion groups or cathartic seminars. Words had seemed like a weak bandage for the unhealed wounds she carried.

But the past had to be healed. The realization shook her now, forcing her back into the dark times, churning up the memory of her father thrown to the ground and beaten, then shoved facedown into a waiting police car. Eighteen years later, she still remembered the streaks of blood on his face as he had tried to sit up and smile at her, cocky and reassuring as he was driven away.

One more act. One more facade in a lifetime full of them.

Nell hunched her shoulders, trembling at the buried memories that began to surface. Struck by a sudden sense of loss and pain, she closed her eyes, squeezed her hands to fists.

And then Nell cried for the first time in longer than she could remember.

From child to teenager to woman, the scars had stayed with her, always pushed deeper and firmly ignored.

All the more reason to face them now.

When the first gusts of rain fell, she stood on the little bridge above the moat, gripping the weathered stone until it bit at her skin, but the pain in her fingers was nothing compared to the pain of remembering.

She wanted her life back. She wanted to remember what living had been like before the world had closed in on her. She was tired of being the constant stranger at the table. She wanted a real future and a life without shadows.

Her face to the driving rain, caught in memories too long ignored, she didn't hear the moan of the wind or the peal of distant church bells, swallowing the growl of a motor coming fast.

DAKOTA TOOK the turn from the village too fast, took the abbey's gravel driveway too fast. He was angry at his orders, angry at being forced into a mission with a civilian.

Not any civilian. Nell. A woman he couldn't ignore or forget.

The price was too high.

Soldiers understood the risks of the job. Their deaths were mourned but accepted. Civilians...hell, civilians shouldn't be involved.

The wind howled as he passed a moat speckled with rain. Two pale shapes that had to be swans drifted on the dark current.

Swans. Moats. Stone turrets.

What kind of place was this?

But he knew the answer. This house belonged to a world filled with money and old power. Nell would feel comfortable in a place like this, he thought grimly. She would be right at home amid the grand antiques and priceless art.

Nell...

Why the hell *couldn't* he get her out of his mind?

Why did he have the feeling that in the end, she was the one who would be hurt most by her father's reckless choices?

When the curve loomed up, Dakota throttled back. Abruptly a gray cat flashed across the road. He pulled hard to the left to miss the cat and his vision blurred. Gravel cracked, kicked up by his tires, and he leaned hard to keep the bike steady.

When he came out of the turn, he saw something else in the rain, motionless on the top of the small bridge. He had a sudden glimpse of the abbey's dark parapets looming at the end of the driveway, but his vision wouldn't clear.

Then he realized it was Nell standing at the far side of the bridge. With her face turned up into the rain, she didn't hear his shout of warning.

CHAPTER NINETEEN

TORN FREE BY THE WIND, leaves sailed over Dakota's head. Only his skill and instant reflexes helped him twist sideways and brake while controlling the skid as he shouted another warning.

Nell spun, her feet slipping on the wet bridge, and Dakota threw his weight to the side, feathering the turn while his leg raked the cobblestones.

It was five in the morning. Why was the woman outside, face to the rain, her clothing soaked?

Bigger question: why hadn't he seen her sooner?

Fury made his hands clench. But the fury was at himself, not Nell. His vision should have offered some color shift to pick her out of the rain, heat against cold, living human form against wind and stone.

But he had seen nothing to warn him. Moments before, the colors of the night had blurred, impossible to read, in a way Dakota had never experienced before. In that one moment's lapse, he could have run her down. Some kind of electrical effect from the storm?

There was no time for answers. Nell was on her knees on the wet cobblestones, coughing as Dakota shoved the motorcycle onto its side and sprinted to cover her with his jacket.

She blinked at him, her eyes dark with confusion and wariness.

"Are you hurt?"

She shook her head.

Dakota didn't believe her. "Look, I'm sorry. I didn't expect anyone to be out here." He bit back a curse. He'd slept on the long flight to England. Then he'd taken every turn from the small military airport near Hastings too fast, but he was trained to drive fast and push the limits of the high-performance Triumph Izzy had located for his use. Rain or not, his driving skills weren't in question.

His vision was at fault, and his vision had never wavered like this since he'd begun his Foxfire training.

Gently, he brushed wet hair from Nell's face. "Are you sure you aren't hurt?"

"I'm f-fine." Her voice was stiff.

"What were you doing out here?"

She looked away, avoiding his eyes. "Nothing that matters."

His hands tightened. Dakota considered the possibility that she had been waiting for someone. She could be buried deeper than they knew, part of a complex level of betrayal in her father's game.

No, he didn't believe it. He would have sensed her guilt and the effort it took for her to hide it. He couldn't pull words from her mind, but he could read intensity and physical response in heat patterns.

He felt that intensity now, felt her struggle to clear her mind.

"Talk to me, Nell. I need to understand." He pulled his jacket tighter around her.

She grimaced and tried to stand. "I was taking a trip down memory lane." Her voice shook. "It wasn't pretty, so I'll spare you the details."

He didn't understand, but right now the blood on her leg was more important than her terse explanation. He cursed himself silently as she put her weight on her right foot and then winced, gripping his arm. Without a word, Dakota slid his arms around her waist and lifted her.

"Hey, I can walk," she protested.

"And I can sew up a torn parachute with dental floss if I have to, but I don't do it unless it's an emergency. Now how much does it hurt?"

She looked away, her mouth in a thin line.

Which meant it hurt like hell.

"Where's your room?" Dakota hunched closer, shielding her against the rain.

"In the gatehouse. Then down the hall to your left."

She didn't argue as he shoved open the big wooden door with his foot. Dakota had time for a quick impression of yellow curtains and blue walls before he set her down on a bed covered with thick down quilts. He didn't waste breath in more apologies. He doubted it would make either of them feel better. Something was wrong and he needed to figure out what.

He grabbed a towel from the bathroom and dried her hair, then sat down beside her. "Slide your leg onto my lap."

She sat stiffly. "I'll take care of any problems later."

"Not later—now." He shoved up her wet skirt and felt a pang of guilt as his fingers slid along her icy skin. "You've got a bad cut on your ankle, and there's gravel in the wound." His hands curved gently around her ankle. "It has to be cleaned, Nell. I've got supplies in my pack."

She stared at him, frowning. "I told you I can manage."

"Is it just *me* that's the problem, or do you brush off help from everyone?"

"I take care of myself. No leaning. It's one of my life rules."

He shook his head. "It's a stupid rule. Everybody can use help sometimes." Frowning, he found a clean washcloth in the spacious bathroom. Armed with alcohol and bandages, he lifted her leg onto his knee and waited for her to protest.

She didn't look at him.

"No more arguments?"

"You seem to know what you're doing."

Dakota leaned closer and cleaned the short gash. "Sorry if I'm hurting you."

"Just finish. I'll survive."

Was a woman ever more prickly? Dakota worked carefully, picking away small bits of gravel while Nell sat stiffly, never speaking. But he heard her breath check, felt her muscles tense. He saw the heat of her body as it warmed, colors shifting, every degree of change clear to him.

No lapses now. Strangely, now that they were inside the abbey his vision seemed better than ever.

"Done." Dakota's pulse seemed loud as he leaned close to wrap a piece of clean gauze around her ankle. "How does it feel?"

"A little throbbing. Forget it."

He couldn't forget it, that was the problem. His reflexes were perfect and his driving skills exceptional, but something had happened to him out in the rain, something that left him adrift in a sea of gray shapes, just for a second. For a man who relied on his special skills to survive in dangerous places, this kind of lapse was unacceptable.

He scanned the room, checking colors and heat signatures. Yellow pillows, blue blanket, condensation on cold windows, all absolutely normal. Everything was just the way it was supposed to look. So what had gone wrong outside?

Nell was sitting very still, staring at him. "Why are you so angry?"

Dakota kept all expression from his face. "Other than the fact that I nearly hit you? That cut's clean now. The gauze should hold for a day." Tense, he stood up and turned away, raising his hands to check the play of colors and heat.

Normal. All normal.

Whatever had happened appeared to be temporary. Problems could develop despite the highest technology that had gone into his enhancements, and considering that he'd been traveling straight through the night, in and out of time zones and weather conditions, maybe...

No way. Dakota had been in tough conditions before, but never with a slip like that. He'd have to report the situation to Izzy. Maybe the Foxfire tech genius could come up with answers.

Meanwhile, there was a mission to plan.

He prowled the room, noticing the quiet good taste and colorful antiques, then turned back to Nell. "Do you need something for the pain? I can ask Draycott if—"

"There's no need. My ankle's not broken. It's happened before, so I'd know." She sat up slowly, keeping one leg straight in front of her. "All in all I'll live. But you still haven't told me what's wrong. You wouldn't race to get here if it wasn't important. Is my father—" Nell hesitated. Her fingers locked on the quilt.

Dakota realized that she was expecting bad news. "It's not your father. As far as we know, he's fine."

He saw her eyes close, body sagging in relief. "I thought…" She ran a hand across her face. "I thought you came to tell me he was dead."

Wind from the open window tossed her hair. When she shoved it back, Dakota saw the faint marks of a dozen old climbing scars on her strong fingers.

He didn't know her at all, he realized. He had seen a laughing woman in the photographs on her wall back in San Francisco. He had seen a brave adventurer on that snowy peak in Scotland. And yet he still didn't have any idea who Nell MacInnes really was.

Finding out suddenly seemed very important.

In the still room the faint scent of lilacs clung to her skin, cool with rain. He watched her work soft strands of hair through her fingers and remembered how they had felt against his chest when he'd carried her inside. The memory was sharp. Too sharp.

He imagined how her hair would feel wrapped around his hand, spilling over his chest. He wanted to feel her that way now, skin to skin, her eyes dark with passion.

His body went absolutely still.

Nothing broke his focus.

Women were a pleasure to be savored then forgotten. When it was required, Dakota had used sensual pleasure to gain a woman's trust or cooperation. Afterward, he had walked away without looking back, his distance intact.

Feeling nothing kept you safe, and being safe, were all that mattered in his uncertain world.

But he wasn't feeling distant now. Impersonal, noisy sex had never been half as intimate as it felt just to look at Nell while his hand traced casual circles on her leg.

His fingers slowed. He skimmed her calf.

There was no mistaking the first stir of her response. He saw the flare of heat at her neck, at her cheeks, across the swell of her breasts pressed against damp cotton. He knew without words what would give her the greatest pleasure because the heat of her body told him.

Heat.

His fingers slid lower.

He didn't intend for his hand to curve over the arch of her foot. He didn't plan to draw her sigh of pleasure as he kneaded a knot of tension at the back of her heel.

But he couldn't look away, watching heat changes

in her skin, flowing eddies of pale yellow and red that gave precise physical messages to an experienced man. And Dakota was very experienced, very patient. He told himself that touching her meant nothing. Only the mission mattered. The mission was what he was.

A lie. He wanted more than this slow glide of fingers. He wanted to slip his hands into her dark hair and lift her until their bodies met with rough lust and brutal honesty. Angry, he ignored the impulse and buried his emotions, clenching his hands as he turned to cross the room.

Stay cold.

Stay distant.

He repeated the words in his mind. "Get changed," he said. "I'm behind schedule and we've got work to do."

"We?" Nell frowned at the sudden edge in his voice. "What kind of work?"

He kept his face impassive. "Whatever I tell you. Your father's in way over his head, Nell. If you want to get him out alive, you'll do whatever it takes."

Color swept her cheeks. His blunt words had cut her, as he'd meant them to. Safer this way, fast and sharp. Better to kill any possible feelings between them right now.

"Don't pretend this is about my father," she said quietly. "You want the art, and nothing else matters. None of you care what happens to my father."

"Is that a question?"

"No."

Dakota didn't tell her she was wrong because she

wasn't. The mission was far bigger than the safety of Jordan MacInnes. In spite of that, Dakota had promised Nicholas Draycott to do everything in his power to bring MacInnes out alive. So he would. No matter who stood in his way.

He didn't tell Nell that, either.

"If we're going to work together, here are the rules," Nell said.

Dakota frowned.

"Don't lie to me, not ever."

"Acceptable." Within security limits, he amended silently.

"Two—when you hear any news about my father, *tell* me. Even if it's…bad." She swallowed. "Very bad."

Guts and brains, he thought. They were always a dangerous combination. "Okay on two. What about three?"

Nell crossed her arms. "When I think of it, I'll tell you." She pulled down a thick robe from the bathroom door. "What do I have to do?"

"We'll start by looking at some photos."

As she took the robe, her wet cotton shirt shifted and brushed every curve. Her breasts were clearly outlined by the movement, smooth and full, shadowed by the thrust of dark nipples.

Dakota wanted her with a savagery that he'd never experienced before. He wondered if his response was somehow connected to his vision lapse on the drive. He wouldn't accept that it was *personal*.

He tossed her a towel, forcing his eyes away. "Dry off. If you get sick, you're no good to me or your father," he said curtly. He glanced out the window at the small parking area behind the abbey. "Is Draycott back from London yet?"

"I didn't hear his car, and I've been working most of the night. He said it might be midday before he finished." Her head tilted. "You've got blood on your hand."

Dakota was surprised to see that she was right. "Must have done it when I braked to avoid you." He dismissed the scrapes after one quick glance. In the overall picture of his life, a few cuts and bruises were a no-show. "It's nothing that matters."

"Everything matters." She frowned at him, still holding the robe awkwardly. "Go take care of those cuts first," she said. "If you get sick, you're no good to me or anyone, Lieutenant."

Dakota almost smiled at the snap in her voice.

Almost.

"Meet me in Draycott's study in ten minutes." He made his voice as cool as he could. The way he saw it, he was doing them both a favor. Nothing good could come out of this awareness that had dogged him since the moment he'd seen her walk out of a Scottish snow-storm, with a rope slung around her shoulder.

He tossed a thick envelope down on the dresser beside her. "Bring those photos along, after you've had a look."

"Exactly what am I looking *for*?" She was still icy, still angry, her fingers gripping the heavy robe.

"Best route of ascent. Call it extreme climbing school."

"What are you talking about?"

"School's in session, Nell. You've got twenty-four hours to teach me how to free-climb a seventy-foot limestone wall and reach a crenellated tower." He smiled tightly. "At night. With armed guards in constant rotation. And without being seen, of course."

Nell simply stared at him.

THE MAN WAS over-the-edge crazy.

"Arrogant as well as crazy," Nell muttered as she saw him run through the rain and lean down to inspect his motorcycle on the drive.

Her leg burned, her ankle throbbed. She was tired from making lists and tired from fighting the demons of her memories. If she'd had a little more time, she might have found some degree of peace. Then Dakota had stormed out of the night, gorgeous and angry and tired, with a hard set to his jaw that hadn't been there the last time she'd seen him in San Francisco.

She'd heard the worry and guilt in his voice when he insisted on carrying her over the gravel driveway. Then had come anger. And finally the anger had faded to hunger, stark and wordless. She hadn't missed the moment. He'd wanted her.

And desire was the last thing she had expected to see in a man who was always contained and controlled.

Nell accepted that men stared at her, studied her legs and made reasons to brush against her in crowded rooms. But then they moved on as fast as they could. Nell didn't know how to be coy. She didn't lure and tease, giving out the clever signals that meant she was interested and available.

Because she *wasn't* available, not on any level. When she was young, Nell had thought that if she fell in love, it would happen in a blinding moment of instinct, without words or games. But the moment had never come. When she realized that love was just another form of leaning, she gave up waiting.

As she unbuttoned her blouse, beads of water ran down her chest. She realized that the damp cotton was nearly transparent from the rain. Dakota would have seen right through her wet shirt and thin silk camisole to her breasts.

They were tight and exquisitely sensitive. Nell had never felt more alive or gripped by desire.

All because of the simple slide of Dakota's hands and the haunted look in his eyes.

She blew out a shaky breath, trying to forget the careful way he'd cleaned her jagged cuts, then stroked her leg, almost as if he didn't realize what he was doing.

She closed her eyes.

Stupid to feel this way.

Stupid to want more, to feel her body coming alive under the brush of his callused fingers. She didn't *want* to be alive that way again.

She shivered as she stripped off her damp clothes. Once she stopped expecting to find one great love, she had settled for an occasional fling, sometimes with a climber, once with an artist whose hands had been careful and experienced. Each time when it was over, Nell had felt cold and empty.

It had been a long time since she'd looked at a man and felt the sharp, blind stir of awareness. She had accepted the loss, even been grateful for it since her life was complicated enough. But tonight in the rain Nell had felt the unmistakable stab of desire return.

She felt it again now, remembering the hunger that had swept his face before he locked the emotion away.

Impossible. They were almost strangers.

Nell jammed a hand through her hair, muttering angrily. Now on top of everything else, she was supposed to give him a crash course in free-climbing?

Okay, he had a deal. If he wanted climbing school, she'd give him climbing school. If he wanted speed, she'd teach him speed. To protect her father, she would do whatever he asked. She'd work him right to the edge, teaching him every trick and move she knew.

She took a quick glance at the photos in the envelope. Limestone walls, just the way he'd said. Weathered towers with stone turrets wrapped in gray mist.

Was her father in that castle along with the stolen art?

Focus.

Nell blew out a breath. It would be a dangerous climb unless all the masonry was stable, which was unlikely in a structure that old. Getting Dakota up safely and fast without ropes or fixed anchors would be a problem.

Distracted by the challenge, she combed her hair and tossed on the first clothes she could find. She had the outline of a plan by the time she reached the viscount's study. Her hair was still damp, her shirt was untucked and she didn't take time to look for socks.

No doubt Dakota wouldn't even notice.

CHAPTER TWENTY

NELL ARRIVED looking breathless, and she wasn't wearing socks.

Dakota slanted her a look. She was four minutes early, but her hair was still damp. He'd have to remember to get a towel from the butler. He couldn't afford for her to be slowed down by a cold.

Because she was too important to the mission. Not for any personal reason.

"There's tea on the sideboard. The butler—I believe he said his name was Marston—just brought some. Drink it while we work."

"Not necessary. Show me what we have to do." All business, she shoved wet hair out of her face with a quick, graceful movement that did something odd to Dakota's throat.

Strength with grace. A mesmerizing combination.

He pointed at the twenty photos lined up on the long oak table. "Those are current exterior shots of the castle in question. I also have copies of the most recent blueprints."

"Where is it located?"

"You don't need to know that. In fact the fewer

details you know, the safer it is." He saw her eyes narrow. "Safer for you and safer for your father, Nell."

She crossed her arms. "I still need to know general location. Is it cold? Will there be rain? What kind of visibility can you expect?"

Smart, he thought. She was asking the right questions. "I'll get you an exact weather forecast shortly. For now, let's focus on the structure. This is a twelfth century fortified castle with moat, towers and battlements. Extensive additions were made under Edward II. Good for them, bad for us."

Nell nodded. "Because they knew how to plan for extended sieges back then."

"Fortified or not, we're breaking in."

"We? I'm going too?" Her voice sharpened.

"Not you. Too dangerous for a civilian. I need you to help me find the fastest route that will offer some cover."

"Oh." The crazy woman actually sounded *disappointed.*

"This isn't a nice, quiet peak in France, Nell. The place will be lousy with private security. Each of those men will be carrying serious firepower, and they will be motivated to use it against any intruder." He studied the photos. "That would be me."

Her eyes darkened. "In that case, you'll have to be fast but silent. Work the corners." She leaned over the table, checking the line of photos, chewing her bottom lip as she studied each one. "Chimney here. Nice crack, nothing off-width. Perfect."

As she spoke, she worked a hand through her hair,

twisting the back out in wild spikes. Restless. Thinking with her whole body.

Dakota could almost see the synapses firing at full force.

"This one could work. A nice jam. Then if you smear over here…."

Dakota looked at the photos, then looked back at Nell, waiting.

She fanned out three photos. "This is a crimp you could use." Abruptly, she tossed the photos back onto the table. "I can't *do* it."

"You have to do it. Or is it me you won't work with?" Dakota reined in his irritation. "If so—"

"It's not *you*." She shoved the photos toward him with one hand. "It's these. If I'm going to send you up a vertical face, you need fixed anchors. Climbing gear."

"No ropes, Nell. Nothing they can see. It's just me and the wall."

"I figured you'd be difficult like that." She rubbed her neck, looking impatient. "Fine, we'll work out a route for a free climb. But to do that, I need more details. I need to know the exact location of every lip, overhang and pocket. I want the precise width of any cracks, because you're going to need every possible hand- and foothold if you plan to get up this face without a rope."

He studied the photos and realized she was absolutely right. While they were clear, they gave too little detail for the kind of route she had to map out. "I'll get Izzy right on it."

"The Denzel look-alike, you mean? Is he good with research details?"

"So I'm told," Dakota said.

The understatement of the century.

"Can he get me something with more depth? Tell him I also need to know the composition of the surface stone and masonry. That will give me an idea how much deterioration to expect from your weight." She glanced over her shoulder. "What is your weight, by the way? And exact height. I want all your measurements, legs, feet, arms and also the length from finger to wrist and across the palm."

Oh, yeah, she was smart. "I'll write them down."

But she was already onto something else. "Don't forget I need updated weather forecasts." She leaned across the table, pulling two photos from the pile. "And it so happens that you're in luck. I climbed a castle like this once, during a commercial for a new line of whisky. My climbing partner, Eric, was supposed to go that day, but at the last minute they wanted a woman." She yawned, stretching a little. "I must have climbed that blasted wall fifty times. No ropes." She studied her palms, frowning as if the memory wasn't entirely pleasant. "Cut the heck out of my hands."

He could imagine Nell, fast and nimble, dancing across the stones, the sea wind on her shoulders.

One day he was going to track down that commercial, Dakota vowed.

Purely for curiosity's sake.

But first he was going to feed her. He put a plate of scones and a cup of tea on the nearest table as she scanned a set of blueprints. "Have some of this."

"What—oh, thanks." Absently, she took a sip of tea and studied the castle layout. "With luck, you can work up this arrow loop and use the top ledge for a foothold. If the surface stone is stable, you could jam here and then go straight into a right traverse." She was talking to herself, studying the photos as she pulled at the air.

Walking her way through the climb, he realized, every movement quick and graceful. This was how she had won third place at Chamonix, free climbing in the Alps.

Dakota watched her reach out with one hand, then edge her foot along the bottom of the table, shoving her fist into an imaginary crack and pulling upward.

"I think I've got it." A quick pull sideways, arm over arm, and then a blinding smile of happiness. "Yeah. This should work."

Amazing, he thought. Her hair was tangled, her eyes edged with dark circles, and all he saw was her energy as she danced from foot to foot.

"Stop that."

"Stop what?"

"Watching me. You're doing it again."

"You take my breath away," he said simply.

He noted the flush of heat, the self-conscious shrug. Wasn't she used to hearing compliments? How was that possible?

"I—I don't know what you mean." She turned, suddenly stiff, the excitement gone. "And…I need to think. There are a lot more details to work out."

No more compliments, Dakota thought. Not if they bothered her so much. But eventually he would find out why.

Marston appeared out in the hall, carrying silverware and a hot platter covered with foil. Dakota took everything and closed the door, so she would have no interruptions.

She was moving again, her back turned as she pantomimed the route.

Dakota realized that she was free when she climbed. It wasn't the adrenaline or the danger that held her, as he'd first thought, but the sense of being away from the ground and completely unfettered. One small piece of Nell MacInnes fell into place as he watched her turn smoothly and wriggle as if she were climbing through a narrow space.

He'd know all there was to know about her before they were done. And if there was a way up the wall, she would find it.

FIFTEEN MINUTES LATER, after some muttering and a few whispered curses, Nell spun around, her eyes shimmering with excitement. "I think I've found a way to get you in."

"That's good news." Dakota put a plate of eggs into her hand. Three cups of tea weren't about to get her through the strenuous afternoon and evening he had planned. "Eat. Then you can give me the details."

"Not hungry. I really don't want—"

"Everything matters, remember?" She was running on empty, too restless, too edgy. If the situation were different, he would have massaged her shoulders to settle her down a bit. But touching her wasn't a good idea. He was smart enough to face that fact. "You need energy or you'll burn out by noon."

"You think?" Her head tilted and she smiled just a little. "Don't go being nice to me, Navy. You'll spoil that hard-ass image you like so much."

Her smile warmed him. Warmed him too much.

Dakota handed her another plate. "Marston made cinnamon scones, and there are fresh strawberries and clotted cream."

Nell took a bite of eggs and then some of a scone, closing her eyes on a low sigh. "Remind me to get a butler when I win the lottery, will you?" She leaned to one side, rubbing her lower back absently and wincing a little.

She must have hurt herself there, when she'd fallen. "What's wrong?"

"Just a little stiff. Nothing major." She winced again.

Quietly, Dakota moved behind her. "Let me do that for you."

"Do what?" Nell stiffened as his hand opened over the small of her back.

"I'm making the tension go away, so you can focus better." His eyes glinted. "As a very wise person once told me, everything matters."

"A compliment?" Her breath caught as he kneaded the knot of tension in her back.

"Let's call it an acknowledgment of superior field awareness. Everything does matter. I'm glad you pointed it out."

Her eyes closed as he worked carefully. For a moment, just a moment, she sagged, leaning back into his hands, her hair soft against his chest, and Dakota caught a hint of the elusive lavender perfume she used.

And then she was Nell again, stiff and stubborn and prickly. She caught a short breath, then stood up. He watched her dig her fingers into her hair and twist it into even greater disorder.

The woman never relaxed. She didn't take care of herself very well, either. He was going to do something about both things before the day was over. "Finish your tea and finish the scone. You'll need the fuel to work."

With a little shrug, she drank some tea, ate more of the scone. "By the way, why 'Dakota'?"

"My parents' home state. But I grew up in the high pines along the northern California coast, in beautiful country."

Nell put her set of photos on the table. "I've never been there."

"You should go someday. Every trail is worth hiking."

Something hung between them, fragile and new, whispering of promises too vague to hold.

Then a phone rang in the back of the house, just as Nicholas Draycott's Mini Cooper purred up the driveway. Whatever had been forming vanished.

Nell cleared her throat. "About the climb."

Back to business.

That was fine with him, Dakota thought irritably. What else was there? "Let's hear it."

"Something has been bothering me." Nell gnawed at her lip. Her sleeves were pushed up above her elbows. Streaks of ballpoint ink ran along her wrists as she braced her elbows on the table. "Here." She carefully overlaid the blueprints with photographs, each in corresponding position.

"There's a problem." She turned, staring at his thighs. "I don't know if you're big enough."

"Big enough?" Dakota raised an eyebrow as she continued to look thoughtfully at his thighs. "You want to explain that?"

Nell was already back at the table, her shoulders hunched over the blueprints.

Dakota was a soldier, but he was also a man, and he wasn't going to have his…anatomy dismissed. Irritated, he leaned over her shoulder, his thighs next to hers. "What's size got to do with it? Experience is what counts."

If there was a smoky, sensual tone to his words, Nell didn't seem to notice. *That* irritated him, too.

"I'm talking about your legs."

As if that explained it.

"Maybe you should try spelling it out."

"The horizontal area here on the facade. You see?"

"I see." Dakota studied the blueprint, catching a hint of her perfume. A hint of cinnamon mixed with lavender and peaches. He cleared his throat, feeling a little dizzy.

A little seduced.

Nothing that he couldn't handle. "What's the problem?"

"You'll have to make a long reach here above the arrow loops, and your legs may not be long enough, if my estimates are right." She was still frowning at the photos. "I need more information. When will your contact have more high-resolution photos for me?"

"Later this afternoon."

Nell stood up and blew out a breath. "I need them *now*. I'm not sending you up there like this. *Not blind*." She stretched, wincing at the movement. "This is the best route, I'm certain of that. But I want exact measurements."

Dakota checked his watch. It would be at least another hour until he expected to hear from Izzy with updated photos. Their climbing gear would arrive about the same time. Meanwhile Nell was pacing, looking worried. Looking as if she'd realized she was now partly responsible for a man's life, along with that of her father.

"What's wrong?" he asked quietly.

"It's dangerous, almost foolhardy. That's what's wrong." Her voice sounded strained as she turned away.

"Nell, this is what I do."

She turned slowly, studying his face. "I saw you in that alley. You were fast, no thinking, just acting. You're not going to get yourself killed on me?"

"Count on it."

"This isn't some cocky navy thing, I hope. Because I'm not going to map everything out if there's no hope that you'll…"

Come back alive.

The words drifted unsaid.

"I'll be coming back, Nell."

She stood rigid, her arms at her sides. Dakota heard her make a small, muffled sound. "I need to know that you'll be safe. But there are no promises, are there? Not in your kind of work."

The air felt heavy. Dakota realized that the careful distance he'd worked to protect was fading fast.

"I'll be safe, Nell. Trust me, you're one hell of a teacher and I'm…" He gave a crooked smile. "I'm a really good student."

"Okay." She managed a partial smile as she paced around the long table. "Okay," she repeated slowly. "We can do this." She reached to pour another cup of tea.

Her seventh cup, Dakota noted. "Why don't you take a break? I'll come get you when I have those new surveillance photos from Izzy."

"I'm good. Really." She rubbed her neck and stretched again. "I don't need—"

"Go take a break. We'll have more to do this afternoon."

She scowled at the table, then frowned at him. "If you're sure there's nothing more I can—"

"I'm sure."

Go somewhere so I don't back you against the wall and kiss you until we're both blind with lust.

She raked her fingers through her hair, hesitated, turned without another word.

CHAPTER TWENTY-ONE

IRRITATED, Nell crossed the courtyard. The problem wasn't how to train Dakota. The problem was her. She didn't *want* to feel. She didn't want to care about this brave stranger with calm gray-blue eyes and gentle hands. She was up to her neck in feelings. Each one gnawed away at her carefully maintained defenses. Why couldn't he have stayed nasty and curt so she could shut him out? Now all she could think about was where he was going, and what would happen to him—and to her father—if her instructions were less than perfect.

Inside her room, Nell closed her eyes, resting her forehead against the wall. How did people stand this kind of responsibility? How did you live with the knowledge that a single mistake could get someone killed?

Nell didn't want that kind of responsibility or anything to do with Dakota Smith. Most of all, she didn't want these sudden churning, twisting emotions that shook her.

He had to climb at night, surrounded by guards, a clear, unprotected target. It wasn't abstract now. The thought paralyzed her.

He's counting on you. Teach him what he has to know.

She rubbed her face. She had to get Dakota into that castle and give him a route back alive.

She glared at the empty room. "I'll find a way."

The curtains billowed out gently at the big French doors. Funny, she could have sworn they'd been closed when she left.

Probably Marston, doing some efficient, butlerish thing.

With a sudden yawn, Nell sank onto the bed, burrowing into the thick down pillow. She'd stretch out, try to scan a journal article on da Vinci's pigments. Not sleep, just rest.

As she began to read, she was oblivious to the great gray cat that ghosted through the open doorway, curling up on the floor nearby.

NICHOLAS DRAYCOTT DROPPED a worn briefcase on his desk and motioned for Dakota to have a seat. Behind the viscount, old crystal and fine silver glinted in the sunlight.

"This is one amazing house," Dakota said. "And your butler, Marston, keeps appearing with whatever we need, even if we don't ask."

"The true sign of a good butler," Nicholas murmured. He steepled his fingers, assessing his guest. "Fortunately, I was able to finish early in London. I see we had the same idea about your route into the castle. This boarded-up stairwell should get you into the main courtyard without triggering any motion sensors. Has Nell worked out your route of ascent yet?"

"She's in the process. But she was up all night, so I told her to get a few hours of rest because Izzy's updates won't be ready until then anyway. Our gear is due to arrive shortly after that, too. Anything from MacInnes?"

The Englishman shook his head. "I do have one bit of good news. The weather in the Western Isles is notoriously fickle, but the rain may hold off for you. A high-pressure front is supposed to move in tonight."

"I'll take all the help I can get."

"Forgive me, Lieutenant, but have you ever *done* any free-climbing before?"

"Only inside, in enclosed spaces, but I'm a fast learner. And I've got an excellent teacher." Dakota glanced out the window. "I'd be happier if I could get started. Sometimes the waiting is the hardest part." He leaned back, crossing his arms. "You'd know about that. I've seen your classified files, including the years you spent in Bhanlai as a prisoner."

Draycott's eyes were unreadable. "My field days are over, Lieutenant. And I've found something that may help you a great deal, I think." The Englishman poured them both tea and began to explain.

AN HOUR LATER Marston's tap on the door brought both men around, frowning at the interruption. "A courier has just arrived, Your Lordship. He is waiting in the blue salon."

"Excellent." Nicholas Draycott stood up. "Where is Nell?"

"Outside. On the south roof, I believe." Marston's face was impassive. "She said something about a crack. Or maybe it was a jam. I didn't understand. She was too fast for me."

"Join the club," Dakota muttered. "She was supposed to be resting. Damn, does the woman *ever* do what she's told?"

Marston cleared his throat. "She told me she couldn't sleep. She said that she was worried about you, Lieutenant."

NELL WAS HALFWAY down the abbey's back wall, her hands covered with chalk and her feet wedged above a narrow ledge over the first-floor windows. Wind whipped at her hair as she studied a set of red chalk lines.

She moved her hands up, searched carefully, then started along a horizontal traverse. She had on a pair of sweatpants and a bulky knit turtleneck, and there was grace in every movement she made.

Nell looked down, saw the two men and dropped lightly to the ground. "Warming up."

"I thought you were going to rest," Dakota said curtly.

"I couldn't. Must be all that tea. I'll catch an hour or two later." She turned her face to the wind. "Beautiful day, isn't it?" She didn't give the men time to answer. "I'll need good gloves. More chalk. You'll need the same."

Dakota pulled two pairs of climbing gloves out of his pocket. "I have the rest of your climbing gear, too."

"*Mine?* How did you—" Nell sighed. "Never mind. I don't want to know. What about climbing shoes?"

Dakota grabbed two big canvas rucksacks sitting by the courtyard steps. "These just arrived."

"Let's get going." Nell turned back to study the wall.

Nicholas Draycott glanced from one to the other. "If you'll excuse me, I'll go talk to the courier."

"Change into something flexible, but not too loose," Nell said briskly after Draycott had gone. "Then come back so I can tape your hands. While you limber up, I want to look at all the high-resolution photos your friend sent."

Four hours later

"NO, NOT THAT WAY. *Watch the wall.* Keep your weight above your feet, always above your feet."

The afternoon sun cast long rays over the distant woods as Nell stared up at Dakota, moving carefully along the stone ledge at the back of the house.

"That's it. Toe in, get your distance, then pull right. Better, much better. How's that tape holding out on your hands?"

"Feels tight."

Nell kept remembering that he had to climb at night. That he would be an exposed target.

She took a sharp breath. Nothing was going to happen to him because he was the best student she'd ever had, and they'd do it and do it again, until he had every movement perfect.

She climbed quickly up the wall, stopping directly to his right. "No, like this. Keep your weight centered. Don't lean back so far. And *read* the rock. Watch for the handholds. They'll show you your next move." She frowned. "Except you can't read the rock, can you? Because it will be night, and there won't *be* any shadows. Damn it," she whispered, dropping back onto the ground. "How can you possibly see to climb without light."

In a few seconds Dakota was on the ground beside her, sweating lightly. "I'll have night-vision goggles," he said quietly. "Stop worrying about this, Nell."

"Worrying?" She paced a little, then gave a short laugh. "No, I'm terrified." She pointed to the red chalk marks drawn on the wall. "Even with your friend's new photos, I don't know exactly what kind of surface you'll have. There's nothing more I can do to help you," she said tightly. "You'll be going in blind."

"You've given me a lot, Nell. Don't forget, I'm trained to think on my feet."

She looked away, then took a hard breath. "Okay, let's try it again. This time stay right beside me and mimic every move. You were clumsy on the last traverse, and I'm worried about the crack. What do you do if your fist is too big to fit inside the opening?"

"I use my fingers. Up to the knuckles, wedged in securely as a hold." Dakota answered the same way he'd answered three times already. He didn't point out the fact because he knew Nell was being ruthlessly thorough.

Just like the best drill instructors he'd had over the years.

She chalked up her hands, then climbed the wall lightly, quickly, not even breathing hard. In fact, she made it look like any child could do it. Dakota knew exactly how hard it was. His muscles were starting to cramp, but the clock was ticking and there was no time to stop.

"Always remember to chalk up first," she called.

"Done. I'm climbing," he answered calmly, keeping his body in line, using the core muscles to hold his position rather than jabbing with his hands. Amazing how much he'd learned from her in four hours.

Izzy's new high-resolution photos had been invaluable. Now Dakota knew what he was up against. It would have been nice to practice on the actual wall, but no way was that happening.

"Get ready for that corner. Get your back against the stone."

Dakota was braced in position, aware of Nell off to his right, when something clattered off the roof, and two more pieces hurtled past him to the ground. He heard Nell gasp as a stone fragment tore off the wall and hit her forehead. She swung free, dangling by three fingers.

She was twenty feet above the ground. "Got a little p-problem here."

Dakota saw the ledge she was holding on to start to buckle. "Hold on, honey."

He estimated the distance to the window above his head, then lunged with one hand and reached the sill. Swinging sideways in a powerful kick, he knocked out the glass and worked his hands over the edge, clearing away glass fragments. Then he pulled his body through.

Inside he ran to the next window above Nell, opened it and leaned out. "Grab my arm. Come on. I'll pull you up."

She was holding on by two fingers now, her face white. But she didn't say a word, focused and controlled as she probed the wall with her foot, searching for a foothold.

"You can do it, Nell. Six more inches. I'm right here."

She jammed her foot against a tiny pocket in the stone, took a deep breath and flung her arm up while she pushed off her foot. Dakota caught her instantly, wrapping both hands around her wrist. He pulled her up to the window just as the ledge of stone tore free, shattering on the ground below.

Nell sank forward, shuddering, while Dakota gripped her shoulders. His fingers brushed her cheeks and then locked in her hair, angling her face toward him. Unable to help himself, he kissed her forehead. "Damn it, Nell."

"I'm fine," she said jerkily. "Thanks to you. The ledge looked stable, but—it happened so fast."

Dakota didn't want to talk. He wanted to feel her body, skin against his skin. His mouth opened on hers as he whispered her name roughly.

Nell leaned into him, shuddering. Her hands opened slowly. She clutched his shirt and kissed him hard, tongue to tongue, whispering his name.

The taste of her was blinding. Dakota felt her nails dig into his back as she shoved up his shirt. "This is g-going nowhere," she muttered.

His hands slid over her waist, rising to cup her breasts. "Damned right," he growled.

"It's stopping—" She shivered as he teased the hard peaks of her nipples. "Right now," she said on a smoky sigh of desire.

"Now," he repeated, shoving off her sweater and dropping it onto the floor. She was sweating lightly, her body flushed and beautiful as he pinned her against the wall. He wanted to look at her, just look, but she dug her nails into his shoulders and breathed his name.

Dakota tongued her high, full breasts until she moaned, cradling his face. His hand slipped under the waistband of her pants.

She slid her fingers deep into his hair. "Forget… what I said."

Dakota opened her legs and spanned his fingers under the lace of her panties, feeling her shudder against him. *"Now,"* Nell said hoarsely.

CHAPTER TWENTY-TWO

NEED SNAPPED and burned.

Nell closed her eyes and fell into the fierce thrill, her hands skimming Dakota's back. His face gave away so little, but right now his body was a map.

Here was strength and courage.

Here was unflinching honor, written in old scars.

And as his hands tangled in her hair, Nell sank deep to find the freedom, the sense of flying with the air in her face and effortless energy in nerve and bone. She held on to his shoulders, hesitated for a second, and remembered all her old rules and old pain.

No trust.

No leaning.

Not ever.

His hand cupped her cheek, feathered softly.

And all Nell's rules toppled, blown away in the hot wind of desire. She was certain that she wanted whatever Dakota offered. More stunning, she was certain that she trusted him.

Something vibrated at her back. Nell blinked, trying to reach her pocket. "My phone—"

"Hold on." Dakota jammed a hand in her back

pocket, pulled the phone out, flipped it open. "Hello," he said tightly. "No, she's not. She'll call you back." He snapped the phone shut and dropped it back into her pocket before she could protest. "It wasn't your father. Anyone else can wait."

His long fingers skimmed her mouth. He nipped her bottom lip and sent up a new wave of heat, rich and maddening. Nell embraced every second, every pang. Needing to be open, needing to be in his arms.

Needing to trust.

Just for now.

She watched the muscles lock at Dakota's jaw as he stripped away the wispy pink panties and murmured rough praise against her skin. She dug her fingers into his shoulders, then slowly rested her face against his chest, hearing the hard, fast drum of his heart. His arms tightened around her and then turned gentle. How long since a man had touched her with such care and patience?

Never.

Never whispering her name, telling her in rough, simple detail how much he wanted her body moving against him, her legs urgent as they slid against his.

Nell ran shaking hands across his chest, learning the rise and fall of every muscle. She bit the rigid line of his shoulder and then leaned down to tongue the warm skin above the waist of his pants.

His stomach muscles tightened. "Nell."

"Too many clothes." She shoved down his pants, shivering when she felt his erection, full and hot against her palms. She cupped him, holding his strength, hot and alive in her hands.

"Nell, don't—"

She smiled at his low curse. "No orders. I want to remember how you taste, Dakota."

Her mouth closed and she explored the length of him, feeling him jerk against her mouth. He was salty with the edge of something smoky and male, a primitive mix that intrigued and seduced. She leaned down to savor more, to take and be taken.

Abruptly his hand fisted in her hair, tugging her upright against his chest. "Damn it, Nell. No more." His voice was hoarse, his mouth relentless on hers. He cupped her hips. Then his fingers slid lower to skim and tease.

Need slammed her up, turned her inside out. Never this hunger, this madness as desire drove her to a blind place she'd never thought to know.

Dakota bit her ear gently. "I could stop now, Nell. The choice is yours."

She managed to open her eyes, blinking up at him, lost in eddies of desire. Trying to understand what he was asking.

"Tell me, Nell. Yes or no. Because you want this the way I do."

Protecting her, she thought. Even when she didn't want to be protected.

"Yes. Your sweat on my skin, your fingers in my hair." She sighed as he sent her heart into a dizzy spiral with another smooth stroke of his callused fingers. Not just because of the madness and the heat, but because he made her feel alive, and Nell wanted every memory to hold when it was over.

Only the hot, demanding *now* mattered. Only the racing madness and the gray-blue eyes that looked at her with something older and darker than hunger. And then she saw the cocky curve of his smile, holding that same fierce light of possession. "You ought to come with a warning, honey. A man could forget everything else touching you like this and wanting more."

For now, just for now, Nell wanted him to forget. His lips brushed her hair. His strong hands tightened.

Holding.

Just holding.

"I thought that I'd lost you." His voice fell. "When that stone came free, I was sure that you…"

He stopped, breathed her name, his pulse very loud.

So close when the stone had broken. It could have been Dakota.

The old nightmare that was every climber's darkest fear bit deep. But Nell willed away the fear and made another memory then, another moment to add to the string of yesterdays she would hold when desire burned away and the world settled back to safe, normal and boring.

But now was not for normal. Now was for speed and fire, for claiming and being claimed. And for trust, even if it was temporary. Her body trusted him, logical or not.

The first peak came, so fast she only had time to follow, her heart pounding. Before the shimmer ended, Dakota braced her against his arms and parted her legs farther, two fingers slipping high, finding her heat while she shattered and the world came apart again.

Then his thumb caressed, working the exquisite point of hot sensation, making her cry out in pleasure as he found his way past her defenses, past all her careful rules, where trust glowed beyond desire, whispering in the play of his hands.

He took her up surely, finding the heat and the yearning, learning what made her gasp, what made her nails rake his back.

"Dakota, you aren't—"

"Shh." His fingers stirred, drove, inflamed.

It started again, tearing at her senses, and Nell reached out for him as the only sure anchor in the spinning world of fresh sensation. While desire keened, she fell into color and heat, her arms around Dakota's rigid shoulders.

She whispered his name without knowing it.

And the sound made Dakota's eyes darken.

This matters, he thought, shaken by her response. She was honest and open in his arms like a long-forgotten dream he'd never hoped to find real and solid. She was all that—along with stubborn and quick and terrifying in her bravery. He didn't want to think about losing her. He *couldn't* lose her. Danger and risk defined his world, willingly faced, and the possibility of death was never more than seconds away. But the thought of Nell plunging from a wall left him shaken.

He realized that all his careful distance was gone. He had crossed a bridge, real but invisible, and now he was caught by an unexplainable need to protect her.

Distance be damned.

Need drove him. As he drank in Nell's ragged cries

of pleasure, felt her slick heat on his hands, Dakota knew he would never have enough of her.

Every rule forgotten, he fed her desire and felt her body rise, driven to the last edge of passion and then falling, falling, while her hair slid through his fingers and her knees gave way.

He wrapped her legs around him, his forehead against hers. Claiming and claimed, he thought grimly. Taking and taken. There would be no forgetting her or any moment of what had just happened. Dakota knew that nothing would ever come close again.

SHE WAS LEANING, Nell thought drowsily.

Her hands were looped around his shoulders, her knees jelly. Her body was braced against his.

Leaning. Trusting.

The two things she'd vowed she would never do.

She felt a laugh bubble through her at the thought of so many broken rules. Yet leaning didn't seem so dangerous now. Was it because of spiking desire and good sex? No, amazing sex, she corrected.

But there had been more than heat and urgency between them. The trust had come with the brush of his hands, gentle and possessing; in the power of his wintry eyes, drinking up the sight of her, hoarding it as if he had too few pleasures.

Nell sensed that Dakota had given up his own pleasures for too many others. She wanted to change that.

Things were suddenly very complicated.

"Back among the living?"

She turned her head and the power of those cool

blue-gray eyes rocked her, as if in their silent force they could read all her secrets.

"I'm…working on it." Something fluttered in her chest when he bent his head, kissing the long welt at her neck.

"Take your time. I'm not complaining."

No going back, Nell thought. But the idea didn't frighten her as much as it should have.

"Dakota, I—"

"We probably should—"

They spoke at once, skirting the force of unanswered questions. Suddenly the possibilities hurt, Dakota thought. Now he understood why Ryker insisted on no families and no personal commitments. Things were going to get messy and complicated.

He also understood why two of his Foxfire team members had broken that rule and faced Ryker without backing down.

"Wait. Let me say this." Nell's fingers played along the taut muscles of his stomach. "You…were amazing. So careful." She smiled at his sharp, indrawn breath as her fingers lingered. "Thank you."

She was thanking *him* for something that had turned his world inside out and made him feel alive again? Dakota frowned, trying to stay focused as her hands shredded his logic. "Trust me, no thanks required, honey."

She leaned her forehead on his chest, smiling crookedly as if she couldn't believe what she was doing. Then she looked down at the phone, at her fallen clothing, at the photo that had dropped out of his pocket.

She took a deep breath. "Dakota, you didn't..." She touched his chest, frowning. "You weren't—"

"No, I didn't. You call that a problem? I needed your heat in my hands and your cries as you slipped over the edge." Something dark and primitive about those memories made him smile. "I hope you aren't complaining now."

"Not me." A ragged laugh. A wave of color streaking her cheeks. "Definitely not me. I just thought—"

"Don't think. Not about this," he said roughly. "We'll think it to death."

After what felt like a long time she nodded. His hands lingered on her cheeks. Then finally he released her.

Though it was the last thing he wanted to do. "Nell, we need to—"

"Yeah. Work." She shivered as his hands lifted, slid through her hair, testing the soft strands. "There's still the problem of the castle you need to break into."

"Lousy timing." He watched color spill through her face, and then he stepped back, holding out her clothes. "So what do you have in mind?"

She took a deep breath. He watched her refocus. "I want to chalk up your moves on a different wall. I'm worried about that traverse."

"Let me do the worrying, Nell. All you have to do is tell me what to climb and how."

"But—"

Dakota brought her palm to his mouth and kissed the scraped skin gently. He saw the broken fingernails, the bloody climbing tape around her palm.

Danger suited her, he thought. But he didn't have to

like it. "There's a new game plan. You're going to relax while I pack up a few things. And this time *really* rest. We could be up all night."

He noted the smudge of blue under her eyes as she straightened her clothes. Running on adrenaline, he thought. He needed her strong, rested and focused. They had one hell of an evening in front of them.

"Stop doing that," she muttered.

"Doing what?"

"Protecting me."

"Afraid I can't stop, honey."

Footsteps echoed outside in the hall. Behind Nell the doorknob turned. Dakota put a finger to her mouth.

"Locked? That's odd." Marston tried the door again, and then his footsteps moved off down the corridor.

"One question." Nell looked up at Dakota. "When are *you* going to sleep?"

"Not a problem. I've got a high metabolism and good genes. I'll sleep later tonight."

"I may have some ideas about tonight, Navy." Her hand opened, warm and firm on his chest. Heat washed her face.

The warm thing moved in his chest, capturing him. If only they had more time…

But his cell phone chimed from the pocket of his pants. He knew the coded ring.

Izzy.

"I've got to take this, Nell."

"Of course you do." She frowned, brushed her fingers across his jaw. "You're too tough for you own good, Lieutenant."

At her touch another part of him fell away, open to her and to possibilities he'd never considered. If he had any sense, he would have been frightened, but instead all he felt was invincible.

He unlocked the door and followed Nell out into the hall. "Don't forget to clean those cuts," he ordered. "Everything matters, remember?"

She dragged a hand through her hair and summoned a smile. "Teach a man a few new climbing tricks and see how he turns insufferable."

"Lie down and rest. That's an order. You're no good to me if you're cross-eyed with exhaustion. We've got a long night of work ahead of us."

"The student's giving orders to the teacher?"

"Damned straight, since the teacher refuses to take care of herself." He pulled out his phone and answered curtly. "Smith here. What have you got?"

"You want the good news or bad news?"

"No," Dakota snapped.

"Too bad. I'll be there in ten."

HE LOOKED INTO her room a few minutes later.

He wasn't taking a chance that she'd sneak out and try to climb another wall, but it appeared that she had actually done what he'd asked for once.

If you could call it sleeping, Dakota thought wryly. The woman was as restless asleep as she was awake. One arm dangled off the bed, the pillow was jammed over her head and the covers were twisted in knots across her shoulder. She muttered something about footholds, swinging out an arm, almost as if she were climbing a wall in her sleep.

He realized that was exactly what she was doing. Warmth nudged at Dakota's chest, drawing out a smile.

He smoothed her sheets, freed her arm, tucked in the blanket that was about to drop on the floor any second. The rich scent of roses drifted through the room, carried on a cool, fresh wind.

Beautiful house, Dakota thought. There was something brooding about the place, as if it had seen too much history, both joys and tragedies.

Too bad he and Nell wouldn't have time to explore it. He closed the door softly as he heard the sound of a car coming up the driveway.

NELL LAY very still, her eyes closed.

His touch awakened her. She knew that he'd come to see she was asleep. He was relentless, focused on every detail; Nell was sure that you didn't get to be a SEAL by being lazy or careless.

But somewhere in the past two hours things had turned personal and she still didn't understand it. She took a deep breath, listening to Dakota's footsteps receding down the hall.

She wasn't shelving her emotions anymore. She wasn't holding her distance. If you were going to break the rules, you might as well break them in a big way by sleeping with a man you barely knew and trusting him with your life.

Most dangerous of all, trusting him with your dreams.

She turned her head into the pillow. Every nerve felt raw, as if it had been short-circuited, and her knees were putty.

She remembered the gentle way he'd straightened her sheets and pulled the blanket around her. Protecting her, even when he thought she was asleep.

But who was going to protect her heart when the job was over?

CHAPTER TWENTY-THREE

IZZY DROPPED two bags on the gravel driveway and stared up at the abbey's chalk-streaked wall. "Looks like bad postmodern graffiti art."

"Try handholds. Nell chalked out the fastest route up, consistent with the dimensions provided from the Glenmor photos." Dakota followed the chalk line upward, frowning.

Izzy followed his gaze. "What?"

"See that ragged line about ten feet from the roof? The damn ledge pulled free. Nell...almost fell."

"That's a twenty foot drop," Izzy said grimly. "She was free-climbing, no ropes?"

Dakota nodded. "She was showing me a move when it happened. I broke a window and got her in time, but I sure as hell didn't like it."

Neither man spoke. Izzy cleared her throat. "She knows what she's doing, Dakota. Right now she's the best teacher you've got."

"Don't you think I know that? Otherwise I wouldn't be here watching her take this kind of risk. She refuses to sit on the ground and give orders. No, she has to be on the wall right beside me."

"Most good teachers teach best in the field." Izzy noted the harsh edge to Dakota's voice.

It was getting personal again. Izzy had seen it enough times with other members of Foxfire to recognize all the signs of impatience, irritation and finally calm acceptance. He *hated* it when things got hot and crossed the line. Why couldn't people be mature and sensible, leaving emotions where they belonged, preferably on a neighboring continent?

"So what's the news you have for me?"

"The auction is set. It's tomorrow night."

Dakota's eyebrow rose. "You're sure?"

"I have people scattered through the pubs near Glenmor Castle. They tell me all of the local staff were fired abruptly, told their services were not needed. According to local staff gossip, a big event is supposed to take place there tomorrow. Cooks, waiters and cleaning staff have been flown in from overseas. I've managed to get someone on the inside working the kitchen, but security is tight. There's no way to do any snooping without raising suspicion."

"Anything more from Jordan MacInnes?"

"Nothing. My contact will make every effort to reach him. If Jordan's being watched closely, we may not hear from him again."

"With so much money at stake, the sellers won't trust anyone. So what's the good news?"

"I'm a little weak on my Scottish history, but Draycott has located a sister castle to Glenmor, renovated by the same man under orders from Edward II. It's nearly an exact match to the structure in Scotland,

and it's less than twenty miles from here. Draycott has cleared your visit with the estate manager, so you and Nell won't be disturbed."

"The owners?"

"Off on a Mediterranean cruise."

Dakota thought it over. Training on a wall with similar design and materials would be a huge help. But even there, he couldn't risk being watched. Surprise was crucial to the success of the mission.

"You're sure no one is there? Not even staff?"

"All taken care of. The staff has been given three days off, according to Nicholas." Izzy pointed to his bags. "I've located an oxygen rebreather unit for your swim in. Judging by the latest thermal and infrared scans from the air, the main water pipe running into the moat is operational."

"Always nice to know I won't be swimming into a blocked tunnel with no way through," Dakota said dryly. "Dynamite might be a little obvious. So what other hardware do you have in your red sack, Santa?"

"Stun gun with waterproof housing. Night-vision goggles as backup. Just covering all the bases." Izzy held out a narrow box of hard plastic with molded edges. "This is for the things you'll bring out. You'll find clips inside and a second casing for water protection."

Gravel crunched behind them, and Nicholas Draycott emerged from the study. "Something tells me I'm going to have nothing but gray hair before this operation is over. Marston told me about the ledge. Nell is safe?"

"A few cuts. Breaking the window was the fastest way inside. Sorry."

"No apologies needed. You saved her life." He shook Izzy's hand. "Nice to have the confusion cleared up, Teague. It's been almost four years since that last business we handled up in Scotland."

"Always a pleasure to visit the abbey," Izzy said. "How's that butler of yours? Still keeping you on a tight leash?"

Right on cue the big carved door to the courtyard opened and Marston appeared. "It's a pleasure to see you again, Mr. Teague. May I offer you something to drink? Keemun was your favorite as I recall. Cream, no sugar. I have already taken the liberty of setting everything out in the library."

Izzy looked at Draycott and raised an eyebrow. "If I ever win the lottery, remind me to spend it on a butler," he muttered.

"HERE'S WHAT WE HAVE." Nicholas gestured at the maps that filled the long oak table in the library. "So far, there's no rain in the thirty-six-hour forecast. That's one bit of good news." He held out a clear plastic envelope to Dakota. "Here are the most recent surveillance photos from Glenmor, including timed shots of guard rotation."

Dakota opened the envelope and studied the photos. "What kind of routine can I expect?"

"No set pattern, I'm afraid." Izzy tapped two of the photos. "The movements look random, which means they know what they're doing. These aren't local renta-cops. I'd guess Gonsalves had them flown in from Macau."

"Too bad." Dakota rubbed his neck. "Predictable rotation would make getting in a whole lot easier. But we expected this." He arranged the photos near a detailed topographical map of the island. "How many security people have you picked up, Draycott?"

"At least sixty according to my spotters. They're keeping random patterns and they're well armed."

"Izzy, what about security once I'm over the wall?"

Izzy opened his briefcase. "There are motion sensors at every corner of the top of the wall. Inside you'll be facing ground surveillance radar units decked out with new hardware from Korea. But there's good news. When the castle was sold five years ago, the buyer brought in a building inspector as part of the appraisal process." Izzy smiled slightly. "I managed to get all his reports."

"Of course you did." Dakota scanned the new set of blueprints Izzy opened on the corner of the table. "Probable location for the art?"

"One of the staff says there are locked rooms in the third floor of the south tower, but I'm discounting that. Old art requires humidity and heat controlled environment and I've found a significant heat anomaly here." Izzy tapped the corner tower at the east side of the castle. "I'd say this indicates sophisticated climate control, the kind you install to protect delicate art. The anomaly only occurs in this part of the castle."

"So that's my target." Dakota committed the detailed architectural designs to memory. "Second floor, east side. I'll go in under the radar, but there's no way to stay silent. Once I tap the art, every alarm in the castle will light up. I'll drop a few flash bangs, but it won't hold them for long."

"Which is why I've planned a little diversion to cut down their response time," Izzy said smugly. He glanced at Draycott, who was listening intently. "You've worked out an arrangement with your people? They stay out until we call them in to mop up?"

Draycott nodded. "They don't like being kept in the dark, but they'll do it."

"Okay. Dakota, you get your package out safely, and we'll take down Gonsalves and his buyers in one swoop. No one is walking out of there except into custody. A whole lot of people want to question Gonsalves about his October Twelfth connections once this is done."

Dakota paced restlessly. "What's the timeline?"

"A chopper is waiting to make your transport to Scotland. You'll be in place, out at sea, by noon tomorrow, ready to go in via the pipe. Radio me when you hit the target location and I'll put on the mother of all light shows for distraction. I'll have my contact inside looking out for MacInnes, too."

"You said you have people in place. I'll need names and photos."

"Already in your briefing bag."

"Twenty-four hours until showtime." Dakota released the blueprints, which snapped together, scattering photos at his feet.

Not bad luck.

No reason to be superstitious.

He picked up the briefing bag from Izzy. "Let's get this thing done, gentlemen."

INSIDE THE GATEHOUSE, Nell dreamed of blue-gray eyes and callused hands. She dreamed of heat and freedom, the air on her face, the rock at her back. Her muscles in the flow, she tackled a sheer wall cut by a thin crack. Hand over hand she rose. Then she heard her father's voice, telling her something was wrong. Telling her to trust no one.

Lines broken. Falling, falling…

Her hands raked cold stone, trying to break the plunge.

"Nell, wake up."

She shot upright, blinking. Instead of cold stone she felt the warm muscles of Dakota's chest. "Dreaming," she said hoarsely.

"A bad one?"

The falling dream was always bad, but there was no point in mentioning that.

Nell glanced through the window and saw the sky streaked with red and purple above the dark woods. "You should have come to get me sooner."

"Soon enough," he said. "We're going to work all night to simulate actual night climbing conditions. Nicholas found a place with a similar layout." Dakota pulled one of her palms into his and studied the cut skin. "Try not to fall, will you? I don't think my heart can take it."

"Not falling will be high on my to-do list, trust me."

Nell reached for her clothes, but Dakota's hands closed around her wrists. "Speaking of trust…you forgot something, didn't you?"

"My phone?" Nell looked around frowning. "My climbing shoes—"

"This," Dakota whispered, leaning down for a slow skim of heat and tongue that warmed and seduced. No speed or fury now, just a silent promise. "Someday you should come up to the California coast. We'll go climbing together." His fingers slid through her hair. "We'll camp out under the stars and watch the sun come up. Five days in the mountains and you'll feel like a brand-new person."

Nell's heart pounded. She didn't do commitment. But maybe for this man, she could change. "So…are you saying there may be an *us*, Dakota? After all this is over?"

His eyes darkened. "Come climbing with me and let's find out. I won't lie to you, Nell. My work—hell, my work has always been my life, 24/7, and I don't know if I can change that. But I'm starting to wonder, to consider the possibilities. You're in all of them." His voice was rough. "What do you say?"

"Oh, I'm open." Nell took a long breath. "Terrified, but open. But just so you know, I hate mosquitoes. And I have to have light to read at night. Don't ask me to give up my books."

"I think we could reach a compromise in that area." Dakota's eyes were smoky. "I'll find something you can do at night—when you don't want to read."

They could find a lot of things to do at night, Nell

thought. Up on a mountain, with only the stars overhead spilled like diamonds over velvet. With bodies urgent and the wind sighing cool through the pines.

The low chime of Dakota's watch made her stiffen.

His face changed, his eyes turning distant.

The mission. The danger he had to face.

Nell pulled away. Before they could think about any kind of future, he had to come back alive. "I—I'd better get dressed."

Dakota nodded. While she grabbed her clothes, he crossed the room and pulled out his phone, speaking quietly.

CHAPTER TWENTY-FOUR

Glenmor Castle
Scotland
North of the Isle of Skye

CLOUDS BLOCKED the horizon. Wind banged at the leaded windows of the castle, dark in the gathering dusk.

A restless young man with cold eyes stood at the crackling fire, beckoning to the American in the doorway. "Come in, Jordan. I have called you to see the new displays. Impressive, are they not?"

Impressive did not do the room justice, Jordan MacInnes thought.

Wind hurled gravel at the windows as the American entered the secure stone room. He gave no sign of uneasiness. Any weakness now would be fatal. Martim Gonsalves always used weakness to his advantage.

MacInnes studied the new construction, noting the three high-tech display cases near the interior wall. Their sleek lights and slim contours seemed starkly out of place in a medieval castle. Higher on the wall he saw the nearly concealed junction of new wiring and the drying paint over metal sheets in the middle of the floor.

Motion sensors on every wall. Pressure-sensitive plates. How much other security had Gonsalves added to this room?

MacInnes gave no sign that he had noticed the new security details. The display lights were off, but he could make out electric wires along the base of the cases. More security.

In answer to his casual questions, the staff had told him that the suites on the third floor had been fitted with new wiring and electronic locks. Based on that information, Jordan had concluded that the stolen da Vinci had been secured somewhere in that part of the castle. No one had mentioned anything about construction in the isolated second-floor tower.

But the proof lay in front of him, awesome even in the partial shadows. In the nearby case he could just make out the haunting outline of a woman's cheek and graceful, folded hands.

Gonsalves's security team had been busy. The high-tech Plexiglas display tubes rose from metal platforms bolted directly into the oak floor. Even a quick glance told MacInnes there would be no way to cut through metal or Plexiglas without a blowtorch or a high-powered saw.

As he walked closer to the displays, Gonsalves fingered a remote. Small lights flashed on, and their diffused golden glow glinted off cushioned bases of pale blue silk, the effect breathtaking in its opulence. On each base a small gilt easel displayed a framed chalk sketch executed on cream linen-rich paper.

Three *identical* pieces?

MacInnes frowned. Three images, each with the graceful lines of the Mona Lisa, smiled back from the cases. The beauty of the trio staggered him, squeezing at his chest, but he struggled to hide his emotions at the treasure before him.

"Well, Jordan? What do you think of my catch?"

"I'm—speechless, Martim."

Grace, glory, eternity—all lay captured within the twelve inches of each fragile chalk sketch; da Vinci's genius had never been more unmistakable.

"Incomparable," he whispered, more moved than he had ever been by a work of art; even the small van Gogh in Boston paled before these. "But you know that already, Martim. Your price will be whatever you ask. No one on my list of buyers will quibble when they see a masterpiece like this."

MacInnes waited, biting back a thousand questions, leaving Gonsalves to explain in his own time.

The younger man nodded thoughtfully. "So far all nine of your buyers have confirmed, just as you predicted. And your idea to convey the auction details via clean, encrypted cell phones has been most helpful. They have been distributed and will be used only once, then disposed of." The second most powerful man in Macau raised an eyebrow. "You have no questions for me?"

"I have a thousand questions. Why are there *three* works, Martim?" Jordan studied each piece in turn. Through the Plexiglas, each seemed to be the original. He turned, frowning. "How is this possible?"

"Amusing, no?" He triggered a remote and one image vanished. Then the other two vanished. Only the empty display cases shimmered in the dim light. "Cameras, my friend. High-resolution video feed. Only one of those cases holds the real da Vinci. Or it *will*, tomorrow."

"Brilliant," Jordan whispered.

Aware of Martim's eyes locked on him in cold, predatory intensity, the American moved calmly from one case to the next. "So all is prepared. I am happy to see it. Although I doubt that any of my chosen buyers would be so stupid as to attempt theft here."

"A precaution nevertheless." Martim triggered the remote and one by one the three haunting faces reappeared. "Should one of your buyers become overeager and manage to access this room, which is most unlikely, which case would they choose? A good question, no? Which one would you steal, my friend?" The question was casual, but the look in Martim's eyes was deadly serious.

MacInnes walked between the three cases, frowning. All three pieces were identical. There was simply no way to choose. Jordan crossed his arms. "To choose is impossible. You know that."

The other man smiled. "If all goes according to plan I will soon be a very rich man—and you will receive your fee of half a million dollars, as we agreed. If you become my partner, I will double that fee."

Jordan met his look squarely. "I am an old man, Martim. One last job, as we agreed, to secure the comforts denied me during my years in prison. But no more. After this, I am going to sit on a white sand beach and drink vintage champagne while I watch the sun set in a beautiful woman's eyes. I am too old and tired for this new world of yours." MacInnes waved a hand at the cases. "You see? Too much technology. Too many new skills to learn. There's no place for a dinosaur like me here."

"You are certain of that?"

"I'm afraid so."

Gonsalves slid the remote back into the pocket of his bespoke Armani suit. "You would not be tempted to betray me, I hope? That would be a very unhealthy choice."

MacInnes pivoted, stiff with anger. "You doubt me still, even after I brought you nine buyers? Each one agreed to come here because of my word and my reputation. If you question my loyalty, why have you used my contacts for the last year?"

Gonsalves raised both palms soothingly. "There is no reason to take offense. If I truly doubted your motives, we would be having this discussion in a manner you would find far more…uncomfortable."

Jordan had no doubt about that. Even Gonsalves's closest guards lived in fear of the man's mood swings. No one was above suspicion, no one entirely safe, not even Gonsalves's own family.

Already two of the security detail had been removed abruptly when Martim discovered them speculating about the secret preparations. Besides Martim, only Jordan and Gonsalves's second in command knew the details of the auction. That secrecy was enforced by security cameras running around the clock throughout the castle and its grounds.

The man trusted no one.

Jordan waved a hand at the three cases. "You questioned *my* loyalty, and now I ask you a question. Do you think you could trick the men I have invited here by taking their money with no intention of giving them the real da Vinci? Maybe you have an excellent forgery ready to transfer after the auction? If so, I must warn you that your life would most certainly be forfeit and mine with it, because I vouched for the art you are to sell. These are dangerous men, Martim. They are also very intelligent men." Anger tightened his voice. "Have you made a secret arrangement to betray them?"

The heir to Macau's largest crime family stared at the display case in cold silence. When he turned, his face was expressionless. "I am hardly so stupid. There will be no surprises tomorrow. Trust me."

MacInnes summoned a smile, pretending to be relieved.

As his cell phone vibrated, Martim answered in rapid-fire Portuguese, then moved to the keypad near the door. Keeping his back to MacInnes, he punched in eight numbers.

The door swung open. Two security guards carried in one of the struggling kitchen staff, his face bloody and his hands bound.

"You have his phone?" Martim demanded, switching to English.

The guard held out a new silver unit. "Two calls

tonight. Both numbers to the same answering service. We couldn't find anything more."

"I think we really should be more persuasive in that case." Gonsalves pulled the remote from his pocket and fingered a button, then slid one end of the unit against the struggling man's neck.

A hum.

The bitter hint of ozone.

The worker made a shrill sound, his body slamming to rigidity as electricity drilled through him.

"Ready to answer yet?"

The man's jaw tightened and he looked away. Silent. Controlled.

Gonsalves frowned. "No? Another sixty thousand volts will change your mind." He leveled another jolt of electricity at the worker's neck, maintaining contact until the man's face filled with color and his legs twitched wildly.

Saliva trickled from the worker's slack mouth. His eyes flickered, then slid over Gonsalves's shoulders. Pain, but nothing else. No answers. No fear.

The behavior would not be tolerated, MacInnes knew. No one crossed Martim Gonsalves.

"Answer me now, damn you." Gonsalves shoved the gagging man back against the stone wall and then pressed the stun device under his chin. With every second his victim's face turned darker.

"Martim, please."

"You protect him, Jordan? You take sides against me?" The stun unit rose, aimed at the American.

"Only because you need this man." Jordan kept his

voice cool, brisk. "If you kill him, you'll never find out who he was contacting. Keep him alive and he will give you valuable information."

Gonsalves considered the idea. "For now." Nodding, he straightened his cuffs and powered down the unit, staring at the worker, who had collapsed and was now held up only by the guards.

Gonsalves kicked the man's leg viciously, again and again, until a bone cracked. "So he will not run." Then he waved to his guards, who dragged the unconscious man outside, leaving a dark line of blood across the freshly polished wood floor. Shaking his head, Gonsalves pulled out a handwoven linen handkerchief and carefully wiped the bloodstains from the floor.

Just your normal average millionaire cleaning up his castle.

Except this millionaire was delusional and ruthless.

When Gonsalves finished, he stared down at the spot where the man had collapsed. "This is a bad thing, my friend. It is all very clear to me."

"I don't understand."

"No? This man was no kitchen worker. He made no protest. He showed no fear. He was a *professional.*" Gonsalves turned slowly, a vein pulsing at his throat. "How did an outsider learn of our auction? I keep asking myself this question."

"One of the buyers may have sent him. They are all careful men."

Gonsalves rubbed his chin. "No, I think there is a different answer." After a final look at the three display units, Gonsalves flipped off the overhead light. "With your help, I will have the truth, my friend. Let us discuss the possibilities upstairs over some cognac."

Although cognac was the last thing MacInnes wanted, he nodded, the picture of affability. No one would guess that he was gripped by pain. "Of course, Martim." MacInnes moved toward the door. "Perhaps you should—"

The sixty-thousand-volt charge hit him full in the neck. His vision exploded in a cascade of white light. Pain slammed through his body as every muscle went rigid.

One second. Two. He fell into an eternity of pain. Jordan MacInnes didn't feel his head strike the floor or two security guards carry him outside in a black plastic bag.

CHAPTER TWENTY-FIVE

SOMETHING WAS WRONG.

Nell shifted, caught in dreams of pale Himalayan snows and finger jams along red Moab cliffs. She thought she heard her father's voice carried on the wind, thready and low, as if from a great distance.

He needed her help.

But there was nothing to see, no one to help, and Nell drifted back into dark images, tossing in her worry.

Warm hands awakened her. She sighed, falling into the surprise of Dakota's mouth and the slide of his tongue. Need raced out into restless discovery.

Dakota whispered her name. Emotion swam through his eyes. Then he put it all away.

Impersonal. Ready to do whatever had to be done.

Nell sat up stiffly. Her muscles ached and her fingers burned from climbing. "Is it time to go?"

He nodded. "No moon. Night climb. One more chance for you to put me through the wringer." He smiled slightly, then raised her palm, tracing the welts and broken skin along her fingers. "Nell, you don't have to—"

"Shut up," she whispered fiercely. "Of course I'm

going and I'll be climbing with you." Desire made her throat dry. "If you'd stop touching me, this would go a lot faster. Safer too."

His eyes narrowed, focused and dangerous. "I never liked playing things safe. I'm telling you now that when this is done, I'm coming for you, Nell. Being *safe* will be the last thing on your mind when I do." His teeth nipped her inner palm. He tongued the sensitive skin at the base of each finger, each touch a silent promise.

And sensual warning.

Nell closed her eyes, her heart fluttering as his fingers trailed over her breasts.

Blindly she reached for her clothes, knowing that if she looked at him she would be lost. When she opened her eyes Dakota was standing at the foot of the bed carrying a nylon backpack. Wind shook the trees outside the gatehouse as she pulled on her jacket and followed him out to the waiting car.

NELL STARED at the classic dark towers rising against the ink-black sky. "In the style of Edward II," she murmured. "Concentric fortified towers, well-defined moat and extensive parapets. The man didn't mess around when it came to crushing the resistance in Wales." Even in the moonless night, the castle walls loomed clearly above them.

Six round towers curved out from the straight castle walls, just as the other towers were built. Nell pressed one palm against the jagged stone, testing the rock face.

No chips fell away. No masonry cracked and tore loose. She prayed Dakota's luck would likewise hold.

"Put these on."

Dakota handed her a pair of night-vision goggles and she slid them on awkwardly. Now when she looked up at the notched teeth at the top of the highest tower, she could calculate height and circumference in the pale green images. The dimensions appeared to match those that Dakota had given her. The climb would be deadly in the dark, and he would be clearly exposed for the last twenty-five feet, a visible target even without any lights to guide him.

Nell wanted to scream with frustration at the reality of what he was preparing to do. But screaming wouldn't help, so she closed down her feelings and focused on the job ahead. She was going to get Dakota up that wall and back down again even if they had to stay here choosing and rejecting footholds all night.

"Will there be any lights at or near the entry wall?"

"None, so far as we can tell."

She pulled out a notebook. "I want exact dimensions of the arrow loops and those lower parapets. I'll chalk out your route while you call out measurements."

"Aye-aye, sir," Dakota murmured.

"Where are the gloves that I made you?"

Dakota reached into his pocket and held up a pair of white mitts carefully constructed of thick athletic tape wrapped to fit his hand.

"Put them on. You're going to need them." She glanced up at the castle wall. "We'll train for the route that we discussed earlier, but I want a second plan in place. There's no telling what you'll find when you get there. Weather, surface deterioration, security lights, anything could go wrong." She took a deep breath, forcing down her uneasiness. "I'm going to give you a plan B."

A good climber always had a plan B, and Nell would know it when she saw it. Dakota was going to memorize both plans until he could do them in his sleep.

She frowned as something vibrated in her pocket. Digging out her phone, she scanned the LED for caller ID and recognized the number of her climbing partner. What time was it back in Utah? she wondered. "Eric? No, everything's fine. I decided to take a few days off. What? Nothing earthshaking." She glanced at Dakota, then looked away. "I'm in Utah. You know how I've been itching to try a new pitch at Bryce."

Her voice carried eerily in the night air. As Dakota chalked up his hands, he watched Nell cradle the phone and speak confidently. He noted the calm, uncomplicated friendliness in her voice.

He was glad that this partner of hers wasn't a lover. That fact had been in Nell's file, but it was nice to have the detail confirmed. Nell's voice would have betrayed her. Dakota could read her too well now.

She paced a little, rubbing one shoulder. "What? No, I'm fine, Eric. I just wanted to get away for a few days and relax. When I finish a painting I'm always a little restless. You know that."

Dakota cleared his throat to catch her attention. The call was harmless, but he didn't want anything distracting her from the work ahead of them.

She gave a little wave and nodded. "Okay, I'll call you tomorrow, Eric. Yes, I promise. Gotta go now." She hung up and shoved the phone back in her pocket. "Sorry. Eric and I have known each other a long time and he gets overprotective if he doesn't hear from me." She opened her notebook and made quick sketches, walking as she wrote. "I'm assuming that you'll be coming in from the back, so let's go take a look."

OUT IN THE SHADOWS beyond the long driveway, Izzy watched them work. The woman was relentless. She kept Dakota moving at a demanding pace, directing him down the wall with clipped and detailed instructions, guiding him every foot of the way.

Watching Nell find a foothold and toe her way up the wall gave Izzy a new respect for the kind of climbing she did. He hadn't expected the grace or the intelligence it required. But what surprised him most was the charged energy between Nell and Dakota. Sometimes she didn't finish a sentence before Dakota completed it. The two were definitely on the same wavelength.

Or something deeper was at work.

He noticed an intensity that had not been there before, from a darkening in Dakota's eyes to the seemingly casual brush of fingers as they unloaded equipment. Unless Izzy was mistaken, another member of Foxfire was about to bite the dust, and Ryker was going to chew dirt when he found out.

Not your business, pal.

If the connection between Nell and Dakota helped

get the job done, then Izzy was all for it. Nell was one of the few people who could get Dakota safely up that wall with only a few hours of training. Getting him down again, safe and in one piece, would be Izzy's problem.

Izzy had a few ideas on how to make that happen, but he wasn't discussing them with anyone until Ryker relayed final mission orders. Meanwhile, he had one more job to do before they left.

AT TWO IN THE MORNING Izzy's dusty Land Rover pulled up the driveway. Nell and Dakota had been training hard, and Nell's fingers were scraped raw, but she couldn't stop thinking about everything that could go wrong.

So she trained harder, always looking for a better pull or a neater jam, showing Dakota cleaner cross movements. More than once she forced him to close his eyes, feeling his way up the wall completely blind. He'd have to read the wall when he made his actual climb under hostile conditions. Nell wanted him prepared to work by touch alone.

Through the long hours, Dakota never complained and barely broke a sweat. As he moved easily up the stone face, Nell marveled that after less than one day of free-climbing, he had tackled moves that had taken her two years to master.

Izzy turned off the Rover and jumped out, watching Dakota toe up the edge of an arrow loop. "He's looking sharp. You've been going at it straight?"

Nell moved over to stand beside him and checked her watch. "Three hours, twenty-two minutes."

"He's ready, Nell." Izzy's eyes were calm, his expression unruffled. "You have to let him go."

Nell shifted from foot to foot. Dakota was ready, but she wasn't. There were still too many things that could go wrong, too many details left to teach him. "You watch them go out, facing heaven knows what kind of risks, not knowing if….if they'll come back. How do you stand it?"

"We all know what we signed up for," Izzy said quietly.

"But what if I missed something? What if Dakota pays the price for my mistakes? How can I live with that?"

"I won't lie to you, Nell. It never gets easier. You just do it. That's all there is. Just go forward."

Just go forward. It sounded so simple.

"What if I taught him the wrong hold? What if he falls and—" Nell's voice tightened.

"You didn't. He won't." Izzy turned, squeezed her shoulder once and released her. "You've both done everything you can. You train hard, do your best, then call it a day. He's ready, Nell. You know it and I know it. It's time to move."

She took a deep breath, thinking of a possibility that she'd hesitated to mention. "I could go in his place, Izzy. I'd be faster, better prepared—"

"No."

"Just consider it. It's the logical thing—"

"*No*. You're a civilian," Izzy said curtly. "You shouldn't be involved at all, but given the situation, you were our best choice for a trainer. And no, you're *not* heading into the fire zone."

"Then what about as backup? I could follow

Dakota and take a different route, drawing attention away from him."

"*No*. It's out of the question."

Nell sighed. She hadn't expected him to agree. Her own skills under fire were negligible, but as a backup climber, she might have helped buy Dakota some time.

"Forget it." Izzy stared at her, eyes narrowed. "You're not going anywhere near the site. Even if I agreed, Dakota never would."

She took a breath. "So how is he going to get down when he's done?"

"Fast rope and a straight drop. He'll anchor on the tower, throw a line over and shoot down. By that point, there will be no more need for concealment, since we assume his cover will be blown once he goes for the art. He'll slip into the water and return the way he came."

Nell knew Izzy was making it sound far easier than it would be. "What about the art?"

"He'll carry waterproof containers to keep it safe."

The climber in Nell liked the plan; the art expert in her shuddered at the thought of one drop of water staining the priceless sketch.

There had to be more questions, but she couldn't think of them. Her mind was spinning. There were so many things that could go wrong and a real possibility that Dakota might not come back.

A single star rose overhead, winking against the moonless sky like a forgotten wish. Nell made a new wish on that faint star, asking for a future with a man who had had too few of his own hopes answered.

Just go forward.

She turned back toward Dakota, summoning her best smile. "Call it a day, Navy. You're as good as I've ever seen. School is out." She glanced back at Izzy. "Your friend here agrees."

"Yeah, but who cares what he thinks?" Dakota dropped lightly to the ground and brushed the extra chalk from his hands. "What I want to know is whether he has a rare steak waiting for me."

Lightness and teasing in the face of death, Nell thought. Not so different from the bravado of climbers.

She took Dakota's arm and shrugged one of the gear bags over her shoulder. "If not, I'll cook the steak myself. What do you say?"

Dakota's eyes narrowed. "If you can cook half as good as you climb, I think I'm a fallen man."

Four in the morning

SO MUCH TO SAY. No time to say it.

Across the hall Nell heard Dakota talking quietly on a cell phone. Through her open windows she smelled the rich perfume of old roses. Restless, she pushed away the covers, thinking about her father and wondering why he hadn't called back.

Barefoot, with a white robe belted against the night's chill, she padded down the hall, where a bar of light shone through the door of Dakota's room. Funny, the man never seemed to sleep. Was that another part of his training?

Nell stopped in the middle of the hall. Dakota was pulling off his shirt, his chest sculpted with lean muscle.

He had an unforgettable body, taut and powerful. She smiled crookedly as she saw the tattoo on his left shoulder.

A tiger, black and red, coiled along one shoulder. Beneath the sleek body were three characters that appeared to be Chinese, though Nell couldn't be sure of that.

As Dakota moved, the tiger seemed to move too, muscles shifting as if sensing danger. It was an arresting sight. Then Nell's smile faded. She saw the old cuts on his back, the welts along his ribs and pale silver scars from old bullet wounds. There were also newer marks, including a bruise on his elbow and one just above his waist. She guessed those had come when he threw the motorcycle to one side to avoid hitting her.

He had looked angry and haunted that night. She didn't know why and probably never would. The man was a walking book of secrets. And their time was nearly gone.

He stretched, rubbing his neck. Opening the nylon bag on the dresser, he pulled out a white tube and applied gel on the cuts at his neck. There was no name on the tube and the heavy blue gel looked unfamiliar. More secrets from the book of Dakota Smith.

Nell didn't care about his shadows as long as he came back alive and brought her father with him.

As Dakota turned, she felt a hot stab of awareness. He wore only a pair of jeans, riding low at his hips. The first button was undone, the denim pulled tight against his stomach. The sight stirred melting memories.

But logic won out over desire. Silently, Nell headed back to bed. The man had to rest.

White curtains danced at the gatehouse windows, and the sudden grip of a hand made her gasp.

"What's wrong, Nell?"

"Nothing—I couldn't sleep. Sorry if I disturbed you."

His eyes were cool and distant. Nell knew he was preparing for the challenges to come.

But she thought of the ways she'd dodged honesty and avoided trust for so many years. So she took a deep breath, choosing honesty over safety. "I want my life back, Dakota. No more shadows and evasions. So here's the rest. I wanted you in Scotland, and I want you now. I can't stop thinking about us. About you inside me."

A muscle tightened at his jaw. "I'd have to say that's a bad idea, honey."

"No kidding." Nell looked away. She'd told him how she felt.

"You *don't* understand." Dakota moved, blocking her way. "Something about this house is wrong. I'm seeing colors I shouldn't see. Movements at the edge of my vision. It's off, and my vision is never off. And then there's the problem with *you*." He cradled her face, his eyes unreadable. "You are doing what no woman has ever done, Nell. I don't like it."

She started to pull away, but his hand slid to the small of her back, driving her flat against his hard, aroused body.

"That's what you do to me. That's how you split my focus. It's never happened to me before. Not even close," he said grimly.

She took a breath. "So what are you going to do about it?"

He edged her back until she was trapped against the wall, then framed her body with his arms. "My first choice? Strip away that robe and take you right here, and then on every other flat surface we can find. Even then I wouldn't have enough of your body, which means that this is out of control. You're going to get hurt if this goes any further, Nell. We both are."

Awareness snapped between them. Nell saw the pulse that beat at his neck, felt the clear pressure of his erection. Yet he didn't move.

She touched his cheek, feeling the locked tension of his arms. *Go forward.* "So what's a little pain? I'm all for the flat surfaces part."

"What about the getting-hurt part?" Dakota was staring at her mouth, looking hungry—and angry about it. "It's a given, damn it."

"I'm a big girl. Let me deal with that."

"I want you to walk away with the feel of my skin, turned inside out with pleasure. Doesn't that frighten you?" Clear in his anger now. Voice rough. Eyes like cold steel.

"Not a bit."

"It *should.*" His fingers fisted in her hair, tugging her down, angling her face toward his. "Fast, impersonal sex doesn't come close to what I want with you. I want hot and noisy and all night. I want to make you scream when you come."

Her hand brushed his cheek, soothing what could never be soothed. "Why are you trying to frighten me, Dakota?"

"Because…"

He swallowed air, scowling.

For all Nell's experience, she knew nothing of the world's darkest places and the ways that people could hurt each other.

There were so many things Dakota could never tell her. His job could never be discussed. When it was important and the order was given, he'd used sex as part of his missions. It hadn't ever made a difference to him one way or another. A different weapon, a practical tool to learn the truth, nothing more. He forgot all about the woman the minute the door was closed.

But now, with Nell, he wanted to remember, not forget. And that wanting left them both at risk. Never before had he wanted to undress a woman and taste her as he did now, leaving a mark so they would both carry the weight of memories.

He wanted to love her.

Dakota went very still.

Love.

When had this deepest of emotions come sneaking in? Love was for movies, pets and children. Love made money for actors and musicians who didn't know anything about how life really worked.

Dakota had seen real love. His parents had known it, the deep and silent kind with glances and fingers that touched when they thought a boy wasn't looking. They'd laughed quietly together in bed at night. He'd heard them often enough.

Then one day they were gone. He'd lost both of them, just as they'd lost each other. So what good had love done them?

But the feeling wouldn't leave. It worked into his chest and locked down hard. *Love* wasn't anywhere in the rule book he had for life.

And yet here it was, a ten-ton gorilla that wasn't going away. Dakota closed his eyes.

"You okay?" Nell's fingers were slow and a little rough, scraped from climbing. She was exhilarating, stubborn and exciting, a woman who gave orders and feared nothing. The woman he wanted to marry and protect and drive to blind, screaming climax.

So little time.

He wasn't close to okay. He was confused, angry, restless. And above everything else Dakota felt invincible, as if he could walk on water. Nell did that, with her glance and her touch.

Nell.

Her breast touched his wrist. He felt the slam of her heart where his hand cradled her ribs. Awareness snapped, like lightning across a summer sky. The next move was going to change everything, and Dakota knew there would be no going back, but he felt as if his whole life had been leading him straight to this moment.

To this woman. To her hands on his face and her body warm against him.

"Sure you don't want to walk away?"

For answer, she opened his palm and slowly bit the callused center. Then she feathered her way slowly over the small bite, using her wet tongue.

When his palm was wet, she guided his hand down over her throat, inside the open collar of her robe.

Across the hot, aroused swell of her breasts, one and then the other, until all he heard was her husky breath and the hammer of his own heart.

Her belt slid free. The robe opened, fell. "Does that feel like I'm going to walk away, or that I'm going to let *you* walk away? Not even close."

CHAPTER-TWENTY-SIX

SHE SHOULD HAVE been terrified, but she wasn't.

Her heart was pounding and her hands shook. Anxious, yes. But also exhilarated.

When Dakota looked at her, she saw wanting and reverence. No man had ever looked at her that way, and she was sure no man would ever look at her that way again.

So only tonight.

Whatever, however, wherever. And when it was done, no looking back.

MacInnes rules.

Only this now *mattered.*

She felt his hand feather through her hair, the slow slide of his tongue along her neck and her ribs. He moved lower, making slow passes over one tight nipple and the other. Heat keened. Sleep was forgotten as carried her back to his room.

Nell didn't want care. She wanted speed, his hunger driving hers. She bit his shoulder, sliding into his arms as he leaned over her on the bed. A question filled his eyes.

She answered by opening the band of his jeans and

finding his erection. The heat and weight of him filled her hand. With any other man she might have hesitated, but not with this one.

Dakota took a harsh breath. "Nell."

She draped one leg around his waist and shoved off his jeans with her toes. One good climbing skill. Her feet were agile and she used them, pressing higher, meeting the hot wedge of skin.

His hand opened, gripping her shoulders. She wanted him inside her, driving deep, but he took his time finding and arousing. His lips were on her forehead when his hand slid between her thighs.

Taking.

Giving.

Nell pushed higher, fitting him against her in reckless welcome, and Dakota cut off her protest with a hungry kiss. She couldn't wait, couldn't think, lost in wanting him.

Blindly she wrapped her legs around his waist, open to him, her hands twisting in his hair, her teeth nipping at his chest. This time Dakota shuddered and held her, just held her.

Unmoving, while sweat skimmed their bodies and need hammered, unappeased.

She was mad with impatience when he drove inside her.

He took her in a long slide of pleasure that blurred her vision and made her heart skip. The only sound in the room came from the curtains shifting in the wind, and then the big duvet toppled onto the floor as Dakota drove her across the bed, thrust by long thrust, carrying her body beneath him with the force of every movement.

Her nails dug into his shoulders.

She felt his skin, slick against hers. Then she tensed, tossed over the edge toward a wall of silver, her legs locked around him, his hands like steel as he held her. Nell bit his neck, muttered his name, wanting more.

Even if it was only for one night.

Her hands pulled at his hair, rough with urgency. She needed the quick heat, the dark loss of reason, and he gave it to her, pushing her across the cool sheets while shock and delight fought through every hard stroke, every low moan.

No time now for promises or gentle questions. Only the ruthless slamming desire of hot, naked skin that left them both clinging to the far side of reason. And then even that ragged line shattered. With Dakota's harsh, erotic praise in her ears, Nell shuddered to a blinding release, dimly feeling his hands fisted in her hair.

His body tensed, driving into her one last time, shoving her against the headboard. He groaned as he claimed her, thigh to thigh. She heard his heart beat wildly against her ear as he held her, then pounded to his own release. Nell felt his heat fill her. Somehow she fell again, lost in his pleasure, every sense unraveled as her hands locked around his neck.

Dimly, she saw the tiger stir on his shoulder. The painted eyes seemed to gleam, shiny in the sweat from Dakota's skin.

SLEEP—WHEN IT FINALLY came, limp and boneless in Dakota's bed—was full of flying and falling. Nell drifted through the wreckage of her life's careful rules and arrived, dreamlike, at a high place where rough gray walls felt like the boundaries of her life.

The wind played through her hair as she stood watching the sea. Beneath her feet the stone shook, just a little. The castle moved as her life moved. Nothing would be the same again.

Nell accepted that, welcomed that. Turning sleepily, her hands opened to meet hard muscle, warm skin.

The body of a warrior.

She smiled sleepily at the thought of the tiger, sated but still dangerous, coiled along his shoulder.

She sighed and pushed closer, her legs tangling with his. She didn't open her eyes when Dakota slipped inside her. Slow heat, silent discoveries. No speed now as he moved deep and turned her inside out, lost in pleasure.

She felt his breath at her cheek.

Heard him whisper her name just before they both fell.

"NELL."

The hand on her shoulder was gentle but insistent. Warm fingers opened, massaging her back.

"Time to go, honey." *Soft dreams.*

A hero's callused hands.

She made an inchoate sound, thinking of rabbit glue and vellum and antique mineral pigments. Da Vinci's strange mirror writing ran through her mind as her eyes fluttered open.

Pale light crept through the abbey's long curtains. She saw Dakota's face, all hard planes, his eyes focused, darker than the shadows at the edge of the room.

Nell sat up. "You're already dressed?"

He nodded and reached out. Their fingers twined. She squeezed hard, as hard as she'd ever touched anything in her life. With all her heart and mind she wanted to stay, wanted to find out every secret in those powerful, focused eyes.

But there was no time.

She threw back the covers and stood up. "There's nothing more I can teach you. Keep your weight centered and read the wall. You're ready for this."

"The rules are carved into my brain."

Nell picked up the dark climbing pants and hooded sweatshirt at the foot of the bed. "I wish there was more that I could do."

"You've already done more than enough. Izzy will take you somewhere safe until it's over." Dakota's fingers skimmed her face, and then he took a step back. "We need to go."

Miles away now. The emotion faded, shoved someplace deep.

She hated the fact that she couldn't do more. As she shouldered her black bag, gathered her notes and took one last look at the beautiful room in the pink-gold light of dawn, something moved, just out of the corner of her eye.

"What was that?"

Dakota turned at the door. "What?"

Nell waited, looking from side to side. "Did you see something by the window?" She frowned, willing the faint shimmer to return. But all she saw was a bar of dawn sunlight, slanting across the abbey's old wooden floor.

"Nothing that I could see."

Probably just her eyes adjusting to the light. Probably jet lag, too much tea and not enough sleep.

When Dakota opened the door, his fingers skimmed Nell's cheek. She thought of the hidden tiger at his shoulder, waiting to be unleashed. He picked up two gear bags and walked out into the clear morning.

Nell followed and did not look back.

THE ABBEY GHOST STOOD in the shadows of the long gallery, his fingers stroking the fur of a great gray cat. Around him the past moved liked cool water. Smells and colors rippled through him, fleeting and vague.

Other lives. Other risks.

Moments torn from days of battle and pain. The stubborn lovers in the gatehouse would not remember that past, but they would remember this present, which was the abbey's gift to them.

"So little I can do," the ghost of Draycott Abbey murmured.

He saw the danger that wrapped around them. But now the risk was overlaid by love. Though the two were only vaguely aware of what was growing between them, Adrian Draycott had intervened to give them a moment out of time, a space between the fear that had passed and the death that was yet to come. He could do no more. Even a ghost's powers were limited.

His fingers tightened on the cat's gray fur.

How damnable to feel so powerless.

Cursed by hand and tongue.

The words seemed to echo coldly in the dawn light while the old house creaked and settled around Adrian, full of memories.

Outside, the black car vanished down the driveway.

CHAPTER TWENTY-SEVEN

DAKOTA DROVE with cool precision, edging the Land Rover over quiet back roads like a native. Nell didn't want to think about leaving as her head slanted against his shoulder.

His fingers opened on her thigh. He turned his head, tucked a strand of hair behind her ear. Then the expression in his eyes faded and the distance returned.

Nell searched for the same distance. "Am I allowed to know your schedule today?"

"Izzy wants me to take one last set of photos at the castle. He has an idea he wants to try that uses texture mapping for 3-D image generation."

Nell didn't follow, but that was expected.

"Izzy will be coming to meet you before I leave." Dakota glanced at his watch. "It's going to be tight, Nell. My chopper is waiting."

She nodded, her heart too full for speech. Fear gnawed at her as she thought of what lay before him.

But Nell forced the fear away. Instead she thought about the tiger curling over his shoulder. Tough man, tough tattoo.

Nell would be tough, too. She closed off her fear. If any man could survive, Dakota could.

FOURTEEN MINUTES LATER, Dakota walked along the castle's gray walls, taking pictures with a heavy white camera. When he was done, he checked the unit and slid it back into his bag.

Nell had to give him one last reminder. "Remember to clean your climbing shoes once you reach the point of ascent. Any mud or grit from the water will ruin your grip."

"Check." Dakota glanced down as his cell phone rang. "Teague, where are you? Fine—we'll meet you there." Dakota put away his phone and stowed his camera bag in the backseat. "Change of plan. Izzy will meet us at the pub back in the village."

"Great. I could use a cup of tea."

When they reached the village pub, Nell paced outside, trying to be calm. The last thing Dakota needed was for her to have a case of nerves just as he was ready to leave.

"I've programmed your phone, Nell. Dial four for Izzy if you need him."

"I'll remember."

"He's supposed to *be* here now." Dakota glanced up the road, looking irritated.

"Look, Dakota—my stomach is pretty upset. I'm going inside to the ladies' room in the pub. Maybe your friend will be here by then."

"He'd better be," Dakota muttered. He scanned the narrow lanes nearby and a field dotted with sleepy sheep. "Go ahead. I'll be right there."

Nell followed a sign to the side entrance of the pub and was halfway down the narrow back corridor when she heard an eager voice behind her.

"Nell? I can't believe I *found* you."

She turned at the familiar sound, amazed to see her climbing partner's clear hazel eyes and lanky frame. "Eric? What are you doing here?"

"Trying to find *you*. Look, I'll explain everything, Nell, but first the good news." He gave her a high five. "I just got a huge endorsement offer, six figures for only three climbs. Can you believe it?"

Nell fought her queasiness, rubbing her stomach. "Great. But why—"

"They want two climbers. Male and female." He squeezed her shoulder. "So, what do you say?"

"I—of course, Eric. But—"

He cut her off, jamming his fingers through his hair. "I know how busy you are, so I'll give them a tentative date." He glanced out the window, frowning. "Our daughter's asthma has gotten worse and the medical bills—well, I *need* this gig, Nell. I need it bad or I wouldn't have bothered you."

"I can squeeze in a climb. But Eric, how did you find me?" He took her arm gently, but Nell pulled free. "No, I want some answers."

"Sorry to bother you like this, Nell. It could make all the difference for me."

He looked tired, she thought. He had lost weight, too. "Eric, what's wrong?"

His eyes flickered over her shoulder. Something closed in his face. For a moment, Nell thought it was guilt.

"I'm sorry, Nell," he whispered. "So damn sorry."

"Why—"

She felt a slight sting at the back of her neck, then the jab of a needle. She whirled, one hand in a fist as a man caught her shoulders tightly. She tried to scream, but only a cracked groan emerged as the drug hit her system.

Her hand clenched, sliding into her pocket. She felt the outline of her cell phone and fumbled until she found the speed dial. "Eric, what—"

Already her words were slurring. Her legs seemed too heavy to move. "What—what was in the—the syringe?" She struggled to force out her words. "*Tell* me."

"I had to help them, Nell. But they won't harm you. They just want information. It's the government, you know. They needed me to watch you for them. Something hush-hush."

"Shut up," the man said flatly. "Tell her nothing."

"W-watch me?" she rasped.

"For three months. Even before Scotland." Her old friend and climbing partner leaned closer, his voice a whisper. "I saw you that night in San Francisco. The men who followed you into that alley weren't part of this. I promise you they weren't."

"*Shut up,*" the other man snapped.

Nell swayed. Her partner's voice seemed to come and go. *Stupid*, she tried to say, her gaze slipping to the deserted field and small service road behind the pub. The sky seemed to fade into gray as the two men pushed her through the door, out toward the grass that bordered the road. When she tried to fight, her knees gave way and they pulled her behind them.

"They promised me, Nell. You won't be in any danger." There was desperation in her partner's voice, as if he was trying to convince himself it was true.

Nell couldn't seem to hear anything more. Her hands shook and the cell phone dropped somewhere in the grass.

Another prick at her ear.

The ground tipped hard.

Cold fingers caught her as she fell.

DAKOTA GLARED at the side door of the pub, then looked back at Izzy. "What is taking her so long?"

"Couldn't tell you. Sometimes women need time for whatever it is they do." Izzy crossed his arms, watching two sheep wander past a little stone fence.

Dakota checked his watch, then strode toward the side door. He heard a plane overhead and the quiet hum of a passing truck.

No screams. No reason for the sudden prickling at the back of his neck.

The corridor inside was empty. He knocked on the bathroom door and called Nell's name, then looked inside.

The bathroom was empty.

DAKOTA SPRINTED back outside, checking the parking lot while he waved to Izzy. "She's gone. Damn it, she was *here* four minutes ago."

"I'll look inside." Teague was already moving. "Check the far side of the building."

Everything looked normal until Dakota came to the back service entrance. He bent down, frowning at the marks of three pairs of shoes in the grass.

One of the prints belonged to Nell.

Beside the print he saw the glint of metal. Her cell phone was still open, and he lifted it carefully, scanned the LED screen and saw that a call was in progress. In seconds he was listening to the muffled, recorded message left on her own voice mail.

Her voice sounded thready and anxious.

"Eric, what was in the syringe…"

Another voice came, this one male. "I had to help them…"

Eric. Her climbing partner.

"Teague, over here."

Dakota scanned the nearby fields. Two furniture trucks lumbered past, half hidden by a tall hedgerow. He jumped the small stone wall as Teague emerged around the side of the pub.

"The furniture trucks."

"I'm on it." Izzy looked down as his cell phone rang. "Yes, sir. Lieutenant Smith is on his way. He'll be at the chopper in ten minutes." He snapped the phone shut. "I'll find her, Dakota. You need to catch that chopper."

Dakota watched a red dairy van turn at the far side of the square. "Teague, she must be—"

Izzy pulled out a Sig Sauer. "Let me do my job, Dakota. You go do *yours*."

Dakota watched him jump in and gun his black Range Rover, fishtail onto the road and race after the furniture trucks. Nell had to be close. He could feel it.

And he had to leave her.

Because the mission always came first.

Fury warred with every feeling. His hands fisted.

And then, though it was the hardest thing he'd ever done, he buried his feelings, grabbed his gear bag and pulled out his keys.

Izzy had forced the two furniture trucks off the road and a police car siren was just sounding in the distance as Dakota drove away to meet his chopper.

As THE OPPOSITE corner of the village, a Federal Air truck moved down a long lane hidden by hedgerows. The driver knew his orders.

The woman's motionless body was hidden beneath a neat layer of baskets and freshly cut flowers. Every box was tagged and invoiced for delivery to a luxury flower shop in London.

Nell's climbing partner appeared to be asleep in the front passenger seat. A single blow to the head had halted his stammering protests.

The driver drove without haste. He was to dump the American man, bound and gagged, at the bend of the river ahead and continue north to meet his waiting transport.

He would be in Scotland with the woman before noon.

CHAPTER TWENTY-EIGHT

"WHAT DO YOU *MEAN* she's not there?" Dakota had been sidelined while the military pilot made preparations for takeoff, checking gauges and completing final paperwork.

Fighting anger, he tried to work through scenarios of what could have happened to Nell. "I saw her, Izzy. It can't be more than ten minutes ago. She said she was going inside for tea."

"They must have been waiting nearby. Maybe they triangulated the cell phone call she received and were watching the area." Izzy's voice was clipped. "She started recording a message and dropped the phone, which was damn smart. It was Eric, her climbing partner. He'd been watching her for several months, even during your climb up in Scotland. He could be reporting to Gonsalves, or someone working for him. Her father might have had second thoughts, or maybe they want her expertise for the auction. She's a one-stop shop for conservation assessment or authentication of the painting."

"Get her back," Dakota said harshly. "I don't want her anywhere *near* that auction."

"Working on it. I've got people at every major inter-section between here and the airport in Hastings."

"The chip," Dakota said. "Her transmitter should still be in place. Why can't you bring up a signal?"

Silence.

"Talk to me, Teague. Damn it, that transmitter was checked out. Ryker said it could withstand direct immersion in water, electrical short circuits and temperature spikes. Why can't you track her?"

"There's no need to yell," Izzy said quietly.

"Who's yelling?" Dakota saw the pilot turn and stare at him oddly. He took a deep breath and lowered his voice. "If anything happens to her—"

"It won't. I won't let it. And her chip signal stopped at the same time she vanished. Hold on."

Dakota heard muffled voices, and Izzy returned. "One of my people reports that a truck driver saw Nell speaking to someone. By the description, it was Eric Burson. She walked out into the parking area with him, a Fed Air truck pulled up, and when our contact glanced back Nell was gone. That's as much as we have. I've got an alert out covering this area and all Fed Air trucks will be stopped. The bad news is that they could have some kind of radio frequency and electrical shielding for their vehicles. We know the Koreans have come up with a powerful portable system."

"Which would explain the loss of her chip signal once she was inside the truck."

But Dakota wasn't thinking about electrical shields or Korean electronics. All he wanted to know was that Nell was safe. He glared at the helicopter, torn between duty and emotion, every soldier's frightening scenario come to life.

He couldn't think about Nell. If the October 12th terrorist group bankrolled thirty-five million into a secret offshore account, there was no telling how many more people would die in bombings and kidnappings. But he couldn't walk away without assurances either. "Teague, she's..." He took a sharp breath. "She's in my life now. Find her."

"I'm on it. Repeat, I *will* track her down. Meanwhile, your orders remain operational. Is that clear?"

Dakota's jaw locked. Fury seethed up. But then he closed down, the way he had to close down.

He knew the facts. No one could do a better job of tracking Nell than Izzy would. Dakota didn't like it, and his mind and being rebelled, but the soldier took charge and forced the man aside. "Understood. I'm boarding now." His voice hardened. "Keep her away from that auction, Teague."

"That's a roger, Navy. I'm on it."

Teague didn't make promises lightly. He would deliver, Dakota knew.

All he could do now was climb aboard the chopper without looking back.

JORDAN MACINNES WOKE with the taste of blood in his mouth. When he tried to sit up, every muscle screamed as if he'd been kicked for a few hours.

Not kicked. Hit with a Taser.

Groggy, he inched onto his side. Images of Martim Gonsalves's remote security device flashed through his muddled mind. What had happened to send the man into a fit? Had the worker really been an embedded spy? And if so, for whom? Brutal and paranoid, Gonsalves had decided to strike first and ask questions later.

His stomach roiling, MacInnes fought his way upright, bracing his back against cold stone. He was in some kind of cell, his hands cuffed. Water trickled nearby.

He heard a small movement and saw a glint of light. A door creaked somewhere beyond his range of vision, and a man peered in, shining a light across the narrow cell.

Jordan saw that there was nothing else in the space. No bed, no chair. No way to escape.

"Let me out. I need to speak to Mr. Gonsalves. I—"

The man walked away without any sign of interest.

MacInnes closed his eyes, sagging against the rough stone wall. They'd taken his shoes and his belt and his watch. He didn't have a clue how long he'd been unconscious. Thankfully he'd hidden his cell phone before he'd gone to see Martim or he'd be dead now.

As his eyes adjusted to the light, he saw the outline of a second cell across from his. A dark form lay unmoving on the floor.

"Hello?"

Silence.

"Can you hear me?"

There was no answer.

Ignoring the burning pain in every muscle, MacInnes struggled to his feet. He reached along the iron bars until he felt the outline of the lock.

Solid metal. With time, he could pick it, but he had no idea when his jailor would return. His fingers moved through the darkness, then closed around the heavy metal chain woven in and out through the steel bars.

No time.

Leaning over, MacInnes began to cough violently, his body rigid. It was easy to make the sound realistic, easy to appear as if he was choking because his pain was real. So was the blood that he coughed up. Quickly, he pried off the porcelain cap at his left molar.

When the outside door opened again, he was huddled in the corner, shaking, struggling to breathe. "I n-need to see Martim. *Now*."

CHAPTER TWENTY-NINE

THEY FOUND the empty express truck abandoned nine miles away from the pub. Izzy's men had responded to a call from a local couple, out walking their Pomeranians when they saw the truck angled into a ditch. The inside of the truck was filled with flowers and boxes, all tagged for delivery, but no businesses existed with the names on the boxes.

The bad news? No sign of Nell.

Izzy was searching the ground near the truck, looking for fallen bits of paper or other clues when his laptop, open inside the Land Rover, whined a noisy alert. He sprinted back to the car, scrolled through two screens and watched a cursor blink, heading northwest.

Nell's chip was broadcasting again. According to Izzy's laptop screen, she was approximately fifteen miles away, somewhere in southern Surrey. Izzy frowned as he checked the GPS and noted her rate of speed—135 miles per hour.

Light aircraft. Probably a small, private charter. Now he had a location. He triggered a receiver plugged into the dashboard of the Land Rover and tuned the unit, listening to the crackle of static. With Nell's chip operational again, he could activate the tiny transceiver in the chip's outer housing.

He worked the dial until the static cleared. Abruptly the drone of motors filled the Rover, followed by the sound of voices, barely audible over the motor's throb. Izzy tinkered a little more, then pulled on headphones to listen.

"She still out back there?"

"Like a zombie. Don't know what they gave her, but it must be heavy-duty stuff. How long till we pass Gatwick?"

"Clear in ten minutes."

"Any contact from the west?"

"Nada. All quiet." A man laughed. *"Easiest money I ever made. With luck, I'll be knocking back a Guinness Extra Stout in Portree by six."*

Static crackled. *"—idea who's paying our tab?"*

The other man cleared his throat. *"Better not to ask. This bunch is touchy about questions. Foreign, that's all I know, but U.S. dollars are U.S. dollars anywhere. What's that engine reading?"*

Izzy flipped a button, replaying the muffled conversation, which soon veered into an argument about whether Manchester United would trounce Sheffield in the following week's playoff games.

Shifting his earphones, he opened an encrypted cell phone, dialing an old friend at the British Department for Transport. In minutes he would have airplane ID and flight plans, along with name of the owner.

Time for Plan B, he thought gravely.

NELL WASN'T ASLEEP, though she hadn't moved for at least twenty minutes. She heard two men talking, their conversation unclear over the whine of the motors. She had woken to find her legs and feet bound, a blanket over her body as she huddled in the cramped backseat of a small plane. She was still dazed from whatever they had given her in the syringe, but with every minute her thoughts grew clearer.

She forced herself to stay calm. Dakota and Izzy would be looking for her, but she wouldn't wait around to be rescued. She had to be headed to Scotland, given the bits of conversation she had picked up. Portree was the capital of the Isle of Skye, so their final destination must be close. Once she was at the castle, she could use her knowledge of the layout to find her father. Assuming that the castle was where they were taking her.

She was still in shock at the memory of her climbing partner's betrayal. Eric had always been easygoing, and he'd never broken any laws that Nell knew about. If anything, he had been overprotective on their many climbs together. *But you never really knew the people around you.*

Nell frowned. She was certain she knew Dakota after only a few days spent together. She knew the force of his will and the weight of his sense of duty. She never doubted that she would see him again or that somehow they would make a future together.

But first she had to escape.

Thunder crackled somewhere to her left. The airplane dipped slightly, then hammered its way north.

CHAPTER THIRTY

The Isle of Skye
Northern Shore

DAKOTA FLOATED in the cold water, one brown speck among hundreds. Wind tossed the gray swells, rocking the ocean kelp bed beneath him.

With a camouflaged pair of Zeiss binoculars at his chest, he rose and fell on the restless waves, watching the castle that loomed above the nearest headland.

The SEAL opened to the patterns of weather and sky, noting the movements of the castle's security teams and timing their rotations, watching late-afternoon cloud patterns and changing tidal flows. All those factors would come into play that night.

Tilting the binoculars, he studied the castle's rear wall. He had climbed the far corner a dozen times in his mind, pulling himself silently up toward the high parapet. Now two guards crossed the crenellated wall, and another guard passed on a lower tower. All carried radios and binoculars and used them frequently, he noted.

Professionals. Dakota turned his head, picking up

high heat readings in two outbuildings attached to the east side of the castle. The heat indicated some kind of heavy equipment in operation there. The doors were guarded by three uniformed men carrying automatic weapons.

He watched every movement at the compound, settling into the terrain, listening to the cries of passing seabirds. He had already verified the best point to enter the water pipes that connected to the moat after making certain neither the pipes nor moat had regular guard surveillance.

The water stirred beneath him, rocking the kelp bed. A thirty-foot basking shark raced past, fin breaching the surface, dragging Dakota along in the force of its wake. The sudden violent turbulence in the water reminded him that nothing was ever final, and the best plans could be shattered in an instant.

He cradled the waterproof binoculars, waiting for the wake to recede. He made his mind still as the gray water and racing clouds, watching his target. There were things he hadn't told Nell or Draycott, under orders from Ryker. The mission was not what she or anyone else believed. Only Izzy knew the full scope of his dangerous assignment.

As Dakota drifted in the cold waters, he thought about his orders and how to negotiate the rocky slope between duty and honor.

NELL CAUGHT the smell of the sea as they carried her out of the airplane. She was careful not to move, feigning sleep while rough hands shoved her into what appeared to be a cold metal compartment. She resisted the urge to fight, knowing it would be useless against the three men she had heard talking after the plane landed.

She heard the roar of a motor and realized she was inside the trunk of a car. Even locked away, she caught the rich tang of the sea. Her elbow hurt and she winced as the car bumped over pitted roads.

When the car finally slowed, Nell made certain that her jacket was pulled up and her hair covered her face. She didn't open her eyes until she was lifted outside. Seabirds wheeled overhead as she took a quick glance and saw gray walls looming on a rocky slope, while the dark curve of the ocean yawned in the distance.

Scotland.

Then she was inside the walls, carried up a long set of steps and tossed onto a small bed.

The heavy wooden door banged shut and a metal lock rang loudly as it was snapped in place.

TWENTY MINUTES LATER two black limousines circled to the end of the castle's gravel driveway. Uniformed guards opened the doors and ushered in the first group of arrivals. None of the well-dressed "guests" seemed surprised that the guards were heavily armed, and no one protested when their bags and bodies were searched for weapons.

NELL'S DOOR SHOOK. She kept her eyes closed as the handle turned.

Hard fingers gripped her hair and yanked her upright. "Time to wake up. Someone wants to see you."

Nell kept her movements slow, as if she was still groggy. She heard the tap of footsteps.

"Nell, wake up. Honey, what have they done to you?"

She stiffened as she heard her father's voice. Opening her eyes, she saw his ashen face. He looked ten years older, gaunt and worried yet trying not to show it.

Nell reached out a trembling hand, unable to speak with the force of her emotions.

"Are you hurt? What did they do?"

She shook her head. "I—I'm fine. A little bruised maybe." Despite all her efforts, her eyes filled with tears. "You're alive," she whispered. "I was so afraid…"

The door closed.

"It's going to be okay. I'm right here, Nell." His arms slid around her. "How did they *find* you?" Her father looked exhausted and there was a bruise along his jaw. "You were supposed to stay with Nicholas."

"Eric—Eric was involved. He called me and maybe they tracked the cell phone calls. I don't know."

"They used Eric?" Her father closed his eyes, stifling a cough.

"Daddy, are you okay? You look…"

"I'm tired, that's all." He gripped her hand, then turned away to pace the small room, which looked like an average servant's bedroom—except for the newly installed metal bars on the door. Abruptly he came back and leaned down, his head beside hers. "We have to convince them we're on different sides." Jordan

MacInnes kept his voice very low. "I don't want him harming you to get at me, do you understand? So we fight. We fight about everything. Hide any emotions but anger from him, Nell."

"Who?"

"The man who controls all of this. They'll be coming soon. If I can create a diversion, I want you to run. Don't wait for me—just go. Do you understand?"

"But what about you?"

I'll be fine, Nell. Just remember what I said. Don't give him *anything* he can use against us."

MORE BLACK LIMOUSINES cruised up the driveway, followed by a silver Aston Martin and a white Rolls-Royce Corniche. Each car was met, each guest was carefully checked for weapons and ushered inside. By eight in the evening. Glenmor Castle's little parking lot was full.

The last car was a black Escalade. The side door opened, a small motorized ramp powered down, and a sleek silver wheelchair buzzed along the ramp. The wizened old man in the chair had mahogany skin and papery white hair and looked around him with cold arrogance.

His name was Bujune Okambe and he had led the military force of his African state until staging a successful coup d'état. That same afternoon Okambe proclaimed himself president and took personal control of his country's newly discovered oil reserves. Now he was one of the wealthiest men in the world.

His aged hands shook on the wheelchair controls

as he submitted to the weapon search. Then with icy impatience he motioned to his striking daughter to follow him up the walk to the castle.

Martim Gonsalves's guest list was now complete. The auction was about to begin.

CHAPTER THIRTY-ONE

THEY CAME for Nell twenty minutes later, two tall men
with scars on their cheeks and leaden eyes. One wore
a blue tie, the other wore green. The stocky one in the
blue tie grabbed her arms when she didn't move fast
enough, shoving her toward the stairs.

"Where are we going?" she snapped.

No answer.

Nell glanced at her father, then looked up as they
were forced into a big service elevator. From the smell
of cooking food, it had to run down near the kitchen
and food service area.

Jordan went in first, followed by the bigger guard,
with Nell close behind. Suddenly her father made a
strangled sound and locked his hands over his chest,
staggering back through the open elevator door.

"Get in, fool." The big guard hauled him back, but
Nell's father groaned, his arms flailing at the guard's
face.

"My heart. Crushing. I can't—*breathe.*"

When the second guard leaned down for a closer
look, Nell dropped her sweater over his head from
behind and yanked the arms in a knot. While her father

grappled with his captor, she ran back down the passage to a small storage closet located beyond the corner. She opened the door a crack, tossing linens onto the floor, then ran down the opposite hallway and waited, crouched behind a cart full of dirty laundry.

Her throat was dry, her heart pounding.

Both guards sprinted along the corridor and the big one stopped at the storage closet, holding up one hand. The second guard nodded and drew a revolver, kicking at the linens.

Silent, Nell crept back toward the elevator along a parallel hallway. Her father was very pale, gesturing upward. Nell climbed the wooden panels inside the elevator, pushed open the small access door at the ceiling and climbed out, then lowered the access door.

She heard footsteps and angry voices below her as she climbed with adrenaline-fuelled grace, hand over hand along the small emergency ladder inside the elevator vault.

Three stories higher the vault ended. Nell hesitated. She pulled the grate from a ventilation duct and crawled inside, her heart pounding.

The elevator creaked and then shot past. When the doors opened, two guards dragged her father out.

"Where is she?"

Her father shrugged. "Women, always making trouble. I told her not to—"

The guard snapped the butt of his gun across MacInnes' jaw. "Where *is* she?" he repeated.

"I told you. I don't—"

Another blow, harder this time. Nell heard her

father's muffled groan followed by the sound of his body hitting the wall.

"Next time I'll shoot you, old man. Where *is* she?"

She spotted a commercial fire extinguisher mounted near the floor opening. As her father was struck again, she pulled the heavy unit free and climbed back onto the elevator. She tossed out the safety pin and waited until it cracked against the floor far below.

The guards shouted, and the elevator began to descend, with Nell clinging to the roof. As the guards struggled in confusion inside, she lifted the emergency access door and dropped the body of the fire extinguisher on the bigger guard.

"Nell, *go*." Her father's voice was harsh. "Don't do this."

She jumped down into the elevator, struggling with the second guard, who kicked her against the wall and then raised a pistol to her father's head.

Nell froze, raising her hands slowly. When the elevator doors opened, three more guards were waiting out in the corridor.

Somewhere in the distance laughter mingled with the sound of harp music.

THE SMALL STONE ROOM where they took her was full of people in formal evening attire.

Three cases gleamed beneath small focused beams. Ten men and one woman circled the cases, watching light play over the delicate face of a woman with a haunting smile. *La Gioconda* had never looked more mysterious.

Three sketches.

Nell caught her breath in awe. Da Vinci's genius shone in the smooth curve of the woman's cheek and the shading of the expressive eyes. Was there smug satisfaction in her gaze or did her face hide some piece of secret knowledge? Scholars had argued about that expression for centuries.

"Gentlemen, and ladies, I am Martim Gonsalves. I welcome you." As a slender man in an Armani suit moved from the back wall, the group parted to make way for him. "This is what you have come to bid on. You are looking at Leonardo's preliminary chalk sketch for the *Mona Lisa*, with probable oversketching by Michelangelo, noticeable in the fine marks at her shoulders and her hands." All other sounds in the room faded. Every face studied the three examples of Renaissance genius.

Martim continued calmly. "The piece was recently discovered in a bank vault in Switzerland. How it came into my possession need not concern us tonight. You see three cases here as a precaution, should one of you plan an act of theft." He eyed the group coldly. "One of the pieces is real. The other two are holographic images. If you have questions about authenticity, I suggest you direct them to Jordan MacInnes and his daughter. Her credentials as a conservator and art expert are a matter of record and you all know Jordan personally, of course." A guard squeezed Nell's arm, holding her in place beside her father.

Martim strolled through the silent group, smiling. "Recently, this sketch was removed from the National

Gallery. As you would expect, all copies of authenticating tests and supporting photographs are available, in addition to those that have already been e-mailed to you. The curator at the museum was most thorough." He smiled thinly.

"Martim, one question." A wheelchair hummed over the wooden floor, steered by an old man with leathery skin. "I respect your experts, of course, but with a price so considerable I require spectroscopy results and pigment analysis. Further, I want proof that these lighter marks belong to Michelangelo. Can you provide these things?"

"Mr. Okambe, shrewd as always." Martim's eyes narrowed. "Here are two experts to answer all your questions."

He motioned to Jordan, who gripped Nell's arm tightly and guided her toward the cases. Heads nodded in recognition and several of the men reached out to shake hands as Nell's father passed.

Several people frowned but no one commented about Nell's rumpled clothes or the bruises on her father's face. Nell realized that this was the shadow world she had imagined for years but had never glimpsed until now.

Her father held out a folder. "My daughter will answer any questions you may have, starting with Mr. Okambe's."

She summoned the calm arrogance that these assembled buyers would respect. The only other female present was a striking African woman with scars in the shape of tears dotting her high cheekbones. The woman studied Nell with disdain, moving closer to the man in the wheelchair, carrying herself like a princess.

In a clear, calm voice Nell explained the results of the various tests, riffling through the folder she had been given. Her host would not know that she had already studied the data line by line, of course.

When she was done, Gonsalves nodded. "An excellent explanation. Now are all the questions answered?" The buyers shuffled and then murmured assent, and their host gestured to his security chief, who punched a number into the keypad. The heavy door opened. "Caviar is now being served in the Blue Ballroom. I will join you there shortly to begin our bidding."

Mr. Okambe gestured to the tall woman—his daughter or his mistress, Nell wasn't sure. "Make Jordan's daughter wait. She must explain the results of the last infrared test."

Martim smiled but shook his head curtly. "Any questions are open to all, Mr. Okambe. It is fairer that way." He gestured to Nell. "Elaborate on the test for us."

Nell ignored the imperious edge to the man's voice and kept her cool smile in place. As she explained how the paper and materials showed results consistent with da Vinci's style and dating, Mr. Okambe listened closely, his chin sunk against his chest. Then he raised one hand, palm up. Nell saw the same set of tear-shaped scars along the base of his wrist. "One moment. I understand that this art is cursed. I do not take such a thing lightly." At his words, excitement snapped through the room.

Nell moved toward the display cases, cutting in front

of the African man's wheelchair. "True. *Maledetto*."
She let the sound roll over her tongue, watching the
reaction to her words. "Legend says it was cursed by
da Vinci after it was stolen from him, possibly by his
disreputable servant. If you buy this piece, you should
understand that harm may come to you."

Martim's jaw locked in a line of fury. He moved
casually beside Nell and took her arm, then his fingers
twisted harshly on her wrist. "A legend, no more, my
dear. We are adults here, not children who cry and run
from shadows."

As Martim's fingers tightened cruelly on her arm,
Nell bit back a gasp.

"You've explained all that we need to know, my
dear." His nails dug into her skin, a painful warning.
"Now you must let our honored guests relax before our
business begins." He glanced at Mr. Okambe. "You are
satisfied?"

The old man nodded, then wheeled outside, with the
regal woman close beside him. In his wake the room
cleared quickly, and as soon as the door closed, Martim
Gonsalves turned and slammed Nell against the wall.
Pulling a small metal unit from his pocket, he drove it
under her chin.

Nell fought to breathe, the world flashing white as
Gonsalves triggered the power on the Taser.

THE MOON WAS A BROKEN sliver against racing clouds
as Dakota neared the base of the castle wall. In a few
smooth strokes he found the mouth of the water pipe.

His rebreather unit hissed quietly against his mask,

the tide driving him forward onto the heavy iron grate at the opening of the pipe. He pried the cover free and slid inside, the water churning up mud in turbid waves around him. Small fish shot from the pipe's bottom as he navigated by the infrared dial of the compass on his wrist.

Abruptly the tunnel opened. Mud gave way to gravel and weeds and drifting sediment as he came to the edge of the castle moat.

He checked his watch.

One minute early.

Inching from the water, he waited, hidden by reeds. Dakota counted out the seconds, following his prearranged schedule. No guards moved over this part of the grounds. There was no flare of heat around him, no movement on the high parapets. Crawling through the reeds, he reached the low grass, his breath loud in his ears, his mask down and rebreather turned off.

Somewhere a bird cried shrilly as Dakota had his first glimpse of the wall he had to climb. Weathered and stark, its stone face loomed up above the loch's edge. He sighted his route, picking out ledges and cracks by the uneven heat patterns that still reflected the afternoon sun.

He read the wall just the way Nell had told him to do, picking out his first three footholds. With his route clear, he eased out of the grass, ready to climb, one foot braced against a ridge of stone.

Then he stopped.

Something she'd said—something important.

The shoes.

Quickly he stripped off his rubber-soled diving boots and stowed them in his pack. Wearing only thin climbing shoes, he grabbed his first hold and toed into small cracks with his weight centered.

Somewhere a car door slammed. The buyers would be inside now.

Find a grip, weight steady. Roll from your feet.

He was already at the arrow loops when a bird shot out of the darkness, diving at his head. Dakota held steady, despite the talons shredding the back of his Neoprene suit. Ignoring the slash of pain at his shoulders, he willed himself to stay motionless.

With a loud cry, the bird soared away into the darkness. Dakota looked up, reading the wall, and reached for the arrow loop. Suddenly the narrow ledge beneath him crumbled.

He swung free, legs dangling. Instantly, he jammed his hand into a crack and held on with two knuckles just the way Nell had shown him.

Near the moat a light cut through the darkness, followed by the static screech of a walkie-talkie.

NELL COULDN'T BREATHE, and the burning pain wouldn't stop.

Her father's voice rose in fury.

"Put your toys away, Martim. It is time for business, *not* ego. I will take care of my difficult daughter."

Time stretched out. Finally the metal box slid away from Nell's neck. Her knees crumpled and she braced her shoulders against the wall to keep from falling.

"Then take care of her now. Otherwise, I will rip the tongue from her throat." Martim smoothed his suit with tight, angry movements. As he punched in the key code he shot a cold look at Nell.

The door slid open. A tall man with silver hair waited in the doorway flanked by two bodyguards. His cool eyes held the confidence of a man well accustomed to giving orders and having them obeyed unquestioningly.

"*Father?*" Martim Gonsalves stood frozen, his face a mask of shock. "How—why have you come here?"

"I am not to visit one of my own homes?" The silverhaired man glanced through the room, noting the three lit cases. "I may not visit my eldest son?" His voice hardened. "Even when he conducts business without advising me?"

"It was…to be a surprise, to show that you can trust me." All Martim's bravado was gone. He moved from foot to foot like a guilty child. "I will explain everything, Father, but not now. Not in front of these outsiders."

"*Now*, I think." The old man ignored his son, walking to the display cases. "So this is the piece of art. Why three, Martim?"

"A precaution to deter any thieves." The younger man triggered the remote with a flourish, and the two outer cases went dark, leaving only the center display lit. "Here is the real work. But Father, my buyers—"

"*Our* buyers," the older man said coldly. "And I believe that they can wait a few more minutes." He never once looked at Nell or her father as he spoke to his son. "I know that this American selected your bidders. Yes, I have my sources, Martim. You kept your secrets well, but not quite well enough." Luis Gonsalves frowned, walking thoughtfully around the case. "What I do not understand is why the man's daughter is here."

"To authenticate the art, Father. I knew there would be questions, and we needed an expert."

The old man frowned. "She is an outsider."

Nell started to answer, but her father's slight headshake stopped her.

"She—" The son cleared his throat. "She is no longer of any importance. After the auction I will make arrangements for her."

Jordan MacInnes cleared his throat. The powerful older criminal turned to study him. "You are the man who stole a Vermeer and three Rembrandts from the Gardner Museum in Boston, I understand."

"Never proved. Never recovered," MacInnes said calmly.

Gonsalves shrugged. "Prison has not been kind to you."

Nell's father met his gaze. "Only to be expected. Now it is my honor to be of service to your son. But one thing first. As one father to another, I ask that my daughter be allowed to leave."

"She was brought here against her will?"

"That need not concern us as long as she leaves now. She is young and arrogant, foolish as young women will be. But family is family, and she is all that I have left."

"Family." The old man nodded slightly. "Always a blessing and sometimes a curse." Luis Gonsalves turned to study the art. "It is the genuine work of da Vinci?"

"Without a doubt," Nell's father said. "The bidders are well chosen, all of them enemies driven by old anger and feuds. They will pay any price to win against each other."

"A good plan." The old man studied the haunting face of the woman in the sketch and then nodded. "Your daughter may go. Her use here has ended."

"But Father—"

"Silence." The order was cold. "She leaves, but the father stays." He turned to Jordan MacInnes. "I have more work for you. This is agreed?"

After a long time Nell's father nodded. "It is agreed."

"No. She will *talk*." Martim hissed. "We can't trust an outsider."

Luis Gonsalves looked at Nell, and she felt the full force of his cold assessment.

"Will you speak of this?"

"No daughter would harm a father," she answered.

"Even if she hates the things he has done—and will do again?" the old man asked shrewdly.

"Even then."

"It is finished." The old man reached into his pocket. "You will be driven to Edinburgh." He pulled out a piece of paper and scrawled a number in ink. "This paper will take you anywhere in the world without harm. The man who answers that phone will see to it. But it may only be used once. You understand the rest—and that your father's life will depend on your silence?"

He'd traded his freedom and future and honor for her, Nell thought. A weight crushed down on her chest. They left him no choice. And now they left *her* no choice but to turn and walk away.

"I…understand."

Her heart was broken. She would probably never see her father again.

"Your driver will meet you outside. Go and leave us to our work."

CHAPTER THIRTY-TWO

DAKOTA PULLED himself into the shadows on the wall as a guard walked behind the castle, playing his flashlight back and forth across the grass.

The walkie-talkie gave another loud burst, and the man stopped. Listening to clipped orders in Portuguese, he glanced out at the sea, then asked a question and waited for an answer.

High above, Dakota locked his fingers in place and hung motionless, listening to the slap of the waves and the low tread of feet below him. The guard raised night-vision binoculars and scanned the moat. The minutes crawled past. Finally satisfied, the guard walked toward the front of the castle and vanished.

Dakota found a toehold, dug in hard and returned to climbing.

Turn. Scan the parapets. Climb the corner.

Hand over hand, he inched higher, watching for lights or motion sensors. A huge seabird raced past his head and he resisted the urge to duck, pushing hard, fingers burning. Just below the lower parapet he stopped, checking for movement. As the silence held, he wedged a foot, pulled up and swung over. Above him was a straight climb seventy feet to the top of the corner tower. Like a shadow he nudged his feet into the next crack, finding the spot where he would be least visible.

Four minutes later he reached the top. Hanging motionless, he watched for thermal patterns and movement nearby.

Thirty seconds.

Sixty.

Two minutes.

Wind gusted in from the sea as he gripped the edge of the high parapet and swung one leg over. Quickly he circled the battlements until he came to a row of windows on the inner wall, facing the center of the castle. The spiral stairs below were boarded up, according to Izzy's last set of building plans. Dakota quietly scored the glass, popped out a pane and bit back a curse when he slid inside.

The stairs were completely gone, collapsed in a mound of rubble and mortar that blocked the inner door at ground level. Aware that he had only minutes to reach his target, Dakota secured a rope and worked his way down, dropping onto the debris at the bottom.

New route.

He checked his watch: fifteen minutes until the auction was due to start. His target was not what he had told Nell. His real objective was locked in a safe inside Martim Gonsalves's secure second-floor office, where a laptop held crucial details of contacts and transactions with terrorist organizations throughout Asia and Europe. Dakota's orders were to copy those files and return the laptop to the safe with no sign of his intrusion.

He gripped the rope and ascended hand over hand along the wall until he could see through the lowest window. To his left light spilled from a marble patio next to the ballroom.

A sharp flare of heat nearby caught his attention. Waves of color radiated off the outbuilding he had noted on his way in. The source appeared to be six feet off the ground, near a box with electrical equipment. An auxiliary power generator? High-volume air-conditioning and heating unit?

The burst of heat troubled him because it was unexpected, and unexpected things had a way of coming back to bite you. But there was no time for him to explore further. His window of time to reach Gonsalves's office was shrinking fast.

Twenty feet above, on the opposite wall, a larger window opened onto the back of the inner courtyard, out of view of the ballroom. Dakota crossed to the stone sill.

Twenty feet of exposed wall between him and the ground.

Four feet below, he saw a row of rough, jutting stones. This was his way down.

He wondered briefly where Izzy was at that moment and whether he had managed to track Nell. But he forced the thought away.

With his eyes on the first toehold, he swung smoothly to the right and toed his way down from hold to hold. Six feet above the ground, he dropped lightly and fell back into the shadows. As he checked his watch, two guards emerged from an underground exterior stairwell, headed right for him.

NELL DIDN'T MOVE.

The old man's promises meant nothing to her. Who was to say this driver of his wouldn't pull off the road and shoot her as soon as they were out of sight of the castle?

Nowhere was safe, but staying wasn't an option either, so Nell decided to take each moment as it came, acting by instinct. Right now her instincts screamed to find the first safe spot and hide.

The stocky guard was holding a walkie-talkie and waiting at the bottom of the stairs. He gestured for Nell to hurry up, then cursed as he glanced out a window. Whatever he saw made him motion to another guard. The two strode across the front hall and vanished outside. When a uniformed worker appeared from a nearby hallway, pushing a cart with fruit on silver trays, Nell walked calmly past the woman and followed the noise toward the kitchen.

Inside the kitchen a sweating chef in a white jacket shouted for her to put on her uniform and get busy. Nell grabbed a uniform from the nearest chair and searched for a place to change. Two women appeared from a door to her right, one of them buttoning her black uniform jacket.

Nell ducked inside.

AT NINETY-TWO, few things impressed Bujune Okambe. The president of a small, oil-rich country, he was also a most impatient man. The drifting harp music and clink of fine crystal were of no interest to him. His cold expression made it clear that all he wanted was for the business to begin. But the thought of spending thirty-five million U.S. dollars left his throat dry.

He beckoned to his daughter, who leaned down, then nodded. More than one man watched Marie Okambe move regally through the brightly lit ballroom toward a waiter carrying a tray of champagne. She shook her head, turning back to point to her father, who needed medicine from her bag in the reception room.

When the waiter motioned for her to follow him, the old man in the wheelchair watched them leave, then cruised impatiently across the room toward Luis Gonsalves and his anxious son.

DAKOTA TOOK OUT the first guard at the edge of the yew hedge, then swung left, rolling the other guard's body back, breaking his wrist. His fingers gripped the man's throat, cutting off his cry of pain before it started. Music drifted from the ballroom as he stowed the bodies out of sight behind the hedge, then followed the tower's curving wall to the exterior stairwell. Calmly Dakota pulled a strip of plastic from his shoe and feathered the lock.

As he opened the door, he checked his watch. Two minutes ahead of schedule. Inside he walked quickly past a communications room, then stopped at the small, ornate doors of a vintage elevator.

When the doors opened, Dakota covered the security

camera with a piece of black cloth and tapped the button for the second floor. The elevator rose slowly and hummed to a halt. Leaving the cloth in place, he headed to the second door on his left, where a new security keypad showed heat patterns from recent contact. Quickly, he read the colors; the hottest key was the one that had been touched most recently. All he had to do was work backward, from warmest to coolest as the order of input. When he punched in the last digit, the heavy metal door slid open with a hiss.

He glanced at his watch. *Right on time.*

The study was pooled in shadow, red velvet curtains cutting off all exterior light. Dakota made his way silently to the desk at the far wall and studied its three locked drawers, assessing which of his tools would open them fastest. He zipped open a pocket on his Neoprene suit, found a narrow sliver of plastic and inserted it carefully.

A sound near the curtains made him lunge sideways, his knife flashing. The serrated assault blade came to rest on a woman's throat.

Meanwhile, her Sig Sauer 9mm was pointed at the center of his forehead. "What took you so long to get here?" the smoky female voice whispered.

CHAPTER THIRTY-THREE

MARIE OKAMBE MOVED with cool grace, keeping Dakota in her sights as she edged around the desk. "Project?"

"Origami," Dakota whispered.

"Code word?"

"Theodore. Izzy swore it was a private joke."

"He's wrong." Her hand tightened, and the gun fell. "I haven't laughed in a very long time, Mr. Smith. Now if you have the hard drive ready for data transfer?"

Dakota unzipped a waterproof pocket in his suit and connected a USB cable to his portable drive. By the time the connection was made, Marie Okambe had powered up Gonsalves's private laptop and slipped in an unlabeled CD. The screen flashed for a moment and booted to a command prompt. Neither spoke as Dakota plugged in the cord and waited for the woman to input commands to dump the hard disk to his drive.

Dakota glanced at the door. "How long?"

"Less than five minutes, assuming that I—*blast*."

"What?"

"He's encrypted one of the partitions. It's asking for a password."

"Do you have one?"

She stared down at the laptop, the light of her tiny penlight reflected back over the intricate scars on her cheeks. "It's unexpected," she muttered, watching lines of text scroll down the screen.

"Then what are we supposed to—"

"Silence, please, Mr. Smith. Unexpected is not impossible." She typed in a string of numbers. "It just takes a little bit longer."

Dakota was certain that Izzy had said the same thing in a prior tense situation. Through a crack in the curtains he saw heat flare across the castle's outer wall, emanating from the same spot as before, and suddenly the walkway lights down in the courtyard exploded.

Every room went dark. The musicians stopped playing and the air-handling system went quiet. The only sound was the angry questions of the guests in the darkened ballroom below.

"What just happened?" Marie Okambe's eyes did not leave the laptop.

"Electricity failure. I'd say there was some kind of major power surge originating across from us on the south wall."

"How would you know the origination point of a power surge?" Marie Okambe's eyes narrowed. "That is not the sort of thing that one can see, surely."

"Just a reasoned deduction. My equipment had already picked up several spikes in that area."

She frowned and turned back to the laptop. "The power here is fine. Gonsalves must have an auxiliary generator prepared."

"Exactly what I would do, given the valuable data stored in here." Dakota leaned over her shoulder. "How much longer?"

"Eighty percent copied." She opened a small pocket sewn to the inside of her skirt and took out a case with a data chip. Opening the cell phone on the desk, she switched the two chips.

"Backup monitoring?"

"Exactly." She dropped the chip into her pocket and secured it.

"Have you seen MacInnes?"

"He was in the display room with the art. He didn't look good. And his daughter—"

Dakota felt cold air brush across his neck. "Nell MacInnes is *here*?"

"There is no doubt it was his daughter. Gonsalves asked her to comment on the art and she complied, but unwillingly. There were welts on her face, as if someone had recently struck her."

Dakota forced down a stab of fury. "Where was she when you last saw her?"

"With her father. They stayed in the display room with Martim after we left, but I do not know if she is still there."

The last time Dakota had spoken to Izzy, Nell's location appeared to be a plane north of Manchester. Izzy had gotten only a few clear hits from her chip before the signal faded again.

He checked his watch. The auction should have started by now, but the lower rooms were still dark. Dakota recalled how all the lightbulbs had exploded at once. "Nonnuclear electromagnetic pulse. Gonsalves could have effectively knocked out all communications from cell phones and PDAs in one stroke. We know the man is paranoid."

"It would require a great burst of power—exactly what you saw. But why do we still have power in here?"

"Probably this office is shielded. With such high stakes, he's taking nothing for granted."

The computer beeped twice. Marie Okambe typed in another command and removed the portable drive. "It is done. Now all we have to do is—"

Footsteps hammered across the floor outside, and an angry voice cut through the silence.

"Hurry up with those locks. I need this door opened now."

BUJUNE OKAMBE'S FINGERS gripped the arm of his wheelchair.

What was the blasted girl *doing?* Only moments earlier the lights had exploded all over the room, and now the old man watched impatiently as guards moved to every exit while waiters carried in lit candles. There was no uneasiness among the staff, as if they had expected the power outage. So their host had arranged this. Possibly to control outside communication?

At the moment he was more concerned about Marie. He didn't think she'd gotten lost. She had the layout of the castle committed to memory. Something had to be keeping her.

The old man powered his chair to the doorway only to find his way blocked by Luis Gonsalves. "It would be better for you to remain here until the power is restored, Mr. Okambe. It may be dangerous to move about in the dark."

"You think I cannot find my own way, that I am a weak, incompetent *fool?*" The old man's voice rose in outrage.

"Nothing like that, and of course I meant no discourtesy. It was merely a precaution. As soon as my son returns—"

"Then call him now!" the old man snapped imperiously. "Enough of our time has been wasted in amateur dramatics and lighting displays. We came here to buy, so let the buying begin."

Gonsalves motioned to one of the guards positioned near the staircase. "My son has gone to his office," he said quietly. "Find him and bring him back here immediately. Then locate Mr. Okambe's daughter for me."

CHAPTER THIRTY-FOUR

THE DOORKNOB SHOOK. Portuguese curses rained down on the hapless guards outside.

Dakota shoved his portable drive and cable into a pocket, secured the zipper, straightened the desk and motioned Marie to the window. She hesitated, glancing back at the door, then leaned over the desk, flipping three switches on a sleek security panel. "The alarm at the exterior is disabled." She watched Dakota pry a screw free from the wooden frame, ease the window open and lean out. Candlelight flickered in the ballroom below, but otherwise every room was dark.

Overhead the notched outline of the parapets jutted out like an angry mouth. Dakota turned back to Marie and pointed up, pulling out a rope.

The doorknob shook. Drilling noises echoed out in the corridor. Marie shook her head, waving him out, her jaw set.

The doorknob spun free and the drilling became a furious whine. There was no more time to argue. Dakota climbed through the window, cast out his doubled rope and caught the edge of the parapet. Glancing back, he saw Marie ease the window shut behind him and then disappear into the shadows near an ornate Victorian settee.

As he reached a notch in the high tower, angry voices rumbled in the room he'd just left. Light spilled through the window. Two shadows moved back and forth like restless moths.

Footsteps crossed the room. Voices rose in muffled argument and then a door slammed. Twenty seconds later the window slowly rose.

Marie Okambe climbed out, gripped the rope and worked her way silently upward hand over hand, her long silk skirt pulled tight at her knees. By the time Dakota helped her up onto the parapet, applause was ringing from the candlelit ballroom.

The bidding had begun.

NELL TOOK a deep breath, listening to staff cross the hall outside the bathroom where she hid.

The outside door swung shut.

Nell waited in the last stall, sweat trickling down her neck.

No shouts. No alarm bells.

Always a good sign. But why had the electricity failed?

Carefully she peeked into the darkness, listening to the drip of water from a faucet. When she was certain the room was empty, she straightened her uniform, picked up a garbage can full of used paper towels and carried it outside, looking as if she was in a hurry.

THE BIDDING WAS FIERCE, but soon the pace slowed in the time lag needed for translation. At twenty million one buyer dropped out. At thirty million two buyers from South America withdrew. Others faded back against the walls of the ballroom as the price kept climbing. Now Okambe was left to bid tensely against a financier representing the head of a South American cartel and a Japanese collector who spoke flawless English.

Suddenly the bidding jumped to fifty million. Okambe made an angry gesture and his fingers tightened on the wheelchair. When he saw his daughter across the noisy room, he gestured sharply and steered his chair toward the door to the patio. Luis Gonsalves looked back as if noting his departure while the bids kept rising.

Nine minutes later Martim's etched silver gavel finally fell. Da Vinci's preliminary chalk sketch for the *Mona Lisa* had commanded a stratospheric price of sixty-seven million dollars from the Japanese buyer, who left the ballroom with Martim to arrange for an immediate wire transfer from an account in Switzerland.

Not everyone was happy with the results of the bidding, and Bujune Okambe was the least happy of all.

Outside low thunder rolled over the loch as the African wheeled toward a group of buyers arguing with Luis Gonsalves and cut in. "I would have paid more if your son had not changed his mind and insisted on an immediate wire transfer. We *all* could have paid, is that not correct?"

The other bidders nodded angrily.

"The auction should be reopened." Okambe banged the arm of his wheelchair. "We are agreed that the rules were both unclear *and* unfair." Amid a chorus of fierce agreement, he glared at Luis Gonsalves. "Call your son back and we will continue."

"It is not possible. My apologies to all of you, but the sale is finished."

"Your son gave us only twenty-four hours to prepare the funds for transfer. *Impossible*." Okambe seemed to sink into his chair, glowering. "Those were not the terms promised to me by Jordan MacInnes. He lied."

As he spoke, MacInnes entered the room with a guard on each side, and Okambe watched him in growing fury. "He knew this would happen. He gave his word that the bidding would be equal for all, do you hear? Either the auction resumes now or Jordan MacInnes pays for his betrayal."

Marie Okambe listened, her eyes narrowed. She turned as a uniformed waitress pushed a cart along the wall and moved directly into Okambe's path. Furious, the old man drew a Browning Hi-Power handgun with Hogue grips from a small space hidden between the spokes of his wheelchair.

The thunder was louder now, low and booming over what might have been the hum of motors.

Nell MacInnes, whom Marie had recognized in spite of the black uniform, gave a sharp cry as the gun rose. The American woman rammed her cart against the wheelchair, but Marie blocked her, shoving her back against the wall.

Jordan turned at his daughter's cry, his face going pale. Then the Browning cracked and while Nell looked on in horror, Okambe triggered four shots in quick succession into her father's chest.

CHAPTER THIRTY-FIVE

BLOOD WELLED over the front of Jordan MacInnes's white shirt as he was thrown back toward the wall. He staggered, clutching his side.

The guards simply watched him fall, their eyes expressionless. No one made a move to help. Nell broke free and ran to him, but her hands came away slick with blood. Her father's eyes did not open.

Someone shouted from the front of the courtyard and then armed soldiers in black gear poured through the castle gatehouse and over the walls, their radios crackling. Nell didn't look up as two soldiers flanked the old man in the wheelchair, who protested loudly as they escorted him away. Nothing seemed to make sense, not the noise or the angry protests. All she could see was her father's lifeless face and the dark stain that covered his chest.

Nell tried to shake him, every movement clumsy. Something told her that if she shook him long enough, he would wake up and smile and tell her the world was a fine place.

But he didn't wake up. She knew he wouldn't ever wake up.

Panic burned in her throat and her low, broken moan

seemed to come from someone else. She tried to grip her father's shirt, but her hands kept pulling free, slick with his blood. The sight made her close her eyes, the room suddenly going black.

A hand brushed across her shoulders. A low voice called her name. Nell looked up to see one of the soldiers leaning down beside her.

"You're safe now, ma'am. Why don't you come with me?" He was American, and something about his calm sense of focus reminded her of Dakota.

Two other men in black lifted her father's body onto a stretcher and carried him toward the courtyard.

"I *can't* leave. He's just unconscious," she whispered hoarsely. But Nell knew it was a lie, knew she would never joke or argue or laugh with her father again. In a matter of seconds everything was cut short. Shaking, she grabbed the wall for support.

It wasn't supposed to be this way. The good guys were supposed to high five and tell loud jokes, walking away with all the glory. But now that glory was gone, and all she would have were pale memories.

"Ma'am, it would be best if you came with me. Are you hurt?"

She looked up slowly. The man in a black tactical suit was speaking slowly, as if she couldn't understand complex sentences. Maybe she couldn't.

The ballroom was empty now. Someone had set up portable lights on the table. All the buyers were grouped outside near one door, surrounded by more men in black uniforms. Nell could hear the staff being questioned in the adjoining service area.

Where was Dakota? She ran a shaky hand across her face. Why was there still no sign of him or the art? She closed her eyes and breathed a prayer for his safety.

"Ma'am, would you like something to drink? Water—a cup of tea?" The tall man was leaning down beside her, his eyes very patient.

"Dakota?" she managed to ask, half-afraid of the answer.

"He's fine, ma'am."

Relief washed over her. Slowly Nell stood up, clumsier than she had ever been. Her thoughts seemed to balloon out and fragment as she followed the soldier through the beautiful old ballroom, past more grim Special Forces troops holding automatic weapons as they questioned the nervous buyers. There was no sign of the old man in the wheelchair. Nell didn't know what she would say to him anyway. She could scream and claw his face, but what good would it do now?

Her father was dead, and nothing would change that. The finality of it crushed her heart.

At the far side of the courtyard, a tall figure emerged from a low door, arguing with one of the British soldiers, and Nell saw that it was Dakota, wearing some kind of black diving suit. The relief hit her again, along with deep emotions that she still didn't have a clear name for.

Then her blank sense of loss returned and she kept walking toward the massive gatehouse, with its arrow loops and portcullis and beautiful mullioned windows, rich with Scottish history.

None of it mattered.

In the darkness, her foot struck an uneven cobblestone. As she stumbled, Nell pressed one hand to the cold stone, her hip thrown against the wall. The sharp contact made her wince and realize there was something in the pocket of her borrowed uniform. She reached down, frowning at the metal shape in her fingers. Long and heavy and very worn.

Nell frowned.

A key?

No key had been in the pocket earlier. She had checked them for a cell phone or a kitchen knife as soon as she'd taken the uniform, but all the pockets had been empty.

The metal felt cold and heavy against her skin. How had it gotten in her uniform? She had been moving constantly since the moment she had changed.

Nell realized that three other big men were surrounding her now in a protective circle. They all had the same quiet sense of authority that Dakota did, and she trusted them immediately.

The nearest man held open the door of a black sedan. "If you would have a seat, someone will take you to a hotel where you can rest. Is there anyone you'd like us to contact for you?"

There was no one. Her father was all the family Nell had.

The man waited for her to answer, calm and polite, but she wanted to explain that any questions could wait, that she needed to be alone so she could cry. But Nell didn't have the strength to answer. Her hands closed tightly around the strange key as the first burning tears coursed down her face.

DAKOTA WATCHED her in the car, saw her white face and frozen expression. Saw the tears she was holding back by sheer will.

He gestured quickly, making sure that the American Foxfire men carrying her father's body took a different route so Nell wouldn't have to watch him being loaded into a van. Then Dakota walked out under the gatehouse arch.

His superior officer, Wolfe Houston, closed the door of the big black sedan and crossed to Dakota. "She's holding up pretty well, considering."

"Don't let them debrief her yet," Dakota said curtly. "Her father just died, damn it. Let Teague fill our counterparts from London in."

Wolfe Houston studied Dakota through narrowed eyes. "That sounds personal, Lieutenant."

Dakota watched the black sedan move down the long gravel driveway and said nothing.

"I figured it was bound to happen someday. Even to you," Houston said wryly. "Let me run interference with Ryker for you."

"Probably a good idea."

Neither man spoke as three members of the Foxfire team carried a Plexiglas case with great care out of the ballroom. The *Mona Lisa* was just as haunting and enigmatic as ever, sealed in her protective world. Would the experts and academics ever resolve the mystery of Michelangelo's connection, or would the theories simply fuel more debate?

Not his problem.

Dakota looked down. His elbow had a four-inch gash, courtesy of a guard he'd dropped on his way down from the tower and he had a few loose ends to tie up, but the mission was materially complete. He would have a final harsh conversation with Okambe and question his daughter before the old man was taken into custody, then head off to meet Ryker's chopper. The hard drive data would provide all of Martim Gonsalves's criminal and terrorist contacts, which Izzy would analyze down to the last passcode and pixel. That information would be priceless to more than one government.

Time to go, pal.

Don't have to like it.

You just have to do it.

Dakota knew it was time and yet he stayed right where he was, feeling the cut along his elbow burn and the blood dry on his scarred hands. He couldn't have managed the climb half as well without Nell's help, and maybe not at all. Given the way things had turned out, he wanted to tell her that and thank her officially on behalf of the British and U.S. governments.

But it wasn't going to happen. She was already heading down the driveway. Wolfe Houston had a good man escorting her to the nearest hotel, and he would remain as her protective escort until Izzy could ask her some final questions.

Across the courtyard, Wolfe Houston called his name, holding up a satellite phone. "Call for you, Smith. It's the man."

Ryker.

Dakota frowned as he watched the black sedan cruise away. No way could he miss a call from Ryker.

Duty warred with emotion, and slowly, painfully duty won. The data secured in his watertight bag mattered more than his own wishes and more than Nell's personal heartache. He swore that someday he would tell her why.

CHAPTER THIRTY-SIX

San Francisco
Two weeks later

WORK KEPT NELL ALIVE and sane. Only the thousand details of jobs to finish gave her the distraction to hold her life together. Now she sleepwalked through the days, forcing all that had happened in Scotland out of her mind, while at night she huddled in her window seat overlooking the bay, sleepless and unable to forget.

The odd key was hidden at the back of a drawer inside her desk. After replaying every minute of the auction night, Nell was almost certain her father had slipped the key inside her pocket before he died, though she hadn't realized it at the time.

From Dakota and Izzy she heard nothing. There had been two calls from Nicholas Draycott, both with invitations for open-ended visits to the abbey. Nell had asked him about the old key, but he was as stumped as she was.

There was no rush. One day she would research the numbers on the worn brass body, then track down the maker for any further information.

One day.

When the bleak memories faded and the huge hole in her life healed—if they ever did.

"Nell, two people are here to see you."

Startled, she looked up from the untouched e-mail on her laptop. Her assistant looked uneasy, glancing back over her shoulder at the reception area. "They won't give their names, but they said to show you this."

The white card had small, official lettering. *FBI. Art Fraud Unit.*

Something punched through the empty gray space where Nell had locked up her emotions since her father's death. She recognized the names on the card, the same people who had harassed her several weeks earlier, the night she'd been stalked through the alley. Like blowflies, they came to feed on her sorrow now.

She strode across the room and shoved open the workroom door, angrier than she'd thought possible. Two agents stood near her front door, as if to block a possible exit.

Except Nell wasn't going anywhere. "What do you want?" she said coldly.

Agent Fuller, tall and icily controlled, crossed her arms and glanced around the neat reception area. "We have some questions to ask you, Ms. MacInnes. It would be easier if we did this at our office downtown."

"Not easier for me. Ask them right here, right now. I have nothing to hide."

It was a lie of course. There were more than a few questions that couldn't be answered. Nicholas had told her to say nothing about what had happened in England and nothing about her father's risky plan.

The woman pulled a notebook from her jacket pocket. "You were gone for several days this month, Ms. MacInnes. Where did you travel?"

"Las Vegas," Nell said curtly. "I wanted to play the slots."

"Hotel name?"

"I stayed with friends."

The cold-faced woman scrawled in her notebook. "Name of your friends and current address?"

Nell crossed her arms. "I don't think I need to answer that. In fact, I think you'd better get some legal documentation before I say another word. Something tells me this is a fishing expedition."

"So you refuse to cooperate, Ms. MacInnes?"

"Bring me a legal document or a search warrant. Then I'll cooperate so much you'll be sick of listening to me." Nell pointed to the door. "Until then, I've got work to do and I'm sure you've got other people to harass."

The woman snapped her notebook shut, tapping it against her knuckles. "We'll be back with a warrant," she said harshly. "You can be certain of that."

Nell didn't listen, walking back to her workroom, her shoulders stiff with fury. Some of her anger was at Dakota and Nicholas Draycott. They should have been clearer about what she couldn't say and who she couldn't say it to. After all, if you couldn't trust agents of your own government, who *could* you trust?

She walked to the big windows overlooking the back alley, rubbing a knot of tension at her neck. Down the block an express courier was delivering packages, and two teenagers hammered by on skateboards, iPods in hand. Nell saw a uniformed man from her security company talking to the baker who worked next door. She'd upgraded her alarm system only a week before, after hearing about a rash of burglaries in the area. Nell couldn't take a chance on losing priceless art released into her care for conservation.

A sound brought her around.

"You think you've won, but you're wrong. You're in way over your head." Agent Fuller was right behind Nell. "I'm going to prove you're dirty if it's the last thing I do."

Did they teach you how to stalk people that way in FBI training? Nell wondered. *Creeping 101?*

Agent Fuller threw her notebook on the table. "My patience is wearing thin, Ms. MacInnes. Either you cooperate now or I'll have your ass locked up in a cell and you won't see daylight for five years. Do we understand each other?"

"Perfectly. And that changes nothing." Nell looked straight forward, her expression stony. "Get the papers. Then I'll be glad to talk to you."

"Where is your father right now, Ms. MacInnes? Out planning another theft?"

She didn't know that he was dead, Nell realized. And Nell wasn't sure how much she was free to reveal, so she chose her words carefully. "I...haven't heard from him in almost two weeks."

"Convenient. Maybe he's working on a new project, some way to divert funds from stolen art to support terrorist organizations. What do you know about your father's involvement with those organizations?"

"*Nothing*. We've been down this path before."

"I can arrange for us to finish this talk in a cell."

Nell felt her face pale, but she strode calmly toward the door. "Leave. You've made enough empty threats."

"Hardly a threat." The agent pulled out a pair of handcuffs. "You are being held as a material witness in a federal terrorist investigation." She stopped as a man crossed the alley, clipboard in hand. He checked his notes, then tapped at the back door. "Ignore it," the agent snapped.

The man knocked harder, his face turned back toward the mouth of the alley. Something about the line of his shoulders made Nell turn and walk quickly to the door, an odd hammering in her ears.

She opened the door, ignoring the agent's low, hissed orders. "Yes?"

His hat was low on his forehead, his jaw hard. "Nell MacInnes? I have a security camera for you. Where do you want it installed?" The eyes were the same clear blue-gray and the angled planes on his face were just as striking.

Nell felt the force of his eyes searching the room behind her, and for no clear reason she could name, she ignored the fact that he was no security company representative and two new cameras had already been installed by the same company whose name was sewn on his fake uniform.

Why was he here, and what was making him look so tense? Nell felt the muscles tighten along her neck and shoulders. "Right over here," she said, pointing to a nearby alcove.

"You can install your cameras later," Agent Fuller snapped. "This woman is under criminal investigation. I'm taking her in for questioning."

"Is that a fact?" Dakota Smith said, his voice very calm.

The agent recognized him then. At a muffled sound from the reception area, the female agent spun around, her hand going to the small of her back, but Dakota moved in fast, gripping her arm so that the small Smith & Wesson slid free. Dakota caught it with one hand, then shoved her against the wall. "Not in this lifetime are you taking her anywhere, Agent Fuller. The only one answering questions from now on will be you." He gripped her wrists together behind her back and snapped on plastic restraints.

A moment later Izzy Teague appeared in the front room, with the other agent similarly cuffed. He studied Nell's new security camera and pursed his lips. "Nice line of sight on that new surveillance video. Set for twenty-four-hour feed, too. What do you think about that, Kolowitz?"

The second FBI agent's eyes flickered back and forth. His bland features tensed. "Her father is a convicted thief and a probable terrorist agent. You're disrupting an official investigation. That's what I think."

"Actually, you're the one disrupting an official investigation, Agent Kolowitz." Izzy gave a cold smile. "That was a bad idea to plant a stolen painting here in Ms. MacInnes's storeroom three nights ago—especially since we have everything nicely captured on high-resolution video feed."

"Painting?" Agent Fuller frowned at her partner. "What are they talking about, Frank?"

"I didn't—" The man cut off an icy answer as he heard the whine of sirens coming up the alley.

"Wrong answer, Agent Kolowitz. We're talking about burglary, aggravated assault and homicide." Izzy pushed the man toward the front door. "He and two other men in your unit played you for a fool, Agent Fuller. How does it feel?"

"I don't *believe* it. You can't—"

She started to say more, but Dakota pushed her toward the back door where two uniformed SFPD officers were waiting.

"Say good-night, Gracie." Dakota watched until the two were transferred to separate cruisers, headed off for interrogation. "That felt good."

Nell looked at the new camera, then at Izzy and last of all at Dakota. "Twenty-four hour feed? I didn't order that on my new system."

Dakota raised an eyebrow at Izzy. "She didn't order that? Impossible. I don't know how a mistake like that could happen, do you? We never make mistakes."

Izzy smiled at Nell and gave a two-finger wave. "Impossible just takes a little longer. Enjoy your week, ma'am." Then he vanished.

Nell was still working through what had just happened. "These people in the FBI unit were involved?"

"Agent Kolowitz and two others had made some deals with people at the National Gallery, and they were all involved with Gonsalves. For now I can't tell you more than that, but it's nasty work. Don't worry, Nell. It's over."

Over.

As Dakota prowled the workroom, she fought an urge to smooth her hair and tug at her sweater. She wasn't going to let this get awkward and messy and— unbearably *personal.* He had come here to finish an assignment; no reason to paint a grand drama out of the event.

"How did Agent Kolowitz and the others—"

"We're still working out the details, but we know they had a contact close to Gonsalves and they were able to tap your father in prison. They were watching for a major piece of art to steal when the *Mona Lisa* sketch was brought in for assessment. When your father didn't show adequate enthusiasm for the job they forced your climbing partner to watch you, as ammunition in case your father wanted out."

"He had no choice, not if he wanted to protect me," Nell said quietly. "Eric—where is he?"

Dakota put his clipboard down on the worktable. "Hospitalized in England." Something crossed his face. "I doubt he'll ever climb again. He was caught in a boat propeller and one hand is badly torn up."

Nell gulped down a breath, fighting nausea. "He didn't think they would hurt me."

"He was wrong, wasn't he?" Dakota's voice was harsh. "He'll have to live with that, along with everything else. Meanwhile, there will be no more police harassment. Izzy and I have taken care of that particular problem."

"But how—"

"Later." Dakota's hands rose, framing Nell's face. He didn't move, simply looked at her. The force of his feelings was almost physical, pulling her in. Closer, always closer. His thumb traced her upper lip. When she trembled, he whispered her name and slid his hands into her hair.

And when he finally leaned down, kissing her as if her mouth held all the air to fill his straining lungs, Nell's world tilted and she knew there would be no going back. Not with a man like this. She sank into the heat of his body, feeling as if she had just come home from a long journey with no signposts except those that she could read in his eyes.

His hands opened, tense against her hips.

Dakota drew a breath, and then kissed her again, gently this time without the desperate greed. There was regret in his eyes when he stood back.

"What's wrong?" Nell brushed his cheek.

"That kiss will have to last us for a day or two."

"Why?"

He smiled faintly. "Get your things. First I'm going to feed you. As usual you're stuck back in the Renaissance, dreaming of spittle and chicken bone glue and linen rag paper. I bet you haven't eaten anything today, have you?"

"No, but I was going to—"

He slid an arm around her shoulders. "Chinese food. I know a great place on Geary. And after I feed you, we're going camping in the mountains."

"But—"

He kissed her hard. *"Later."*

CHAPTER THIRTY-SEVEN

DAKOTA DIDN'T TELL her the rest.

The mountains he mentioned *happened* to be in France, not California.

All the details were arranged. After a brief stop at Nell's apartment for her climbing clothes and gear, the hours of travel flashed past in a sleepy haze. Nell drowsed off and on during the flight. Whenever she woke, she looked down to find her hands intertwined with Dakota's. He didn't push her with questions or make small talk. The solid strength of his presence was enough.

For two nights they traveled, each day passing farther from civilization, cars and noise. On the second night they stayed in the old gatehouse of a vineyard owned by a friend of Nicholas Draycott. Nell got a little drunk from their exceptional wine, and Dakota said very little as he pulled her back into the curve of his arm. He spoke to their host for a long time, discussing trails over a set of topo maps, and they left at dawn the next morning after a short, restless sleep.

Sleep and nothing more.

There was something he wanted to show her,

Dakota had said. Something important. Everything else could wait.

On the third night they sat on the peak of a mountain in the Luberon and watched sunset fade from pink to purple. When the first star winked to life, Dakota spread out a sleeping bag and two pillows.

And there in the darkness he simply held her, arms tight, her head against his chest while the stars glittered over their heads. After her return from Scotland, Nell had a thousand questions to ask him.

Now, with his arms around her and the night's beauty sweet and heavy as a dream, there were no questions worth asking.

SHE AWOKE to a breeze ruffling her hair and the distant cry of an owl. She blinked, disoriented, and felt hard fingers curve around her waist.

"It's just an owl." Dakota murmured. "Go back to sleep."

Sleep? Nell realized she was draped across him like a blanket, her fingers worked under the waist of his jeans.

Warm skin.

Lean muscle.

Heat fluttered through her chest, and she tried to pull her hand away, but he rolled onto his side, trapping her hand right where it was. And then the irritating man went right back to sleep, while Nell's body shot to full alert. He hadn't done more than skim her cheek or kiss her since his arrival in San Francisco, and now her body jolted to three-alarm, head-swimming arousal.

Nell frowned. She tried to pull her hand surreptitiously from beneath his waistband.

"No need to move. It's fine where it is," Dakota murmured.

Not for *her*, it wasn't. Every movement was torture and every breath he took thrummed across her nerves, inciting reckless possibilities.

"I can't sleep."

He moved slightly, drawing her against his chest. "You were sleeping fine a few minutes ago."

"Then I woke up." Now she was far too awake for comfort and her hand kept wanting to slide lower until she curved around his wonderfully sensuous heat.

Goaded to her limit, she rolled across him. "Doesn't it *bother* you?"

"What?" He sounded sleepy and absolutely calm.

"Our bodies together like this. Your fingers on my breast and my hand in your jeans. Without…whatever."

And *whatever* was exactly what Nell had in mind. Whatever Dakota wanted. Whenever and however he wanted it, under the high cold fire of the stars.

"Anywhere you want to touch is fine with me, honey. Go right ahead." He rolled a little, sliding his fingers into her hair. The movement drove their thighs together and sent Nell's hand even lower beneath his jeans.

It wasn't *fair*. He was cool and absolutely controlled while she was losing her mind. At least the man should squirm a little.

She remembered their few wonderful hours in the big soft bed at Draycott Abbey. He hadn't been calm and controlled then. The air had snapped with hot awareness as they'd tangled the sheets and lost all reason, locked in each other's arms. But the thought of Draycott Abbey brought other memories, along with the slick feel of her father's blood. How could she think of life when his death was still so close?

Nell sank back, half-sprawled against Dakota's chest, and tried to slip her hand free.

No luck.

He had her trapped, caught in heat and desire.

Wind played through the cypress trees. Nell watched a cloud drift over the moon, her heart too heavy to speak.

"Why don't you tell me what's wrong?"

She wanted to be open with him. She'd sworn not to erect walls around her emotions, but she didn't know where to start. Even if she did know, why should she bother Dakota with her pain? He had enough stress and uncertainty in his life. So Nell shoved down the hurt and lay very still, watching the clouds make their way south to the Mediterranean.

"Nell?"

"I'm fine. Just tired from climbing." She manufactured a yawn. "Probably I can sleep now. Why don't you just turn a little so I can move my hand?"

Dakota frowned in the darkness. Like *hell* she was fine. Before he was done, they were going to talk about her father and whatever else was worrying her.

Slowly he brushed her lip with his thumb. "Sorry, but I'm not moving. You'll have to get used to it."

"Get used to what?"

"Feeling me," he said quietly. "Having my hands in your hair and my leg over yours. I'm going to be doing that a lot from now on, honey. I know that what happened will never go away and you're still hurting, so I won't push you, but I'll be here. Someday I'll be as close as forever. Someday—whenever you're ready." There was more Dakota could have said, more promises that clamored to be spoken, but he would start with this.

Nell pushed to one elbow and stared at him. "You think I can sleep after that? You think I *want* to sleep?" She gave a muffled sound of irritation. "My hand is getting hot, you know. Not *just* my hand," she snapped.

"Good to hear it." Dakota moved a little, making her fingers even hotter, sliding his thigh over hers. "Sleeping wasn't really what I had in mind." His voice was low and rough. "You are a part of my life now, Nell. This isn't about a few hours of reckless sex under the stars, with our future put on hold. We're not going to run from all the possibilities."

Not a question.

An irrevocable statement of fact. He wanted that absolutely clear to her before things went any further. Which things were going to do very soon, Dakota swore.

Nell caught a sharp breath. "Reckless sex under the stars sounds pretty good to me," she whispered. As the wind skimmed the slope, she had a sudden sense of bigger connections. Her father was gone, but his memories were clear, alive in her. Later she would have a torrent of questions for Dakota, but now the air was rich with quiet promise and infinite expectations and touching his lean, tough body beneath a sky full of stars seemed to be the greatest miracle of her unpredictable life.

She wasn't about to let that miracle escape. It seemed natural to trace the hard line of his jaw and then bite his mouth gently. "Giving me orders already, Navy?"

"Not orders." He frowned. "I will not push you. I want that clear, Nell—"

"Oh, everything's clear. Beautifully clear." Nell felt a crooked grin form as she slid her hand lower into his jeans, opening her fingers around his rigid length. Need mixed with a nearly electrical sense of rightness, as if they fit together in deeper levels that she had barely begun to sense.

Dakota kissed the curve at her neck. "You want to explain what's clear? I'm getting a little…distracted here."

"Later." She rolled over, pinning him beneath her. The words would come later. Now was for taking and being taken, for feeling his breath catch as her fingers explored his thighs and tugged his jeans lower.

Trust flowed over Nell in a rush, stealing all speech. She'd never expected to find it, yet here it was.

Dakota's hands opened on her hips, then rose to cup her breasts and heat washed up, settling in her chest until she couldn't breathe. When his lips closed around her breast, desire flared white-hot, and hotter still when his fingers cupped her stomach and feathered between her thighs. Slow and clever, they found her, slipped deep and made her quiver in breathless discovery. His lips were on her cheek when the first wave ripped through her and Nell dug her hands into his back, thinking of the tiger that coiled over his shoulder, as beautifully dangerous as Dakota was.

The stars seemed to tilt overhead.

"Dakota, I—want all of this, everything we can share. All the possibilities. Nothing's been half so good in my life as what I've found with you."

"Me too, honey." His hands tightened. "Hold on because it's going to get even better." He cupped her hips and lifted her to meet his swift entering and Nell gasped at the unexpected heat and force of him inside her. His eyes never left her face as he let her down slowly inch by inch, then drew her back to meet his strokes, while her body came fully alive against him.

Racked by pleasure, Nell closed her eyes, tightening around him. The stars tilted and danced as she bit his shoulder, wanting more speed, more heat, touching the center of all that he was.

He whispered her name. She fell then, lost in the granite strength of his body and the mystery of the pleasure he made her feel. She saw the warrior's eyes narrow, saw the tiger crouch and twist on his flexed shoulder, the image unbearably erotic as his fingers moved, driving her up in a white burn of pleasure.

Coming home, she thought.

Finding a haven she had never planned to find.

She cradled his face, making her own fierce promises

in a language deeper than words, and her breath caught when he made the fire jolt up again, pushing her beyond thought or fear, making her feel more loved and cherished than she believed possible. And her heart, so long girded, spun free, fell like a star along with her shuddering body.

Forever, she vowed. She'd fallen that way. Forever would not be enough time to share his life, to light his dreams.

As the sage-rich wind played over their heated skin, Nell rocked against him, then cried out, consumed in the fire made between them.

Even then Dakota held her, kissed the warm skin at her neck, smoothed her shoulders with slow, fierce control.

Delaying his own pleasure to savor the beauty of hers.

Her eyes opened. Still shuddering in her pleasure, she gripped his shoulder where the tiger stirred. "Dakota, you didn't—"

"There's time. We'll have all the time in the world," he said roughly. Ignoring the heat of her body, he pulled her against his chest, thigh to thigh, skin still intimately cradled, the pleasure nearly unbearable.

"But I—"

He kissed her hungrily. "My own fantasy," he said. "Soaking up the touch of your skin. Hearing the breathless sounds you make when you fall." He moved inside her in a long, smooth slide of heat. "And here's the rest of my fantasy."

The tiger came unleashed then, as their bodies met hungrily. Sweat gleamed on Dakota's shoulders and

Nell locked her thighs around him, drawing him as deep as he could go.

Their hands twined. He breathed her name. They fell together.

THERE WERE QUESTIONS in the darkness after the stars burned away. There were promises in the bluish-gray light that came before the dawn. Most important of all were the quiet plans for a way to tie their lives together despite demanding jobs and uncertain times.

"It won't be easy," Dakota warned. "The work I do isn't nine-to-five. Bad guys keep bad hours," he said dryly.

Nell traced the tiger, once again at rest on his motionless shoulder. "We'll work something out. Lucky for us I'm not a white-picket-fence kind of girl."

"Yeah, in a day or two you'll be bored out of your head, setting off in search of red ochre pigment or vintage rabbit glue."

She gave his jaw a mock punch. "Don't knock the rabbit glue, pal. It's a prime tool in the restorer's arsenal."

"I'll be sure to remember that."

Sated from the night's excess, Nell traced her fingers down his chest. "I found a key in my pocket when I left the castle. Strange, but I still can't figure how it got there. I made a color photo and sent it to Izzy."

"If an answer exists, the man will find it. He loves impossible challenges."

"Probably isn't important. I'd just like to...tie things up." She took a deep breath.

"You miss him."

Nell nodded slowly. "Every hour I'll remember an outrageous story he told me about his travels or some reckless adventure he took me on. I'd forgotten the good things over the years. Now I'm trying hard to keep the good things close. I guess that makes me naive."

"It means you're doing what it takes to heal. It means," he said gently, "that he was a very lucky man to have a daughter like you. Somehow I think he knew that."

Nell sighed as his fingers cupped her cheek. "We didn't get much climbing done today."

"There's always tomorrow. And five long days after that."

"A week of heaven in France." Nell stretched lazily. "Give me another week to train you and you'll take first place at Chamonix next year, Navy."

"Somehow I don't see a climbing competition in my future," Dakota said. "I get paid to be invisible, Nell. I get the job done and then leave. People don't remember my face." His voice turned serious. "That's who I am. Most of what I do I can't discuss and I'll never have a set schedule. Can you live with that kind of uncertainty?"

"Just as long as it's me you come back to when the danger is done. I'll make sympathetic noises while I bandage you up." She leaned on one elbow, nodding thoughtfully. "Or anything else you want me to do."

"Anything?" Heat glinted in his eyes. "No limits?" His hand skimmed her neck, then feathered lower, brushing every curve and hollow. Slowly, too slowly.

Nell's patience began to unravel. "Do you and your

tiger have something dangerous in mind?" Her hand cupped his length.

"Anything I do with you feels dangerous." His eyes turned serious and he pulled her against his chest. "This is feeling a whole lot like forever for me, Nell."

"I know what you mean. Funny, I never expected that." *A month maybe,* she thought. *Not forever. But forever it was going to be.*

An owl called out again in the darkness. Nell wriggled higher, her thighs opening to his, her body pinning his warm chest.

She whispered a breathless protest when he rolled free to tongue her breasts. Her fingers tugged at his hair as he moved down her flat stomach, tasting until she quivered and strained. His mouth settled over her wet heat, taking her fast until the pleasure left her blind.

Driven now, she twisted, bringing him closer, sighing as his thighs cradled her. His fingers worked a deep rhythm of pleasure, sending her up, breathless and lost, but this time her nails raked his chest and she moved against his heat, taking him deeper. In the dim gray light the tattoo on Dakota's shoulder seemed to wake and stretch luxuriously, looking hungry. Nell closed her eyes as the heat filled her, driving deep and pulling her with him, better than any dream she'd ever known.

He lifted them both in high, driving thrusts with Nell's legs wrapped around him and her hands locked in his hair. The heat in his eyes spilled into his heart as her fingers linked with his, both of them caught on the razor edge of oblivion.

Tight.

Tighter.

She smiled with the fierce promise of a woman who understood the challenges that distance and danger and forced silences would create.

A woman who knew and wasn't afraid.

Was that part of the smile on the face of the *Mona Lisa*, a woman confident in her world and herself?

The question didn't matter. All that mattered was *now* as the pleasure snapped over Nell and she rode his length. The sight of his body in the moonlight was a clean sweep of need that could no longer be resisted. When he drove up, filled her, his very being poured into the hot, still center where their bodies met, and they made the long, breathless leap to pleasure together.

In the next days their fingers met and twined often. When they sat, their backs touched; when they walked, their shoulders brushed, side by side. Without looking, they always knew where the other was.

On the day that they had to pack and climb down the mountain, Dakota stopped Nell at the top of the trail. He touched her hair and brushed a smudge of climbing chalk from her cheek.

"I won't be able to discuss a lot of things, Nell. Sometimes I'll be distant and cold, a stranger that you won't even recognize. I'll always watch the shadows and when the phone rings I'll grab my pack and go. No explanations, no delays, no matter what we're doing. You can't expect answers and you can never talk about what I do with anyone."

"You'll talk when you're ready and I'll make your life miserable until you remember you're not a stranger."

After a long time he smiled. "Promise?"

"Count on it, Navy."

If he hadn't been so moved, Dakota might have smiled at the thought of their future and how his life had tilted 180 degrees in just a few weeks. But now it was time to leave.

The wind lingered, then scattered small stones that caught the hot sunlight as they started back down the trail.

CHAPTER THIRTY-EIGHT

Macau
Two weeks later

THE BLUE COVES and limestone cliffs of China glittered across the bay. Oblivious to the hot sun and the beauty around him, Dakota kept a silent vigil outside the well-guarded mansion on the hilltop. Sometimes crime paid *very* well, he thought grimly.

Between lush red hibiscus and jade plants, silent guards moved in low-profile rotations, and Dakota maintained his alert position near the car. He would have preferred to be inside, but the discussion taking place in the hilltop palace was to be heard by only two people. Even Izzy Teague's usual surveillance equipment was useless here.

Some kind of new shielding was in place. Izzy already had a line on a source, and the Foxfire team would have a prototype within weeks, if his research went as planned.

But Dakota didn't like being in the dark. He glanced impatiently at his watch. If Teague wasn't out in five more minutes, he was going in after him. He didn't trust

Luis Gonsalves for a second, despite the careful groundwork Izzy and Ryker had laid.

Abruptly the big carved door opened. Luis Gonsalves, looking twenty years older than he'd appeared in Scotland, walked Izzy out to the curving driveway. The two men shook hands and then Izzy strode toward the car, his expression completely masked.

Dakota slid behind the wheel. "Where to next?"

"The airport. I'm finished here." Izzy set his briefcase on the backseat and stared out the window. "Take the long route, will you? There's a bad smell in the air and I want to clear it out before I board the plane."

Dakota drove past more estates that hugged the curves of the hills overlooking the water. He knew what had been discussed and shared Izzy's uneasiness.

Ten minutes later Izzy opened his window and breathed in the sea air. "It's done. Luis Gonsalves will turn over all his son's remaining records to our intelligence people. He claims to be shocked at the terrorist connections his son was involved with. The man deals in smuggling, racketeering, extortion and gambling. No terrorism, he swears that."

"You believe him?"

"If I didn't, we wouldn't have come here. I checked him out, and the details back him up. He may be a thug and a vicious racketeer, but now he's *our* thug and vicious racketeer."

"What about his son?"

"Luis made sure the plug was pulled as far as Martim is concerned. I don't like this outcome, but Ryker had the final call. Since the son is no longer a player, the father may be an asset in the future. His extensive contacts in Asia will be invaluable to our government."

"You really think he can be trusted?" Dakota was still uncomfortable with what had been arranged.

"About as much as I trust a grizzly on steroids. But the deal is done, and it's way above our pay grade, pal. At least Ryker will be satisfied." Izzy took a deep breath. "The son will be a virtual prisoner, watched at all times. In return for Gonsalves's freedom, we get the evidence to connect all the people Martim was working with. We were right about the October Twelfth group."

"You're sure?"

Izzy nodded. "The group was a fiction, run by Agent Fuller's partner. He was the insider that Jordan MacInnes had long suspected. There are records of cell calls between Kolowitz and Martim. Martim has also been laundering money for known terrorist financiers for the last four years. All in all he had a nice, full-service operation going on over here, and Frank Kolowitz fit right into the deal. Except his motive was greed, pure and simple." Izzy rubbed his neck and stared out the window. "This was probably the right thing to do, but it still makes me feel dirty. I like things black and white, not shifting shades of gray. Gonsalves and his son should be put away."

"You do what you can do," Dakota said. "Somebody made the call and they thought it was right. I'm just glad that I don't have to sit at a desk and make the policy decisions. Sometimes being the guy who slogs through the mud has its advantages."

Neither spoke as they crawled through heavy morning traffic until they reached the airport.

Izzy grabbed his briefcase from the backseat as soon as they pulled up. "Let me contact Ryker, then let's get the hell out of Dodge."

"Roger that."

EPILOGUE

Southern France

NELL STOOD IN THE French sunlight, listening to the wind sigh through the pine trees. The scent of lavender filled the sunny courtyard of the old stone house, its gray walls dappled by shadow. A pair of black dogs sprawled on the patio, asleep in the heat of afternoon.

Her hand trembled as she faced the mystery of her father's final gift. When she slid the cool metal into the old-fashioned lock, the big door opened with the whisper of well-oiled hinges.

"Is anyone home? *Y a-t-il quelqu'un là?*" She felt rude, like an intruder, but this was the right place. The letter from Nicholas Draycott had been very clear.

Drive through the first village. Pass the church and turn left at the olive mill. Watch for a pair of old stone lions at the little gravel drive.

Nicholas had refused all further explanation. Nell had read the cryptic directions a dozen times since her plane landed, and a dozen more times during the train ride from Paris.

"Trust me, Nell. You'll understand it all when you reach the village. Just be sure to take your key."

And now here she stood, her heart pounding in the hot silence of afternoon while the sharp scent of lavender filled her head. When there was no sound from the house, she knocked once again for good measure, then walked under the low door frame. Inside the small half-timbered foyer, time stood still.

Instantly Nell was surrounded by color—fuchsia to persimmon to turquoise. At her right was a Picasso sketch, followed by a Modigliani and what looked like—but surely *couldn't* be—an original Renoir. From canvases that filled every wall her gaze fell to an antique farm table holding a set of blue-and-white Chinese porcelain bowls and a Tang Dynasty ceramic horse caught in midstride. Even the carpet beneath her feet was antique, its reds and blues muted by centuries.

As she stared at the old stone walls, Nell knew she was in the home of someone with great wealth and impeccable taste. But none of her questions had been answered.

One of the dogs trotted in from the back of the house, tail wagging. Moments later a housekeeper in a spotless black uniform appeared. Her lined cheeks creased in a smile. "*Enfin*. You come. It is good, very good. Monsieur told me you would come one day and that I should always be ready. Everything clean and dusted, *comme il faut*."

"I'm sorry, but—do you *know* me?"

"*Bien sûr*. Here, you are in the photo, you see? He tells me to wait and so I do." When the housekeeper held out a gilt-framed photo, Nell caught a breath, shocked to see her own face, over two decades before, breathless with excitement. Behind her stood a taller figure with laughing eyes and a perfectly tailored tweed jacket.

Her father.

"*This* is your employer?" Nell didn't understand. This was her father's house? Had he built a secret identity here, in a place he would be safe? If so, he'd never mentioned a word about it to Nell.

"Certainly he is. And you are his daughter. He told me one day you would come with the key. You have it there in your hand, no?"

The puzzle began to fall into place. The key was his final gift to her, passing on his last secrets at his death.

Nell couldn't seem to breathe.

"But come, mademoiselle. You must be tired and you'll want to see your room. There's a fine view out over the lavender fields. On a good day you can see just a bit of the Mediterranean." Sunlight flashed with sparks of color against old mullioned windows, open to the lavender-scented breeze as the old woman bustled through the room, opening the shutters. "When you've rested, I'll bring the white peaches he said you'd like, along with merlot from your grapes in the back. It is all yours, just as he meant it to be. Every painting, every chair, all to make you smile and feel like home."

Nell shook her head. "You must be wrong. He—he never told me anything about this house. Not a word."

"He always did love his secrets." The old woman

nodded, her eyes softening as if in memory. "But it is yours. I have the deed if you wish for proof."

"I'll take your word." Nell turned away, pain blocking her throat with the sting of tears. "Even if it doesn't make sense."

The housekeeper made a clicking noise. "The answers must be here, no? Look around you and see them."

Nell turned slowly. In her shock at the sight of so many valuable paintings she had missed the other walls. Their rough gray limestone was dotted with a dozen framed photos of her father laughing, head back and arms open wide.

One with a gracious, aging movie star. Another with a former president. Two photos with a long-legged British photographer known for her stunning safari scenes—and her equally stunning love affairs.

Jordan MacInnes looked at ease in every one, a man with no cares in the world. Younger, confident, as he'd been before his arrest.

Nell gripped the heavy key, her heart filled to full measure, drinking in her father's happiness. With her emotions rising as fast as her tears, she ran her fingers along the old frames and pristine glass, savoring the sight of her father's joy.

It made the pain of his loss easier, to remember how happy he had been.

Something hummed near the door. Nell realized it was her cell phone, shoved deep in her big leather travel bag.

The housekeeper bustled to the kitchen as Nell dug the phone free.

"Hello?"

"Nell, it's Nicholas. Are you all right? You sound out of breath."

"I'm fine. I'm here at the address you gave me, Nicholas. It's a beautifully restored French farmhouse, and there are pictures of my father everywhere. I still can't take it all in."

"Sit down and breathe. You'll be fine." He sounded very calm, Nell thought.

"Did you know?" she asked suddenly. "Did he tell you about this place?"

"Not a word. I found out when Izzy Teague tracked the key. The company had not produced that kind of lock in fifty years, but they kept the owner's records from a previous renovation, so they were able to trace the address in Provence. All the same, I'm not surprised that Jordan had a refuge where no one would look. It was his way to be cautious."

"But this art—is it…stolen?"

"Definitely not. He was a shrewd businessman, Nell. He kept flipping the art, always getting something he loved more. They are yours, legal and clean."

So her father had told no one about this place. Yes, being careful was a habit for him, Nell thought. There were a thousand more questions, but she couldn't seem to focus on them. She was mesmerized by the smile in her father's photographs and the people who had once been a part of his life. She smiled at a photo of her mother, walking through a field of lavender with a white rose in her hair. Next to that was a picture of Nell, chasing a kitten over a smooth green lawn back in California.

So much love, all of it his final gift to her.

"I'll let you go, then. I just wanted to be sure everything worked out. Ring me if you need anything."

"Of course, Nicholas." A bee droned through the sunlight at the open door. Nell turned at the sound, then froze as a figure appeared in the doorway. The face was unfamiliar, heavily wrinkled beneath a shining bald curve.

No one that Nell knew. But when the eyes twinkled in apology and excitement, she couldn't look away. "Do I know you?"

"Oh, definitely."

The voice caught at her. Then the eyes.

Even through the thick glasses she knew those eyes, knew that cocky gleam. *It couldn't be.*

Nell gripped the huge wooden farm table as her legs went weak, the phone call forgotten. "You?"

His face was in shadow, but his voice was resonant and deep. "So it is, my dearest girl." He came closer, circling the peaceful room, straightening a vase and adjusting a flower with an owner's care. "Forgive the little piece of drama. It was necessary, I'm afraid."

The words rolled over Nell as she stood frozen, pinned to a bar of sunlight. "But how?" she whispered.

Jordan MacInnes smiled. "Thanks to Izzy Teague and your Dakota. They knew that my death was the only way I'd be free of the past." His voice wavered. "I'm sorry for all the pain it caused you, sorry for every tear. Believe that." He reached out a hand that trembled. "I love you so much."

Overwhelmed, Nell closed her eyes and hugged him

while the rich, ripe scent of lavender filled the air and the beaming housekeeper carried tea and lemonade outside to the stone patio.

"ARE YOU SURE?" Nell said. "Absolutely sure? You're finally free of them, and they'll never know the truth?"

"I'm sure. Jordan MacInnes is dead on every government record. Everyone important in my old world saw me 'die' in Scotland, and the word has spread. No one will be bothering either of us now."

A Bluefaced Leicester sheep wandered in from the meadow, rosemary sprigs matted in its thick fleece. "Now," Jordan MacInnes said, refilling Nell's glass of lemonade, "tell me about your man Dakota."

There was a father's clear curiosity in the question, along with the refusal to believe that *any* man was good enough for his daughter.

Nell cleared her throat. She didn't have neat and tidy answers. She'd spoken to Dakota only twice since their climbing trip, and both calls had been short.

"It's serious, then?"

All she could do was nod.

"About time," her father said calmly.

Bolder now, the sheep moved across the patio to nuzzle her hand while Nell pulled out the captive rosemary stems gently. Her fingers tangled in the soft wool.

She raised her face to the liquid sunlight. Suddenly her life was full of possibilities.

She turned to look at her father. "You aren't going to ask me what he does or what our plans are?"

"Why should I? The glow you have right now is answer enough. You need a good man in your life, Nell. And if Dakota doesn't marry you, I'll have to shoot him."

Suddenly the two dogs raced down the gravel drive, barking wildly. A car motor whined, circling up from the highway.

Nell stood up quickly, trying to see past the banked roses. "I'd better go clean up. It's been a long trip and I doubt I'd be good company for your visitors."

She started to move away, but her father took her hand tightly. "I think this is someone you should see, my love."

Footsteps crunched over the gravel, and one of the dogs shot over the low stone wall, tail wagging. Behind him Dakota Smith appeared, a travel bag over his shoulder, a bunch of freshly gathered lavender mounded in his arms. "So the secret's out." He nodded at Jordan MacInnes and then his gaze lingered on Nell's face. "You look beautiful. And a little overwhelmed."

"I am." Nell took a shaky breath. "You and Nicholas planned this to protect him?"

"Draycott had the idea first." Dakota dropped his bag and shoved his hands into his pockets. "Izzy and I helped put all the pieces together." He reached out to shake her father's hand. "Good to see you, sir. I'd say the cosmetic implants were a success. I wouldn't have recognized you, which is the whole idea, of course." He turned, prowling the room. "I like the Chinese clay horse. My uncle used to tell me how they were made, with running glazes and bodies so real you expected them to fly. I can see that he was right."

"You know about Chinese ceramics?" Nell's father sounded pleased by the possibility.

"Not much. Just that I like them."

The housekeeper bustled in. "The tea is arranged outside, if you would like."

Jordan MacInnes glanced out the back window and smiled. "I see that Izzy Teague has arrived and is already helping himself. Probably he's charmed his way into samples of my best Bordeaux, as well. I'd better go check. No doubt you two have things to discuss anyway." As he turned toward the kitchen, his movements were stiff and awkward, and Nell realized that he was in pain. For all his bravado the sickness must be growing worse.

How long did he have?

But she fought a sense of panic with the reminder that she'd had one wish granted, and that other miracles might be possible, too.

Find your grip.

Go forward.

The last thing her father would want was to see her cry.

"You okay?" Dakota's hand brushed her cheek.

"Fine. Jet lag…and everything. You look good." Their hands met, fingers curving together as if they'd been apart for only five minutes instead of almost three months.

"How about we go somewhere and talk?" Dakota said.

"Don't leave on my account," Jordan MacInnes called over his shoulder. "Izzy and I have work to do outside and we don't want to be disturbed."

"What kind of work?" Nell asked suspiciously.

"I've got a piece of art for him to return—anonymously of course."

"These pieces?" Nell stared at the treasury of art around her.

"I'm afraid the Renoir will have to go." He looked a little sad, then brightened. "All the rest are yours, Nell. All were purchased quite honestly, even if my name doesn't appear on any documents. After the arrangements are made, Izzy and I are going to check the security system at the National Gallery loading dock. I've found a few weaknesses, and Izzy will see that they're corrected. We'll also implement some new procedures for tracking art between departments." Jordan's eyes narrowed, magnified by the thick glasses. "No one is going to carry out another theft at the National Gallery like the last one." One eyebrow rose. "After all, the notorious Jordan MacInnes, the master thief who specialized in stealing Renaissance art, is dead. Or haven't you two heard?"

CLOUDS BRUSHED an endless azure sky over fields of lavender, while two unruly dogs herded a dozen Leicester sheep. Nell savored the color and motion as she walked with Dakota's arm around her shoulders.

At the center of everything was her father, back in the flesh, striding through the sunlight to joke with his housekeeper and argue with Izzy, presiding over all with generosity and wit. Watching him, Nell finally began to accept that she wasn't dreaming.

Which left only the small problem of her own future to be resolved.

Before she could bring up the subject, Dakota's palm moved up her bare arm and slid into the disordered strands at her neck. "I'm glad you know, Nell. I don't need to tell you that this secret has to stay between us."

Nell nodded, realizing how far Dakota and his friend had gone out on a limb to orchestrate the "death" in Scotland, creating her father's new identity. "Thank you," she whispered, pulling him down for a hard, fast kiss that left her toes curling.

"Don't thank me yet, honey. We still have things to discuss." He pulled her under the shade of a towering linden tree, yellow-white blooms spilling down around them.

"I'm listening." Nell wished she could read his face.

"Your homeless friend from San Francisco sends his regards. Izzy and I found a group home run by a Vietnam Vet, and he's doing great there."

"Thank you." It was hard to talk for the lump in her throat. "Now I know he'll be safe."

"No problem. He's one tough guy. He kept telling us how he could have used you when they stormed Hue. I told him he was probably right." Leaning down, Dakota brushed linden blossoms from Nell's hair. "We didn't finish our talk up in the mountains. It's time to do that now."

Nell's heart fluttered.

Find your grip.

Move forward.

"What did you have in mind?" She ran a hand along his shoulder. "I can make suggestions if you want them." She felt his heat and the play of muscles beneath his cotton shirt, then the sharp slam of his heart. She imagined the tiger, stirring on his muscled arm, coming to life.

"I'll give you my list first." He opened her hand, slipped something over her finger. "A vow, a promise. Two rings. This one belonged to my mother." The ring felt warm on Nell's finger, sliding into place. "Marry me, Nell. I promise to make you smile. I promise I'll guard your dreams. Your face will be home, wherever we are. All the rest we can make up as we go along."

Nell traced his mouth with her finger, seeing flashes of their future. She let the warmth of belonging flow over her, awed that fate had brought them together.

"I haven't heard a yes yet." Dakota frowned at her. "I haven't even heard a *maybe*. Now would be a good time for either, honey."

The man sounded just a little nervous. Since he was *never* nervous, Nell decided to savor the moment. "I'm thinking."

"Take your time." He glanced down at his watch. "You have about twenty more seconds until I start playing hardball."

"Then I'll give you my list. One, we'll go climbing together."

"As often as possible."

"And we'll go back to Draycott Abbey again soon. Nicholas has a Constable that may need restoration work, and he wants me to have a look."

"I'd consider it a pleasure. There's something about the place that leaves you with questions. It's the light or the age—or both."

Nell knew exactly what he meant. The abbey rooms

had a unique mix of light and shadows, marked by a distracting sense of movement just out of the corner of your eye. Probably it came from the play of light through antique, handmade glass used in the mullioned windows. At least, Nell told herself the phenomenon had a solid, physical source. It had to be explainable and scientific. She simply didn't believe in ghosts.

On the other hand, Draycott would be a prime candidate to change her mind.

Her hands circled Dakota's neck. "I keep wondering about that night you arrived in the rain. You said there was something wrong with your vision."

"I remember."

"Did you figure out what it was?" Nell knew his vision was special. She'd seen him measuring precise holds at the abbey when there was barely enough light for her to see. Any man who could do that had abilities far beyond what she'd consider normal.

Dakota seemed to choose his words carefully. "Not entirely. That's why I'd like to go back. Izzy has some theories. I won't bore you with the details, but they factor in stress and jet lag, combined with sudden changes in humidity. I'd like to see if he's right—or if there's something more we should consider."

Nell sensed the possibility was more important than he indicated. But she didn't ask him for more explanations. If there were things he could tell her, he would.

"I'll talk to Draycott about a date." His hands tightened on her shoulders. "Sometime after our honeymoon, assuming you give me an answer before I start sweating."

Nell smiled slowly. "You know my answer. You

have my heart and my future. I'll even throw in free climbing lessons."

Dakota's face eased into a grin. He raised her hand and studied the ring that glinted in the sunlight. Then he brought her palm to his chest and turned, looking at the blue valley that stretched beneath them.

He seemed content, Nell thought. Relaxed as she rarely had seen him.

"Izzy tells me there's some spectacular climbing around here." His arms circled her waist. "I'm ready when you are."

Nell's heart was pounding. "How many days do you have?"

"Five. Enough to get drunk on your father's excellent champagne. Enough to climb all morning and eat olives in the hot afternoon. Enough to get married." When he turned, his eyes were like fire inside smoky glass. "Marry me, Nell. Marry me today or tomorrow. In fact, marry me every day I'm here, so we can have the honeymoon all over again."

Up the hill they heard Izzy and her father arguing companionably about wiring schematics and alarm systems. Then Jordan's voice boomed through the sudden silence. "I want grandkids, blast it. Hurry up, you two."

Nell flushed. "Let's go find someplace without two arguing busybodies."

The scent of lavender spilled through the air as they walked through the afternoon sunlight.

THEY WERE MARRIED in the little church at the bottom of the valley. The mayor was able to waive the usual residency interval, thanks to Izzy's prearrangements. Nell wore a dress of vintage silk noile with a spray of pink roses.

Dakota was the handsomest man she'd ever seen.

Nicholas Draycott came for the wedding, along with two of Dakota's friends, the same big men that Nell remembered seeing briefly in Scotland. They teased Dakota for thinking that a mountain-climbing trip was any kind of proper honeymoon, but Nell told them it suited her perfectly. Half the village turned out to share almond buttercream cake, then toasted with vintage champagne and danced to her father's Edith Piaf records.

Then it was time to go.

Dakota pulled up on a dusty Triumph motorcycle with well-filled saddlebags, prepared for a trip wandering through Provence.

Jordan watched them go, looking thoughtful and unusually quiet.

"Don't worry. She'll be in good hands." Izzy crossed his arms. "Dakota's a good man."

"I'm certain of it. Otherwise I would have done everything to stop her. Not that I would have succeeded. My daughter is as stubborn as I am." As the motorcycle disappeared, he held out a glass of champagne to Izzy. "I must say, Bujune Okambe seemed more irritable than usual when I saw him last in Scotland. And his voice seemed deeper than I remember. I don't suppose you could explain that, could you?"

"Haven't got a clue." Izzy sipped his champagne and watched the sun set. "The man's a terror. So is that long-legged daughter of his."

Jordan's eyes narrowed. "Every man in the room was mesmerized by her, as I recall."

"Not me," Izzy said curtly.

"Of course not. You were too busy trying to keep that pistol hidden inside the wheelchair. But you did manage his accent beautifully. He's still in the hospital, I take it?"

"He's recovering. I doubt he'll hear about the impersonation. If he does, Marie will tackle the fallout." He frowned and then finished his champagne. "Enough about Okambe and his irritating daughter. I've got some schematics I want to show you. My people were pleased with your suggestions, and they have some questions for me to ask you."

"Ask away. It's the least I can do."

Within minutes the two were hunched over Izzy's notebook, studying new wiring schematics meant for the Freer Gallery.

Draycott Abbey

THE HILLS ABOVE the moat were red in the fading sunlight. Somewhere an animal slid behind the banked roses of Draycott Abbey's east face, hunting silently.

Nicholas Draycott and his wife and daughter did not notice, busy making plans to travel to London for a quick visit. Even Marston, the abbey's meticulous and all-seeing butler, was too busy to notice.

But the figure that stood in the shadow of the stone parapets watched his beloved roses move, noting the gray shape that followed the wall and vanished into the shadows of twilight.

When the cat appeared at his feet a few minutes later, Adrian Draycott looked pleased. "Restless, are you? Bored? I see, you've nothing to do." The abbey ghost studied the growing shadows over the home wood. "Enjoy your boredom, my friend. I intend to do so. I have every hope that the curse has been shifted now that the Italian's art has found its way to safe haven in a museum. Anywhere but here."

Somewhere a bird cried out in the darkness.

The cat listened, its powerful body tense.

"Yes, go to your hunting. I'll occupy myself in my own memories tonight. I've a mind to look through the old notebook again."

At his feet the cat's eyes gleamed.

"Of course it's in a safe place. No one will find it until I choose for it to be found."

The cat's long tail flicked from side to side.

"No, I won't be lonely. There's no need to keep me company."

The cat stretched lazily, then vanished into the shadows on the roof. As the moon rose from the horizon, the abbey ghost turned, lace fluttering at a phantom cuff. Wind stirred the last of the season's roses, the perfume like a dream of summer's richness.

His roses. His gift to this old house he had always loved, not wisely but too well.

A single star glittered to the southeast, somewhere over France.

The ghost of Draycott Abbey smiled at a vision of uncanny joy and promise, savoring the knowledge of a job well done.

AUTHOR NOTE

I hoped you enjoyed your time with Nell and Dakota.
I am certain that their adventures are just beginning!

Do you love old houses with mullioned windows?
Weathered stone walls where the sense of history is as
heavy as a physical touch? Maybe you've even visited
castles that echo with age and phantom sounds. If so,
you'll feel right at home at Draycott Abbey, with its
shadowed rooms overhung with fragrant roses. One
day on a visit to England, the swans on the moat floated
into my mind, followed in short order by the imperious guardian ghost and his faithful cat Gideon.

There are more secrets to come in this place of
magic and beauty.

To read more about Draycott Abbey, I'd suggest
starting with the first novella, "Enchantment," after
twelve years finally available again as a reprint in *The
Draycott Legacy: Enchantment & Bridge of Dreams*
(Toronto: HQN Books, 2007). This novella begins the
Draycott Abbey series with the story of Nicholas
Draycott—and the abbey's brooding ghost, Adrian.
Follow up with Adrian's haunting story in "What
Dreams May Come." This long-out-of-print novella

appears in a special compendium edition entitled *Draycott Eternal*, available in early 2008.

If you'd like a signed bookplate to go with your book, please drop me a note at bookplates@christinas-kye.com. If you have a reading group, let me know and I'll send you special materials for your group.

I'm frequently asked if my books have to be read in order. Definitely not! Each book is written to stand alone, and all stories are self-contained. But if you choose to read all the Draycott Abbey books in order of their publication, here is the sequence:

Hour of the Rose
Bridge of Dreams
Bride of the Mist
Key to Forever
Season of Wishes
Christmas Knight
The Perfect Gift

Enjoy! And be sure to visit www.draycottabbey.com for new abbey videos, interviews, travelogues and sketches of new stories in the making. (Warning— Adrian is already into new trouble!)

I know you'll be interested in art crime after meeting Nell's father! For a closer look at the shadowy world of art theft, read *Museum of the Missing: A History of Art Theft* by Simon Houpt (Toronto: Madison Press, 2006). *Stolen Masterpiece Tracker* by legendary FBI art theft investigator Thomas McShane (Fort Lee, New Jersey: Barricade, 2006) is a memoir of an undercover agent who successfully tracked down stolen Rembrandts and van Goghs for almost four decades. Jonathan Harr's *The Lost Painting: The Quest for a Caravaggio Masterpiece* (New York: Random House, 2005) traces the complex detective work required to recover missing art.

For a look at the high-stakes world of art forgery, pick up *False Impressions: The Hunt for Big-Time Art Fakes,* by Thomas Hoving (New York: Touchstone, 1997). The former director of New York's Metropolitan Museum of Art dishes up an insider's look at the creative ways highly trained forgers try to make a killing.

But art experts today use extensive scientific techniques to verify authenticity of art and to carry out conservation work. You'll find a closer look at Nell's world and the training required in *Conservation Skills: Judgement, Method and Decision Making* by Chris Caple (London and New York: Routledge, 2000). Protecting art from the ravages of time and natural decay is an ongoing battle, but the conservator's arsenal keeps growing. *Art, Biology, and Conservation: Biodeterioration of Works of Art,* edited by Robert J. Koestler et al. (New York: Metropolitan Museum of Art, 2004) gives a detailed look at cutting-edge techniques that keep masterpieces safe.

Centuries after his death, Leonardo da Vinci continues to fascinate viewers with his genius. The illegitimate son of a notary, Leonardo went on to unmatched triumphs as painter, scientist, engineer and inventor. Thousands of sketches preserve his insatiable quest to understand the workings of human anatomy and the natural world.

His incorrigible servant, Salai, was well known as a liar, thief and manipulator. The rest of his contribution to this story is speculation, as is the curse on the stolen sketch. Does such a preparatory sketch for the *Mona Lisa* actually exist? I'll leave that answer to Adrian Draycott.

What fun to see another SEAL meet his match! To learn more about Nell's free-climbing skills, check out *Rock Climbing: Mastering Basic Skills* by Craig Luebben (Seattle: Mountaineers Books, 2004). For a closer look at the gonzo techniques that make up parkour, check out the amazing videos on YouTube, in case you missed examples in the recent James Bond installment, "Casino Royale."

Find your grip.

Go forward, as Nell likes to say.

Finally, I know that Izzy's on your mind! Judging by your constant e-mails, you want this charming hunk to have his own book. I'm working on it, believe me, but the man is one tough customer.

For a special look into Izzy's shadowy past and his secret case files describing past and future books, log on to www.christinaskye.com/izzyfiles. If you're among the first fifty readers to log in to access Izzy's secret case notes, you'll win a special, limited edition T-shirt with Izzy's signature, along with access to an audio story that will not be available in stores. So get your iPod or MP3 player charged up and ready to roll.

Hey, Izzy's a techno kind of guy! He also says thanks to Nick and Celeste from NJ for the da Vinci help.

Meanwhile, savor the abbey's moonlight. Smell the perfume from its old roses. Above all, enjoy its promise of beauty and unending love as new mysteries unfold.

Until your next visit...happy reading.

Christina

REQUEST YOUR FREE BOOKS!

2 FREE NOVELS
FROM THE ROMANCE/SUSPENSE
COLLECTION PLUS 2 FREE GIFTS!

YES! Please send me 2 FREE novels from the Romance/Suspense Collection and my 2 FREE gifts (gifts are worth about $10). After receiving them, if I don't wish to receive any more books, I can return the shipping statement marked "cancel." If I don't cancel, I will receive 4 brand-new novels every month and be billed just $5.49 per book in the U.S. or $5.99 per book in Canada, plus 25¢ shipping and handling per book plus applicable taxes, if any*. That's a savings of at least 20% off the cover price! I understand that accepting the 2 free books and gifts places me under no obligation to buy anything. I can always return a shipment and cancel at any time. Even if I never buy another book from the Reader Service, the two free books and gifts are mine to keep forever.

185 MDN EF5Y 385 MDN EF6C

Name	(PLEASE PRINT)	
Address		Apt. #
City	State/Prov.	Zip/Postal Code

Signature (if under 18, a parent or guardian must sign)

Mail to **The Reader Service:**
IN U.S.A.: P.O. Box 1867, Buffalo, NY 14240-1867
IN CANADA: P.O. Box 609, Fort Erie, Ontario L2A 5X3

Not valid to current subscribers to the Romance Collection,
the Suspense Collection or the Romance/Suspense Collection.

Want to try two free books from another line?
Call 1-800-873-8635 or visit www.morefreebooks.com.

* Terms and prices subject to change without notice. N.Y. residents add applicable sales tax. Canadian residents will be charged applicable provincial taxes and GST. Offer not valid in Quebec. This offer is limited to one order per household. All orders subject to approval. Credit or debit balances in a customer's account(s) may be offset by any other outstanding balance owed by or to the customer. Please allow 4 to 6 weeks for delivery. Offer available while quantities last.

Your Privacy: Harlequin is committed to protecting your privacy. Our Privacy Policy is available online at www.eHarlequin.com or upon request from the Reader Service. From time to time we make our lists of customers available to reputable third parties who may have a product or service of interest to you. If you would prefer we not share your name and address, please check here. ☐

BOB08R